I0552852

VIKINGS FROM MARS

JAMIE BEGLEY

Young Ink Press Publication
YoungInkPress.com

Copyright © 2022 by Jamie Begley & Sarah Brianne

Edited by CD Editing, Erin Toland,
& Diamond in the Rough Editing
Cover Art by Cover Couture

All rights reserved.

No part of this book may be reproduced in any form or by any electronic
or mechanical means including information storage and retrieval
systems, without permission in writing from the author. The only
exception is by a reviewer, who may quote short excerpts in a review.

This book is a work of fiction. Names, characters, places, and incidents
either are products of the author's imagination or are used fictitiously.
Any resemblance to actual persons, living or dead, events, or locales is
entirely coincidental.

Connect with Jamie,
facebook.com/AuthorJamieBegley
Instagram.com/authorjamiebegley
JamieBegley.net

PROLOGUE

RAINE

"What's with the long face?" Raine spared a moment to ask the woman who took the booth next to her in the teller line, delaying asking the next customer to step forward.

"Late night."

Giving Brinn a sympathetic glance, Raine called out for the next customer. Then, as she keyed the customer's information into her computer to cash a check, Raine noticed her bank manager talking to the security guard. Frowning, Raine had to force herself to concentrate on the computer monitor when she saw Dobbs rush away and head out the front door.

She had to wait until she had counted out the money and the customer had left before she turned toward Brinn, who was still trying to log in to her computer.

"I should have called in sick today," Brinn said sulkily when another attempt failed.

"It must be the Internet. My computer was lagging on the last two transactions. I'll call Lucas over."

Raine pressed the button on her computer, which

would notify the manager on duty that they needed assistance.

Looking over to where she could see Lucas through the glass wall of his office, she saw he was now talking to the head teller.

"What's taking him so long?" Brinn complained as several customers came through the front door at once.

"I have no idea."

As she took another customer in the swelling line, Raine started to grow concerned when Olivia frantically rushed from Lucas' office, heading toward the back room, only to come back a minute later with her purse, leaving without a word to any of the tellers who were trying to get her attention.

Raine finished the transaction she was working on and turned back to Brinn.

"What in the world is going on? Olivia just left."

"I saw." Brinn frowned, looking just as concerned as her.

That was when a commotion in the lobby had them both turning and staring as a huge crowd started fighting to get inside the bank.

"This isn't good." Brinn gave her concerned glance as she tried to log in once again.

"Go ask Lucas what's going on," Raine suggested, motioning a customer forward. All the other tellers looked just as disturbed as her, yet they continued to work, despite being afraid a riot would break out at any minute.

Raine saw Brinn barge into Lucas' office, though he was on the phone.

"How can I help you today, Mrs. Johnson?" Raine asked the elderly woman whom she had grown familiar with during the year she had worked for the bank.

"I need to make a withdrawal." Mrs. Johnson slid a withdrawal slip under the plexiglass shield with her gnarled hand.

Raine keyed in Mrs. Johnson's information then asked, "Are you sure? That will leave you five dollars in your account." The elderly woman had never withdrawn more than fifty dollars a week since she had known her.

"I'm sure," she insisted. "Please hurry. I need to get home to my dogs. I'd like my money in tens."

Raine counted out the requested five hundred dollars as Brinn returned. From the pallor on her coworker's face, Raine was afraid Lucas had fired Brinn for barging into his office.

"Have a good day, Mrs. Johnson."

The elderly woman gave her a strange look before hurrying away.

Before Raine could take another customer, Brinn touched her shoulder.

"Lucas wants to talk with you. He told me to work your station."

No one ever worked at another station without logging off and counting and taking the drawer of money.

Seeing another teller had been called into Lucas' office after Brinn had left and the huge crowd in the bank clamoring to get waited on, Raine didn't argue. The tension in the bank was waiting for a spark to ignite whatever situation was occurring, and the only way she could find out what was going on was to go to Lucas' office.

Stepping away from her station, Raine hurriedly walked to Lucas' office, her heart starting to pound in her chest, when Tayla came out, looking just as pale as Brinn had.

"What's going on?" Raine asked Lucas as she walked through the door.

"The news reported a nuclear bomb was launched toward Hawaii."

Raine grabbed the back of chair, sitting in front of Lucas' desk.

"If this is a joke, it isn't funny," Raine managed to get out.

"Do I look like I'm joking?"

No, the unflappable manager seemed just as calm and collected as he always did, and the serious gaze Lucas was giving had her heart racing faster.

"That's why everyone wants to get cash?"

"Yes. Not only that, but there are more reports coming in that, when we launched one back, several more bombs were deployed for other parts of the United States."

"Any coming here?" I asked shakily, aware that bad news was going to keep coming.

"After the United States launched their missile, other countries did the same, and then their allies launched theirs. It's become a fucking shooting range out there."

"Jesus."

"I'm afraid it's too late for prayers to be any use. I'm telling everyone who wants to leave to go. I don't expect you to stay here."

"You're not going?" Raine couldn't believe Lucas was still here and wasn't already rushing home to his kid sister.

"I sent Dobbs after Piper. I plan to ride out whatever happens in the vault. You can stay or go. I'm going to gather what food and water we have in the bank and move it down to the vault. Piper is bringing what supplies she can from our apartment."

Raine felt her legs trying to buckle at the decision she needed to make. The only family she had was a brother, who lived hundreds of miles away in another state. She guessed it was too late to catch a flight out.

Getting a firmer grip on the back of the chair to keep herself from sinking to the floor, Raine came to a quick decision. She lived alone, without even a cat or dog to keep herself company. If she was going to die, she didn't want to do it alone in a high-rise, which could come crashing down with her in it if a bomb struck nearby.

"I'll stay."

Lucas didn't try to talk her out of it. "I know this is a lot to ask, but can you keep working until it's time to go down to the vault? People are terrified enough. I want to keep everyone calm until I can get the doors locked. Having their money handy makes people feel they can weather anything."

"Not usually when there is a nuclear warhead heading in your direction," Raine disagreed. "The problem is the computers are lagging. Brinn can't even get on hers."

"Just give them the money they are asking for."

Shit was definitely hitting the fan for Lucas to break protocol.

"Just give the money they are asking for regardless? You'll lose your job, go to prison. Your career will be destroyed!" Raine tried to get him to reconsider.

"If we come out of this alive, I'll happily dance my way to prison. When Dobbs gets back with Piper, I'll have him start bringing up the cash from the vault to make it more accessible."

"Okay. Do we know when...?"

"In the next hour and a half."

"Nothing like being given a timeline of when you're about to get nuked."

"Tell me about it. They keep shortening the timetable as

5

each new warhead is detected." Lucas straightened his tie. "Can you send Karina in?"

Wishing she could share his calm demeanor, Raine forced herself to release the support of the chair and return to her station.

"You're not leaving?" Brinn asked as she changed spots with Raine.

"No. I'm surprised you're not leaving to be with your fiancé."

"Harris is picking me up here, and then we're going to his parents' house twenty minutes away. I told Lucas I would stay until he gets here."

Both of them rapidly started dispensing the cash the customers requested. Intermittently, Raine would catch sight of Lucas as he went back and forth from the office's breakroom to carry what he could find to the vault, dropping off bags of cash to each of the remaining tellers along his trek.

She could see the relief on his face when his sister, Piper, showed up with Dobbs. Setting the two cases of soda down by the breakroom, he went to the side to open the side door, which would allow them behind the counter. He took the plastic bags from his sister, and they followed Lucas down to the lower level.

When thirty minutes had passed and Brinn's fiancé hadn't shown up, she become more and more distressed.

"If you want to go outside and wait for him, you can," Raine offered, not knowing what else to say to the woman.

"He's not coming."

"It has to be crazy out there," Raine offered.

"Lucas lives farther away than our apartment, and Dobbs got Piper here," Brinn said with a catch in her throat. "He's gone to his parents' without me."

She had only met Harris a couple of times during the bank holiday parties, and he had never impressed her with his overbearing attitude toward Brinn.

"You don't know that."

"Maybe not, but we both know Harris is all about *his* wants and needs, which is why I put off setting a date for the wedding."

Screams suddenly filled the air, and people began running out of the bank. What had sent everyone running?

"Get to the basement, everyone—hurry!" Lucas yelled from the door to the stairs.

All the tellers began running at once.

Raine bumped into someone coming up behind her, and a shot of pain went through her hip when she collided with the head teller's desk.

Emma managed to catch her. "Are you alright?"

"I think so. You go ahead. I'm coming."

"Lean on me." Emma pulled her arm over her shoulder. The only woman at the bank who had actually made an effort to become a friend to her refused to leave her side.

Raine knew it would be futile arguing with her friend. So, she forced herself to ignore the stabbing pain and head down on the stairs.

As they entered the vault, Raine was amazed to find how much Lucas had managed to gather.

"He even emptied the refrigerator." Raine gave a pain-filled laugh, trying not to become hysterical, like a couple of the women in the vault.

Emma helped her to sit down on the concrete floor before sitting down next to her.

"He raided the vending machines, too. I saw him steal Hoyt's private stash, too."

"I don't know which is going to be worse for him to deal with if he survives—the Federal Reserve or Hoyt."

"Definitely Hoyt." Emma snagged one of the cushions Lucas had brought down from his office to place it behind her back. "Here, try sitting on this."

Raine gave her a thankful smile. "You're always so concerned with how everyone is doing. If you weren't shaking as bad as me, I'd never know you're as scared as I am."

"Oh, I wouldn't say scared. More like terrified," she countered, smiling nervously before letting her gaze slide away to take in what Lucas had managed to do in the brief time he'd had. "I never thought I'd be grateful for not taking the new position the bank offered me at another branch office."

"The new branch wouldn't have the vault in the basement that's over a hundred years old, that's for sure," Raine agreed.

"I was thinking more about how Lucas has set us for the time we'd have to stay in here. I wouldn't been able to bring myself to take the cash bags out."

"Me neither," Raine admitted. "How long do you think we'll have to stay in here?"

"I have no idea ..." Emma broke off to listen to the radio that Dobbs had brought from Lucas' home.

Raine felt Emma take her hand as they listened to the world they knew come to a crashing end. In that one moment of shocked silence, everyone in the vault stared at each other in stunned dismay as they listened to the Earth being destroyed by grown men using nuclear bombs as if they were Styrofoam darts.

As everyone's worst nightmare played out, horrifying accounts of the total devastation were being broadcast over the wind-up radio. Descriptions erupted in the aftermath—chaos, radiation, millions of fatalities. And if that wasn't bad enough, other reports slowly began trickling in from the survivors having to contend with unbelievable objects appearing in sky and creatures hunting down and killing survivors still coping with a scorched Earth. The nightmare they had been living in had transcending into a true terror. A threshold had been breached from the manmade war, leaving Earth easy prey from a greater threat.

Aliens had arrived.

CHAPTER 1
RAINE

The sounds of a vicious fight taking place just feet from where she hid had Raine scooting over the debris of the building she was hiding behind to get a better viewpoint.

Scrupulously raising her head, Raine watched as a type of alien she had never seen before was being violently beaten. She bit her lip and lowered her head back down, unable to watch.

Why did she care it was six against one? If he died, it was one less alien she had to hide from.

Curling into a ball, she covered her ears to mask the sounds of the attack. She had lost all hope of the world ever going back to normal three days after the nuclear warheads had been sent from the heads of different nations without mercy for the human lives that would be lost or how those who did would survive.

When other civilizations, watching from other planets, had made their own strike on Earth, taking advantage of the devastation left behind to attack those who had managed to survive, the different nations had used all their

11

bombs on each other. Therefore, when the aliens had attacked, they had been met with little to no resistance, conquering Earth within twenty-four hours. Survivors from the nuclear war were now running for their lives, trying to stay out of the aliens' reach.

Raine didn't want to know what happened to those who were taken. Not for the first time, she regretted living through the bombing.

Playing back that fateful day still had her second-guessing the decision she had made. She should have gone home. *If you had*, Raine told herself, *you would be just another rotting corpse filling the air with the stench of death*. On the other hand, she wouldn't be out here, terrified and hungry, on the search for food to bring back to the nine others.

There had been eleven, but they had lost Dobbs on the first day the aliens had arrived. Unaware of the threat waiting for them, Lucas and Dobbs had gone out to check the damage. Lucas was the only one who had made it back.

After that, Lucas had ventured out alone, scavenging what he could find for them to eat, until a week ago when he had been hurt fighting off a couple of aliens who had sighted him. After that, each day, the rest of them took turns going out. Unfortunately, today was hers.

She had never been a particularly brave person, and listening to the godawful fight taking place cemented that belief. A bully had once pushed her to the ground when she had been in grade school. Raine remembered squealing as if she had been mortally wounded. No, enduring pain wasn't her strong suit.

Holding the pitifully small canvas bag close to her chest, she refused to return until she had more than two cans of chili beans and a jar of salsa. Karina had gone out yesterday and had come back with even less. Raine had wanted to find enough supplies so Brinn wouldn't have to go out for a couple of days.

She had high hopes for today after Karina had returned yesterday, saying the different types of aliens seemed to be withdrawing from the city in large droves. Karina had been right. She hadn't needed to hide from any of the aliens since leaving the bank... until now.

Those who she saw beating the grotesque alien were unfamiliar to her. What was surprising was the ones providing the beating were different types of aliens, who had been fighting each other over their spoils ever since they had arrived. They had banded together to beat the grotesque one.

All the aliens were fierce and terrifying-looking, but the one being beaten was a different caliber. He gave ugly a bad name. From their forages outside, they had seen some who were an ugly shade of green with a mismatched features that looked as if their mouths and noses had been squished together. They were the smallest but the most vicious ones. Emma had joked that it had been their looks that made them so hostile. They didn't take human captives, killing humans on sight.

Then there were the black and grey ones who looked as if they had been burnt and charred. Lucas, unfortunately, had gotten close enough to one, saying they appeared to have scales. They were above normal in height compared to human size, varying in height and stature.

Then there were the aliens she feared the most—light red with features that were the most human, yet they weren't. They had protruding foreheads of various colors with hair that looked like spikes. When they were chasing humans, they didn't use weapons; they would drop onto their hands and run like a high-powered K-9. The red ones were also the ones who were taking the most humans captives.

If those three groups of aliens that were battling each over superiority weren't bad enough, the dark purple ones drove a stake in any hope no more would be coming. Large and menacing, they reached seven feet tall and had the size and shape of bears. With claws for nails, they could kill humans with one swipe. The bear-like creatures could climb, too, scaling the side of a building to be able to see for miles around them. If that weren't worrying enough, they could leap to buildings nearby.

Unable to keep her curiosity at bay any longer, Raine uncurled herself to chance another glance at the same moment when the green alien raised a wicked-looking dagger, plunging it into the chest of the one lying on the ground.

Raine couldn't understand the garbled-sounding conversation coming from the aliens, but when they scattered, leaving their victim behind, Raine reasoned they weren't happy that the green one had stabbed him.

Ducking back down out of sight, she was afraid to move, afraid one of them would come back. Minutes clicked past before she was brave enough to look again.

She gingerly scooted to the side of the wall to get a better viewpoint. When she saw no one around, she slowly got to her feet, about to take off and run, when she heard a low moan come from the wounded alien.

Ignoring the sound, Raine took off, yet only managing to take a couple of steps before her conscience struck.

Don't do it, she silently yelled at herself as she abruptly stopped. *Do not do it.*

Ugh. She was going to do it. She had never been able to leave anyone in pain.

She cautiously edged toward the large alien lying on the ground. Her stomach reeled when she saw the repulsive alien up close.

"Are you alive?" she whispered, afraid other aliens could hear if they were near. Then Raine rolled her eyes at her own words. She probably wouldn't be able to understand him if he could answer.

Dammit, she was going to have to touch the repulsive being.

Bending down, she warily touched it on the shoulder.

Another low moan came out.

Looking around to make sure no one else was close, Raine hunkered down next to it.

What are you doing? she blasted herself. What did she know about alien anatomy? Zip, zilch, nada. What if it ate her? It was her worst fear; because of her ample size, she would become food for a family of four aliens.

Not happy being considered a buffet for the aliens, she turned her thoughts back to the male alien. Hell, as far as she knew, it could be a female. She scanned the repulsive creature, noticing blood seeping through a slit in its chest. The blood was red. She had imagined their blood would be a different color. Was red blood universal?

Glancing around, she became even more concerned that another alien would come across them out in the open. *Just leave it and go*, she told herself. Instead, she reached into the canvas bag hanging from her shoulder to take out a box of gauze pads. Cautiously, she pressed down hard on the wound, trying to stop the bleeding. As she did, its skin started slipping off to the side with a sucking sound.

Falling backward onto her bottom, she tried not to vomit at the sound. Had she killed the alien by touching it? Squeamish, she forced herself to look back at the alien, expecting to see the repulsive insides. Instead, what she saw had her going to her knees and crawling closer, her mind slow to process what she was seeing.

"What the hell?"

The tanned skin of a human had been revealed, instead of the gory insides of an alien.

Slowly, she reached out to touch the flesh that had come loose. It felt like leather. The human must have either killed or found dead aliens and skinned them to make himself appear like one of them.

"Why didn't we think about doing that?" she thought out loud. It was a sound plan, which was in direct contrast to the way they had been dealing with the aliens—they ran. In all their searches for food and supplies, they had yet to come across any weapons that could be used to defend themselves.

On the other hand, wearing the suit was probably why he had been attacked. It was kind of a big *fuck you* from the aliens he had killed to make the suit.

Had the man lying on the ground made the suit for protection in an effort to blend in among the aliens, or was it a callous disregard to the lives he had taken?

Raine estimated his height to be above six feet as she gingerly reached out to move his blond, tousled hair away from his face to get a better look at his features.

Sucking in a deep breath, she saw the masculine beauty of his features, though the lower part of his face was hidden beneath a massive moustache and beard. Curiously, he had parted the beard with each half braided, tying each end of the beard with what seemed like a leather tong. Above the beard, his facial features were breathtaking, with an aquiline nose and a sculpted jawline.

Dragging her eyes away from the man's face, Raine took

out another clean gauze pad to press down on the bleeding wound. The clothes he wore under the alien skin had the feel of a supple leather, fitting his body like they had been made for him.

Feeling guilty taking advantage of him being unconscious, she traveled her eyes down to the broad shoulders and massive chest. Embarrassed, her eyes flew over the bulge of his crotch to move down the long length of his legs.

Holy moly, he was a big dude. No wonder the aliens had ganged up on him.

Her concern grew that they could be sighted out in the open. She rose to stand over the unconscious man. Taking him by his feet, Raine then started dragging him to the spot where she had been hiding during his beating.

Dropping back down to the ground after she came back from getting the skins and covering the trail of blood he had left behind, she situated him as best as she could out of sight. Then she reassumed pressing down on his wound.

"What should I do?" Raine asked the unconscious man. "I can't drag you all the way back with me. The aliens could come back to the city at any minute. If they find us, they'll finish you off and either kill me or take me captive. I don't know what to do."

Uncertain, she continued putting pressure on the wound, intermittently checking to see if the bleeding had stopped. Time passed with no further sound or movement from the man. Finally seeing the bleeding had stopped, Raine began assessing her next move.

There were three buildings surrounding them, which she hadn't yet searched. She would go through them to find what she could then come back to check on him. She desperately needed more bandages after using the ones she had found for Lucas. He had been injured while searching for supplies. One of the purple ones had slashed his back before he had been able to escape. He was getting worse, and unless one of them were able to find antibiotics soon, she was afraid he would die.

"I need to go look for food and supplies. I'll come back and check on you." Raine placed a soft hand on his skin, checking for a fever. The feel of his skin sent a heat wave through her, as if she had been shocked by an electric surge.

"Don't be afraid. I'll hurry."

Or at least I will try. She added the last part to herself.

Earth was no longer a place where certainties could be counted on. Instead, uncertainty ruled every moment while you wait for the next batch of aliens to arrive.

Earth's downfall must be the new hot topic in outer space. She wished she knew their method so she could figure out which ones were carnivores.

Milly, the customer service representative at the bank, who was the most hated employee even before the bombings, liked to torment her by saying you could tell which aliens ate humans by their size. Milly never offered to go with anyone except her to search for supplies, rudely saying she would be safe accompanying her because the aliens wouldn't waste time chasing after an appetizer when they could feed their army with her.

She really detested Milly and would always lose her right away, afraid the *witch* would deliberately draw the aliens' attention to her just so she would be eaten.

Pushing the nasty thought aside that she wouldn't be upset if one of the aliens found Milly and ate her, she patted the man comfortingly, promising to protect him.

"Don't worry; I'll won't let them eat you."

CHAPTER 2

RAINE

C rawling to the side of the building, she poked her head out to make sure no one was around before taking off at a run to the building across the street from the one they were in.

She entered the building, and as she surveyed the gloomy interior, she became afraid it would crumble down around her at any moment. Taking out a small pocket flashlight, Raine began searching the rooms. It appeared to have been an office building. She wanted to cry when all she found was a box of K-cups. This building had already been picked over.

Biting her lip, she debated going up a flight of stairs she had discovered. She flashed the beam of light up the metal stairway, which had a good deal of debris on it, and started to climb over the mound of rocks. It took several attempts before reaching the top. At least going down would be much easier.

A metal door had two rocks propped up against it, blocking it from opening. With raising hopes that no one had searched this part of the building, she started trying to shift the rocks.

It took all her strength just to open the door wide enough for her to squeeze through. The only good thing about having nuclear bombs detonated and being invaded by aliens meant that it was a surefire method of losing weight.

She had no idea how much weight she had lost, but her size-twenty pants were barely hanging on. Why couldn't a clothing store or homes have been close by where she worked? If she didn't find some clothes to fit her soon, she would be flashing everyone in the vault every time she moved.

Gaping at what she found on the other side of the door, it took all her willpower not to fall on her knees and cry. The floor was a lunchroom and cafeteria.

Other survivors must have been too afraid to go past the first floor, in fear of the aliens. She wouldn't have chanced it either if they didn't desperately need the food.

Biting back a scream when rats started fleeing from her flashlight scanning the area, she gathered her courage and started searching for any items they could use.

She couldn't hold back her tears at the number of canned foods she found in the kitchen area and the walk-in. However, there was no way she could carry it all back by herself. The cans were huge and were meant to serve several portions. Guilt ate at her for losing Milly. Not only could she have helped carry the food but the unconscious man.

She chose a large can of peaches and baked beans; it hurt her soul to leave the over twenty cans sitting on the shelves.

Leaving the walk-in, she opened a door to the side and

saw it was a locker room. Setting the heavy canvas bag down, she started opening employee lockers. In one, she found a jacket. She tied the tight jacket around her waist rather than carrying it and opened the next locker. By the time she reached the end of the row, she had managed to find another jacket and a pair of sneakers that was too large for her. Disappointment turned to joy when she noticed the backpack hanging inside. She would be able to fit another can of food in the backpack. Unzipping it, she saw a pair of jeans and a computer.

Of course, the jeans weren't her size either and, while the clothes wouldn't benefit her, they would benefit someone in their group. Leaving the computer, she returned to the kitchen to shove a can of chili in the backpack.

She shrugged the pack on before she hid several cans of the food around the kitchen from other searchers. Tomorrow, if the aliens weren't around, she would bring others in their group to carry as much as they could back to the vault. If they could carry it back, it would be enough to hold them over for a couple of months if they rationed their meals.

Becoming worried about the wounded man she had left, Raine flashed the beam of light around, looking for a first-aid kit. Accidents invariably happened around a kitchen ...

Raine struck her forehead with the palm of her head at her stupidity. She moved to the metal drawers, found the knife drawer, and picked up five of them to put in the bulging backpack. The knifes would be the first ones they had managed to find since the bombing. Lucas was going to be ecstatic at her find. Snatching a can opener, she shoved it into the backpack.

Determined to find the first-aid kit, she was about to

give up when she found a doorway she hadn't noticed before. Slowly going through the door, she felt tiny feet scurrying out of the dark interior. When she jumped back, her flashlight briefly shone on the side of the wall. Instantly recognizing the bright red and white symbol on the case hanging on the wall, Raine snatched it, as if afraid someone would steal it.

Not bothering to open the case, she looked around the room. It was someone's office.

Opening the drawers, she found a pair of scissors, a single-serve can of chicken noodle soup, a bottled water, and a bottle of Tylenol. While it wasn't the antibiotics Lucas desperately needed, the Tylenol might make a small dent in the pain he was feeling.

Raine moved back to the door in the stairwell; she hated to leave without taking more, but she was too afraid to overburden herself in case she had to take off in a run if any of the aliens spotted her.

Sliding down the rubble-strewn staircase was much easier than climbing upward. Tugging her baggy dress pants back up, she cautiously made her way back to the opening of the building. Finding the street empty, Raine made the dash across the street.

Dropping down next to the wounded man, she took a gasping breath of air, unaware she had been holding her breath. She placed a shaking hand on his chest to check if he was still breathing.

"I was afraid they would find you while I was gone," she murmured, keeping her voice low. Then, pulling the bottled water and soup out of the backpack, she tried to rouse the unconscious man.

"Please wake up. The aliens who attacked you could

come back. I have a place I can hide you if you're able to move. You're too heavy for me to carry."

Raine sighed. He didn't move. What should she do?

"It's starting to get dark," Raine spoke out loud to the man, even though she knew he was unable to hear. "If I leave you alone, you might not make it. If I don't go back, my friends will worry about me," she reasoned. When no input was forthcoming, Raine decided to stay.

"I can't leave you helpless." Raine took off the jacket tied around her waist, then took the other one out of the backpack. Placing one behind his head, she then made sure he hadn't started bleeding again. Then she covered what she could of his chest and shoulders, which wasn't much. The jacket seemed like a child's article of clothing against his muscular frame.

Scooting closer to him, she shivered, trying to get warm as the temperature began to drop. While the days in Sunset, Nevada were warm this time of the year, the nights were chilly during the spring months. It would be a few more few months before the nights would warm up, as the days grew excruciatingly hot.

Ignoring the growling of her stomach, she took a couple of sips from the water bottle, wanting to save the majority of it for the man. He could have gone without water and be in desperate need when he woke up.

As the night grew colder and darker, Raine had a hard time staying awake. Giving up the battle, she lay down next to the man, snuggling up to his side.

"This is going to be extremely embarrassing when you wake up, but I'm freezing."

Placing her hands under his back for warmth, she wondered again about the texture of the clothes he was wearing. She tried to place the material, but drew a blank.

He must have bought the clothes before the bombing or found a higher-end store, because the feel against her skin was amazing.

Uncomfortable with her head on the ground, she rested it on his shoulder. Then, not hearing any sounds in their vicinity, she relaxed against him, closing her eyes.

"Don't worry; I'll protect you if they come back."

Rubbing her cheek against his shoulder, Raine fell asleep, feeling safer than even before the bombings without knowing why. The man wouldn't be able to defend himself from the aliens, much less her, if they came back. Despite that realization, she managed to sink into a deep sleep next to him, basically outdoors, where she wouldn't be surrounded by nine others in a metal vault. Either she had accepted dying was a forgone conclusion, or the man she had found had unknowingly just given her a reason to live.

CHAPTER 3

SKARS

Opening his eyes, Skars stared down at the human woman sleeping trustfully next to him.

Slightly lifting the shoulder her head was lying on, he monitored her reaction to make sure she was truly asleep. Just the small movement had him gasping for air. Seeing no movement from the human, he experimentally drew in a deep breath.

Devil's piss, his lungs were burning like fire. Getting used to Earth's atmosphere was taking even longer than he had anticipated. Thank Odin that he had listened to his instinct that their computer was off on the amount of time it would take to acclimate to the atmosphere on Earth. He had argued back and forth with his brother that the meteor shower they had gone through had affected the computer's readings.

Skars cursed again at the meteor shower that had prevented them from arriving before humans destroyed their planet and the other species beat them to ravage what was left. Giving a snort of disgust at the devastation he had found, he quickly looked to make sure he hadn't woken the woman.

Exhaustion showed on her sleeping face, even in her deep sleep. Hesitantly, he reached out to touch the wisp of hair curled on her pale cheek. The rest of her mahogany hair had been pulled back into a braid, exposing the delicate face next to his. He shook his head at the woman who had approached him after the Sorn, Volzon, Olggan, and Ferajorin had attacked him.

None of them would have been capable of downing him on their own without dealing a death blow. Instead, they had banded together, despite being sworn enemies. Dead, he was worthless. Alive, he was invaluable.

The only one who had shown true courage was the woman who had thought she was saving his life. If he had been at his full strength, he would have dealt with the Sorn, Volzon, Olggan, and Ferajorin viciously, but until his lungs adapted to the atmosphere, he was only at a fourth of his strength, which was why he was playing unconscious to the woman. He didn't trust that she wouldn't use the opportunity to slit his throat when she realized he wasn't a human male. If she succeeded, his soul would have been lost forever, never to grace the halls of Valhalla.

He touched the wound that was barely a scratch, yet the woman treated it like a death blow. Skars excused the woman for not knowing better. Human males were frail, useless creatures. For several moons, they had watched the weaklings incapably battle the distant species running amok on their planet then resorting to hiding at their failed attempts. None of them had been able to find the weakness, which would have sent the invaders running.

The woman let out a small whimper, snuggling to his

side for more warmth. Why had she discarded the skins? Fur lined the inside; they would have provided the warmth she needed.

Taking in another gasp of air, he was beginning to feel the tightness in his chest begin to loosen. In a few more hours, he should be able to breathe easier and return to full strength. If he hadn't convinced Thorsten to let him come first, before the others in the clan, they would have lost many of their best fighters. As soon as he regained his strength, he would return to the ship, and they could prepare to take what spoils hadn't yet been taken on Earth.

Experimentally touching her cheek again, he felt her soft skin under his finger. The touch set off a hunger inside of him that he had never felt before.

He removed his hand quickly, as if his brother could see him from the sky above, violating the law of their people. While, if he wanted to take anything from Earth that he wanted of value for merely wanting it, because he was first to land, and alone, that didn't include women.

Twining a curl of hair around his finger, he figured he technically had not violated their law. Even in the dark of the night, he could see from her hair color that she wasn't of Viking descent; therefore, he wouldn't be punished unless she met Reva, the clan's seeress, and the woman's bloodline was established as Viking.

The woman would go back with him, he arrogantly determined. She was now his. The woman had saved his life, hadn't she? The knife wound might only be a scratch, but she hadn't known that. She had thought she had saved his life, and that was what counted.

To him.

When the Martians had kidnapped his ancestors from

Earth for breeding purposes, they had mainly taken the males. It was only after they had returned to their planet of Mars that they had realized their mistake. Human males weren't the ones who produced the babies. What few women they had taken from them were able to birth their offspring, but once they were past the childbearing age, the women were returned to live among the Viking males. The Vikings who had been starved for the females fought among themselves, killing each other off, determined to have the women for their own. However, planning on escaping the Martians when the means became available to them, they couldn't face the loss of any of their males.

It was their original chieftain who had come up with two bygone laws. In a ritual, each woman would choose who would be given the honor of being her husband. Only those Vikings who wanted the woman would take part in the ritual. The other law took into account the women's bravery. This gave the women the opportunity to take a Viking who had not wanted to take part in the ritual. If a woman saved a Viking's life, they were now considered wed.

To find himself wed brought great joy and sorrow. His days of leading the men in battle would be over once their official marriage ceremony was completed by their current chieftain. Once the ceremony was over, the male was expected to give up his place as a warrior to settle down and make a home with his bride. They were also expected to be faithful husbands and ensure the protection of their wives, to assure future generations of Vikings would be born.

Having to deal with a human woman just as they were about to battle the different species that had taken over

Earth would be difficult, but not insurmountable. She would remain on the ship until he was ready to ask for Thorsen to perform the ceremony.

As the tightness in his chest eased, he carefully reached over the sleeping woman to drag the dried alien skins closer, draping them over her. His own body didn't need the added warmth. To him, it was a refreshing change from the hotter temperatures he was used to.

Listening for any sounds of approaching enemies, he spent the remainder of the night on watch. He would see what she planned to do come daylight before he opened his eyes. So far, he had been able to hide that he wasn't from Earth, but once she realized the whites of his eyes were red, she would run. Until his lungs were fully recovered, he wouldn't be able to give chase if she managed to escape his hold.

The small carrier he had used to come to Earth was a distance away. He needed to be at full strength in case he came upon more attackers. He could not face another shame if he was beaten twice, even if he had been in a weakened state.

While he wasn't ready to complete the ceremony to make their marriage official, he wasn't willing to risk the safety of his wife. If a male from another species captured her, especially if she did have Viking blood, despite his thinking she didn't, he wouldn't be able to ransom her back until it could be determined if she was meant to be trumated to one of their men. The clan wouldn't even be allowed to battle for her to keep her from being traded off.

"What?"

He heard her startled mumble as she sat upright, jerking the skins off her.

"*Ew* ... I must have reached for them when I was sleeping."

Remaining still, he felt her hand on his wound.

"No bleeding. You're going to have a wicked scar when that bad boy heals."

Did she know he was only pretending to be unconscious? Was that why she was talking to him?

"At least you slept through our cuddle time. I didn't want you to think I was taking advantage of you sleeping. On the other hand, it would make it much easier if you would wake up. I need to take the food back to the others, and even if I left the food behind, there's no way I could get you to where we're hiding by myself.

"I don't want to leave you here unprotected, either. You're not exactly in any shape to fight anyone if you're found. I could go and be back in a couple of hours with the others to help and get the rest of the food that I wasn't able to carry."

Reassured that she believed he was still unconscious, Skars listened to her ramble about what to do.

She had others nearby? How many? Thorsen would want to know if there was a big encampment of survivors. If he pretended to wake, she would never lead him to where they were hiding.

Changing his plan, he continued to pretend to be unconscious. He would give her a few minutes head start then follow behind her and send a transmission to Thorsen to come.

"I hate to leave you, but I have no choice."

Skars felt her gentle breath on his face as she leaned in closer.

"My friends will be worried sick I'm not back. I left food and water for when you wake. I'll hurry back."

Waiting until he heard sounds on the other side of the wall, Skars opened his eyes, seeing dawn about to break. He surveyed the area to make sure she was no longer around, then grabbed his cloak to swing it around his shoulders. He pressed a small button, and the cape melded to his body like a second skin.

Crouching by a gap in the wall, he saw the woman running around a building.

Turd of rat, he cursed. He hadn't expected her to run so fast.

His lungs started burning again as his long legs ate the distance between them. He should have just taken her, but he hadn't wanted to turn her against him if she refused to reveal the location of the encampment, and Thorsen wouldn't be gentle in his methods to retrieve the information. Skars didn't want the woman to look unfavorably on his brother until their ceremony was completed, nor did he want Thorsen to refuse to perform the ceremony. Until the ceremony was completed, his wife wouldn't truly belong to their clan and wouldn't be accorded the same courtesy and protection as other Viking wives. He already chanced that Thorsen would allow the ceremony, using an ancient law to steal the woman from Earth. That was if he could catch her. The woman ran with the speed of a gazelle.

Slowing, Skars hesitated before moving around another corner, not wanting to be spotted if he ventured closer. Tilting his head forward, he looked around the corner. What he saw had him charging forward, regardless if he was seen or not.

Two Olggans were perched on the side of the building she had just run past. His wife didn't even notice the danger she was in.

Rushing forward, Skars managed to grab one from

behind as it dropped to the ground. Claws extended to grab the sack she was carrying on her back, unaware Skars was behind him. The other Olggan stopped in his preparation of the net to spring on the woman, noticing his companion being attacked.

An overwhelming need to protect his wife had Skars pushing past the pain in his lungs at the exertion he had to use on the Olggan.

Taking on the two by himself would have been nothing if he had his ax. He would have cleaved them into small bits of slop for the animals on board his ship. Even during the heat of the battle, Skars could only marvel over how obtuse the woman was at the struggle taking place behind her.

Managing to snap the neck of the one he was holding, Skars expertly avoided a claw meant to rip his face off. Letting the Olggan he had just killed drop to the ground, he grabbed the remaining one by the wrist and, with a quick snap, broke it. A painful howl rented the air before the Olggan could slash him with his other claw. Skars grabbed it, breaking it also. The Olggan dropped to its knees, howling in pain. Picking up the net, he quickly wound it around the injured Olggan, leaving it to be collected by their kin.

That the two younglings were allowed out on their own without a more seasoned warrior showed that Jurzed believed the battle for Earth to be over. Once the king of the Olggan heard of his appearance on Earth, the younglings would be sent back to their ship and the more seasoned warriors would return.

Satan's balls, he should have taken his wife back to the ship.

Belatedly, he searched for the woman who he had protected from being taken only to discover she was no longer within sight. Running without regard of whether she would see him, Skars went to where he had last seen her. Searching through a couple of the buildings nearby was met with no success.

His wife had disappeared.

CHAPTER 4
SKARS

Frustrated at himself for letting the woman slip out of sight, Skars sent a transmission to Thorsen to send a nejim. The small carrier would allow him to search the small alleys she had escaped through. It would also have a thermal radar that would detect humans within buildings or underground.

After continuing the search for several more minutes, Skars had to admit failure. Backtracking to the spot his wife had left him lying, he noticed the water and some type of food left behind. That she had spared needed necessities for a complete stranger brought warmth to his chest. Her bravery and compassion showed she was going to be an asset to their clan.

Feeling the slight vibration on his shoulder where the skins were attached, he stepped out of the destroyed building as a much larger ship than he had requested landed. Inwardly groaning at Thorsen for not following his instructions, he walked up the metal ramp.

"You came too quickly," Skars grumbled once the door slid closed.

His brother arched an arrogant brow at him. "Is that any way to treat a brother concerned about your well-being?"

"Sorry, brother, I beg forgiveness."

"Forgiven. I'm too relieved to see you. When you didn't respond when I tried to contact you on your ship, I grew concerned."

"My ship crashed when I lost consciousness," Skars informed his brother.

"The computer stats were wrong." Thorsen's expression became grim.

Skars' expression matched his brother's. "As I cautioned you, the meteor shower damage was more intensive than we believed."

"If I hadn't heeded your warning and granted you permission to go first, our clan losses would have been heavy. When you regained consciousness, why didn't you contact me on your transmitter?"

"My ship going down was seen by those on the ground. I had to contend with an Olggan, a Volzon, and a Sorn."

Thorsen scowled.

"They banded together?"

"Já. I was surprised as well. They were younglings."

"Ahh ... That explains much."

"Já, they believed me helpless."

Thorsen broke into laughter. "It would take more than four younglings to accomplish that feat."

Skars didn't minimize how close he had come to being taken.

"A babe would have been able to accomplish the task. My lungs hadn't adjusted to Earth's atmosphere during the time limit the computer estimated they would. I wasn't able to fight them off. They started arguing among themselves who would take me captive and went to get their ships. I was gone before they came back."

"How did you escape?"

As he recounted the situation he had found himself in to Thorsen, the clan members accompanying his brother listened raptly.

"A human woman dragged me to safety. It was several hours before I regained my full strength."

Thorsen's face showed his shock. "A human woman helped? Where is this woman? I would thank her."

Embarrassed at being unable to produce the woman, Skars admitted the embarrassing truth. "I lost her when I had to prevent two Olggans from attacking her."

Thorsen grew concerned. "She escaped unharmed?"

"Já."

Thorsen slapped him on the back. "All is well, then. We'll return to the ship and return with the rest of the warriors."

Skars steeled himself for opposing his brother's plan. "I wish to stay. I need to find my wife."

Thorsen's jaw dropped. "Did I hear you correctly? *Wife*?"

Skars nodded. "I have claimed her as my wife. She saved my life. We are wed."

Thorsen looked at him in confusion. "You're invoking an ancient law we no longer follow?"

"Já."

Skars stood straight and tall, feeling the eyes of warriors waiting for Thorsen's reaction.

Thorsen looked thoughtful. "Did she at least appear to be of Viking descent? Is that why you're making the claim, so no other Viking could claim her?"

Skars jaw tautened. "Neinn. If she had appeared Viking,

I would have waited until Reva made her determination."

"Why would you want to claim the woman as wife when we may find your tru-mate here on Earth?"

"There is no law against me taking two wives."

"There is no law," Thorsen conceded. "However, human women would oppose it, especially your tru-mate. They are known to becoming unhappy when their mate turns to another. An unhappy tru-mate will make strife in the home."

Skars wasn't going to be swayed. He knew what he had felt when he'd touched the woman. She might not be his tru-mate, but his body didn't care.

"The chances of me finding my tru-mate are small. We both are aware of that fact, but if I do happen to find one, I will see to the happiness of both."

Laughter filled the ship.

Thorsen gave him a brotherly slap on the back. "I have no doubt you can." He laughed. "I will not deny you the woman ... if you find her."

"*I'll find her,*" Skars vowed.

"How did she react you not being from Earth?"

The question came from behind him.

Skars turned his head to see Ulf. "I pretended to be unconscious. I didn't want her running away from me before I regained my strength. She believed me to be human, like her."

Laughter broke out again.

"The great Viking Skars lost his woman!" Ulf roared out.

The others looked at him in sympathy but joined in the laughter.

Skars hung his head in shame. "Two Olggans were about to attack her. She disappeared while I was dealing with them."

"Did you let them get away, too?" Bjorn asked.

"I killed one; the other, I maimed his claws. He had Jurzed's mark upon his chest. I used his net to contain him. I'm sure he has been retrieved by now."

The Viking men stopped laughing.

"Wise decision, brother," Thorsen approved. "King Jurzed won't be pleased you killed one of his young, but if you were attacked first, then it will be excused. But if you killed one who belonged to his household, we would lose much time in our search for Xioarius."

Skars made a disgusted face. "The computer hasn't been able to track his whereabouts on the planet?"

"Neinn," Thorsen said.

"Devil's balls, I had hoped that you would have at least accomplished that during my absence."

Thorsen's expression grew fierce. "As did I. Thane was the only one who knew how to work the blasted machine. Erik is useless. Not only did the computer cause us to lose Xioarius and give him time to make it to Earth before the destruction, it did not warn us about the meteor shower, which hindered our kin from the chance to find their mates. And what valuables to be had, there isn't much left."

"I assumed as much," Skars grumbled in irritation. "That explains why the others pulled back when we arrived. There was no use fighting over a dead carcass."

Thorsen wasn't ready to admit failure. "We will search for the female descendants we can find, and perhaps then we will be able to bargain with King Jurzed and the High Archuru for those females who weren't tru-mated to any of their warriors. I will give that duty to you since you will be on the search for the wife you have claimed. I will search for Xioarius."

Skars flinched at the cold tone in Thorsen's voice as their enemy's name passed his lips.

"I will accept the duty. You will make the seeress available to me? There will be no need of me transporting the women I find back to your ship if they aren't tru-mates."

"Agreed." Thorsen gave him a fierce frown. "Reva's safety rests in your hands."

"I will keep her safe, or my life will be forfeited," he swore.

Thorsen nodded.

"My wife planned to bring back others to help me. I will find her, and hopefully, there could be a tru-mate among them." Skars tried to interject confidence in his words while, inwardly, he felt finding any potential tru-mates for his Viking brothers wasn't likely.

If there were any tru-mates to be found on Earth, the Olggans or the Ferajorins would have already found them.

"I pray to the gods this is so." Weariness and the responsibility for his clan showed on Thorsen's face. "It is the only hope many of the men have left. Many of them are only holding out to find out what tru-mates can be found on Earth. I do not want to lose another clansman like I had to lose Thane."

"Your wife won't be happy if we take those within her group without their consent," Njal warned. "You watched the movies, as I have. She will not understand our ways, nor will she understand if you take another wife."

"I have no need to tell her if the circumstances do not occur. Which they will not. Reva's visions are never wrong. She told me a Viking tru-mate was not in my future. I will be content with a wife who will give me daughters regardless of her ancestry. My daughters will be part Viking and with the God's blessings one day become a tru-mate."

"True, brother." Thorsen nodded. "Perhaps it would be cautious not to tell your wife we look for tru-mates. Offer all who are with her my protection. Transport them to your ship that we shall send for your use. If Reva finds any of them are tru-mates, it will be easier to allay their fears once they are on our ship."

Skars didn't want to start his marriage off with a deception, but he could understand Thorsen's reasoning. He also didn't believe they would find any tru-mates. The Olggans and the Ferajorins wouldn't have let any slip through their fingers.

"Thank you, Chieftain. I will assure her of their well-being."

Thorsen slapped him on the shoulder. "Damn, I will miss having you as my deputy once I perform your marriage."

This was what Skars had feared.

"I thought we could wait until we left Earth before the ceremony was performed."

Thorsen laughed. "Which are you more afraid of missing out on? The pillaging or the opportunity of finding Xioarius yourself on your search for tru-mates for the clan?"

"I will need to build a home for my wife, as well as making it comfortable for her."

"I see a problem with your reasoning."

Skars raised a questioning brow at his brother.

"With your bride not being a tru-mate, you're going to have to convince her the old-fashioned way."

"You doubt my abilities?"

"Never." Thorsen laughed at his confidence then grew serious. "How may I assist you further?"

"A nejim would be useful."

"I will send for several immediately. You may take Ulf,

Bjorn, Njal, and Arne in your search."

"Thank you, Chieftain. I will repay your kindness. I will give you first choice of those spoils I find on my own."

Thorsen snorted. "If there is any left. We need to find someone capable of repairing our computer before leaving Earth. Thanes' passing to Valhalla has left us vulnerable. I won't jeopardize the men by leaving Earth until I am assured the computer is fixed."

"How are you going to convince one of the humans to help us?" Skars questioned.

"Easily." Thorsen shrugged. "Their lives will be hung in the balance, as well as ours. The humans have proven to be cowards; they will fix the computer rather than dying."

Skars didn't disagree. If the humans had been afraid of the other species and run, the Vikings would terrify them. Most of the alien species preferred dragging their victims back to their camps to torture and kill out of sight, while the Vikings didn't want their victims to suffer and killed those who stood in their way immediately. Their Vikings' cousins were even more cold-blooded than them.

"I will find someone to fix our computer as I search for Xioarius, while you retrieve your wife." Thorsen continued, "If you need more warriors, contact me."

"Four men is more than I will need." Skars rolled his eyes at his brother. "How much trouble could finding her be?"

Thorsen gave him a warning glance.

"Careful, the gods will hear you. Erik is already claiming our bad luck is due to the gods' interference."

"I will make a sacrifice before I begin my search for my wife. Send Erik with the nejim."

Thorsen gave him a wry look. "You'll have to think of someone else to sacrifice. Erik is mine."

CHAPTER 5
RAINE

Raine looked around the corner carefully. What she was attempting to do was crazy. No, take that back. It was deranged.

Determined to make it back to where she had left the unconscious man more than two weeks ago, she had snuck out of the vault while everyone was sleeping. Without a doubt, the poor guy was certainly long gone or dead.

Her stomach lurched in dread when she saw the shelled building. When she had tried to return with Emma and Tayla, whom she had met up with during their search of him, there had been a spaceship hovering nearby. Frightened, Emma and Tayla had made her return to the vault without getting closer to the building.

Each day, she had tried to venture out, but Lucas had stopped her. Becoming weaker by the day, he had warned them from going out when each attempt they made resulted in them nearly getting caught. Aliens were swarming the areas close by and were coming closer to where they were hiding. The days she had to sit in the vault, she imagined the worst for the stranger whom she had left helpless, while watching their food supply dwindle until there was only a day's portion remaining. Seeing her resolve, Piper and Tayla had followed after her when they saw her sneaking out while the others were sleeping.

"I shouldn't have let you come with me." Disgusted with herself, Raine couldn't help but think this was just one big clusterfuck waiting to happen. If something could go wrong, it always did with her.

The first week she had worked at the bank, she had somehow managed to shut down all the terminals when she would log on to her station. A jinx was one of the nicer terms she'd been called behind her back.

The area around the shelled building and the other one where she had found the food was empty, yet it held an eerie silence, which she didn't trust.

"Quit feeling guilty. We weren't going to let you go out alone. Besides, it's not like we gave you a choice," Piper whispered next to her, poking her own head around the side of the building they were hiding behind. "You might be searching for a hunk of burning love, but all Tayla and I have on our minds is one thing—food."

"I wasn't sneaking out for a man. I was going for the food," Raine denied.

"Yeah, right." Tayla snorted. "We've had to listen for the last two weeks about how good looking he was. He might have been unconscious, but he made a hell of an impression on you."

"I feel terrible that I left him defenseless."

"I would, too, if he was as good looking as you said he was." Tayla squished closer to look over her head. "Coast is clear. Are we going to do this or hide here all day?"

"Which building should we go in first?" Piper asked, leaving the decision-making to them.

Raine stared at the dainty woman. Piper was Lucas' younger sister, whom he had brought to the bank when the alert had gone off about the incoming bombs.

Piper, being the youngest of their group, hadn't been able to leave the vault before. None of the women had been prepared for the new world they had found themselves confronted with, but Piper's health condition made her particularly vulnerable. Lucas was going to kill her and Tayla for letting Piper come with them. If she hadn't been determined to retrieve the canned food she had left behind, she would have never agreed to let her come, regardless of how much she wanted to discover if the man she had left behind had survived.

"You and Tayla go to that one and wait for me, while I check out the other building to see if he is still there."

Piper gave her a sympathetic glance. "Are you sure you don't won't us to go with you? What if he died?"

Raine's stomach lurched as she imagined the grotesque way a decomposing body could be all that was left of the handsome man she had left behind the crumbled wall.

She shook her head. "No, there isn't any reason to subject you guys to what I'll probably find."

"I'm sure you won't find anything." Tayla's sensible pragmatism had Raine partially agreeing with her.

"It'll probably be a waste of time, but if it keeps you from being a gloomy mess anymore, then it'll be worth the holdup. Raine and I are both dead meat, anyway, when we get back to the vault. Lucas is going to kill us."

"No, he won't," Piper protested. "I'm going to tell him that I snuck out after you guys left."

"Yeah, like that's gonna make a difference." Raine rolled her eyes at the fragile blonde who looked as if a hard wind would blow her away. "There's no need arguing about it anymore; what's done is done. Hopefully, if the food is still there that I couldn't carry, it might alleviate some of his anger."

"Only one way to find out." Tayla tensed behind her. "No one is around. On the count three, let's get our rear in gear. I'm giving you two minutes, Raine," she warned. "Get in and get out, whatever you find. Our first priority is to get the food."

"I'm ready." Raine nodded.

"Me, too." Piper didn't sound as sure, but she was determined not to be left behind.

"Go!" Tayla whisper-shouted.

The three of them took off running; Tayla and Piper in one direction and Raine in the other. *This is crazy as hell.* Inwardly shouting at herself, she ducked behind a crumbled brick wall. Frantic, her eyes went to the spot where she had left the defenseless man lying on the ground. A relieved sigh left her when she saw the bare ground.

Should she call out for him? Afraid the sound would alert any aliens that could possibly be around, she had to be content that at least he wasn't dead and go help Tayla and Piper gather the food they desperately needed.

Ignoring the sense of dejection of the man not being there, she turned to poke her head out of the building to see if it was clear when a hand covered her mouth and pulled her back to a hard chest.

A muffled scream was the only sound she was able to get through the hand pressed against her mouth. Frenziedly, she started fighting the other hand around her waist, desperate to escape his hold.

"Still. You will only hurt yourself."

She stopped fighting, her fear abating somewhat as she realized the person holding her was human from his voice.

She was unable to talk with the hand over her mouth, and her relief became short-lived when the man holding her started walking out of the building without any regard that there could be aliens nearby.

What in the hell? Was he trying to get them killed? Her eyes widened when she noticed three men, dressed like the unconscious man she had helped two weeks ago, stealthily slide around the building that Piper and Tayla were inside of.

Raine began fighting again. She had to help them. *Dear God, why did I allow them to come with me?* Thrashing her legs backward, Raine was frantic to escape to help them.

"Be calm, wife. My men will not harm your friends."

Wife? What the hell? Jerking her head backward, Raine lifted her eyes upward to see the man holding her. He was the one she had been searching for. Had he lost his mind during the fight with the aliens and had amnesia?

Her panic-stricken thoughts finally caught up with what she had missed when she had first looked up and realized who was holding her. She closed her eyes in self-hatred at her stupidity. Her being a jinx had doomed the women.

The man holding her might appear human at first glance... until it clicked what was different about him. The whites of his eyes were red. He was an alien, and she had led Tayla and Piper right to them.

Held captive, all Raine could do was watch as the three aliens stealthily entered the building where Tayla and Piper were waiting for her. Hearing startled screams come from within had Raine turning in her captor's arms, trying to gouge his red eyes out. Fury provided the fuel she needed at the unexpectedness of her attack. If she had to maim him to provide the opportunity to reach

Tayla and Piper, she was willing to be as vicious at it took.

Startled, he released her, and at the suddenness of his loosening hold, Raine found herself sitting on the broken sidewalk. She immediately jumped to her feet and started running toward the building just as Piper and Tayla came out, walking awkwardly, as if they were puppets on a string. At their unusual gait, Raine couldn't understand why they weren't running when the men she had seen sneaking into the building came striding out, holding something in their hands that was pointed at Piper and Tayla. Spotting something blinking on the front of their shirts, she had a sinking feeling they were under the men's control.

"Let them go!" Raine screamed as they continued pointing at the women, who had come to a stop.

"Quiet her, Skars! The Olggan and Ferajorin are nearing." The shout had come from the side of the building as a fourth man appeared.

Raine realized the name of the one who she had helped after his beating must be Skars when he attempted to grab her again. Feeling the material of her top tear, Raine managed to jerk herself away before he could touch her again. The other male aliens quickly did something to the devices they were holding, instantly silencing Tayla's and Piper's screams.

Running toward the first one she came to, Raine raised a fist to strike the device out of his hand when a long arm came to the top of her head to hold her back.

"Skars, control your woman."

"I'm not his," Raine spat. "Let them go!"

All the men laughed at her.

Confused and angered at their amusement, Raine

moved the trajectory of her aim to strike a hit to his face. Stymied at not being able to reach the gloating face, she switched methods. Being held at arm's length didn't prevent her from kicking out, and Raine prayed the aliens basically had the same anatomy as human males as she drove her foot into where his groin should be. Satisfied to see the alien sink to his knees like lead, she snatched the electronic device out of his hand and pressed the buttons she could see were lighted. Piper started screaming and jerking the object off her chest to throw it into the air, as if frightened it would latch on to her again.

"Go!" Raine shouted, throwing the electronic device at an advancing Skars.

Without waiting to see if Piper was following her order, Raine turned her attention to the alien holding Tayla's device. What little she could see of the alien's face from the alien skin he was wearing didn't bode well for her success.

Witnessing how she had attacked his friend, he cast her a warning glare with his red eyes. "Wife of Skars, Bjorn and Skars may make allowances for you, but I will not. If you strike out at me, I will return in kind."

"Let her go, and I won't hurt you!" Flushed with her success so far at taking the aliens on, Raine was too furious to care about the warning.

Preparing to kick the alien, she found herself snatched up again by the one called Skars.

"Is this the only way you can get a woman? By sneaking up on her?" Raine yelled, swinging her fist upward and aiming for the side of his face.

"Ulf means what he says, wife. We do not seek to hurt you, nor your friends." His attempt at calming her failed.

"If that's true, then all you had to do was talk to us, not

grab me or put electronic dog leashes on my friends," Raine countered.

"We wanted to get you safely secured on our ship. I have been searching for you for many days. I didn't want to take the chance of you slipping away again. There are many Olggans and Ferajorins in the area," Skars countered. "We were concerned for your safety first, unlike you, who are shouting loud enough that they will be able to hear from twenty paces away."

Her arms pinned under his, she used all her strength to raise his arms high enough to bite him. Sinking her teeth into his flesh as hard as she could, Raine let herself go limp until she was able to slip out of his slackened hold. To hell with talking; her only focus was on distracting the aliens so Piper could get away.

Picking up large chunks of rumble from the ground, she started throwing them at the back of the head of the one chasing after the young girl. Raine gave it a mean glare when it turned back to her before giving the one holding her a fake smile.

"Leave her be, and I'll lower my voice, and we can talk like reasonable adults."

Spinning, she stared at Skars. "I'm willing to go on your ship. I'll stop fighting if you let my friends leave." Raine attempted a smile, as if she was eager to go along with him.

The alien smiled back, and Raine was struck by how handsome he was, despite the bright-red eyes. Unlike the others, he didn't have the top part of the alien skin pulled over his head.

Raine almost regretted lying, but she had to take into consideration the safety of the other two women. They would still have been in the vault if she hadn't sneaked out, concerned for this ... alien.

You didn't know he wasn't a man. Her lack of knowledge didn't make her feel better.

"Do you care about your friends?"

Raine frowned, taken aback by his question. Obviously, whichever planet he came from didn't create geniuses. "Yes. That's why I want you to let them go."

"Then come with us. The three of you will be safer with us." Skars held out his hand.

She met Tayla's eyes in mutual understanding at her being mentally ready for something to happen. Then, pretending to take his hand, Raine spun on her feet to dart forward. Smashing her foot into the alien's crotch who was holding Tayla's device, she waited with her breath stuck in her throat for his reaction. Unlike the alien she had managed to wrest Piper's device from, the one whose nuts she had just tried to crush held on to Tayla's, refusing to relinquish it.

Dammit, why couldn't one thing be easy dealing with these aliens?

"Dammit, let go..." Struggling to wrest the device from his hard grip, she spied Piper trying to sneak back.

"Don't you dare!" she screamed at the young girl.

None of the three aliens tried to go after her, leaving it to the fourth one to do so.

She slapped at the three aliens like a windmill, but they were determined for her not to get Tayla's device, too consumed with what they were doing to notice what was going around them until several grey and black aliens began dropping from the buildings behind their backs.

Stunned, Raine debated the wisdom of warning them when the one who had chased after Piper saw them and gave out a warning shout.

Continuing to try to rip the device out the alien's hand, she saw Piper find a hiding space inside a burnt-out car.

"Let it fucking go!" Unconcerned with her own escape, she snarled at the one holding the device, kicking at the alien's chest. She almost flew over his shoulder when he jerked it backward. Held in place by the other two aliens she was fighting off, she turned her head to the side and saw Tayla staring wide-eyed at a grey and black alien that had dropped down inches from her side and was throwing a net over the immobile woman.

Automatically, she stopped fighting for the device, seeing the grey and black one was about to swoop in and steal Tayla away.

"Aren't you going to stop them?" She glared at the men she had been fighting with as if they were somehow responsible. Then Raine slapped at Skars' chest. "Please don't let him take her," she begged.

"You will stop fighting us?"

"Yes! Just help Tayla, and we'll do anything you say."

Skars didn't appear to believe her, yet he nodded at the other three. "Ulf, keep them safe," he ordered.

Her mouth dropped open when the men pushed at something on their shoulders, and the skin they were wearing became a cape. Despite what she had just witnessed as unusual, what had a cold shiver running up her back were the axes they pulled out from inside of the capes.

Her brain in hyperdrive mode, it took a minute to grasp what they were about to do. While they were quickly becoming outnumbered, when they started swinging their axes, the number of the grey and black aliens didn't increase ...

Because they were being chopped into bits.

Raine covered her mouth when body parts started flying in the air, and it took her several minutes to get her gag reflex under control.

Ulf had used a blade to remove the net from Tayla, whose blanched face showed she was trying to vomit, but the device on her shirt was preventing her.

"Do something!" Raine tore at the device, attempting to remove it without hurting Tayla. "She needs to vomit before she chokes to death!"

Able to see the same thing for himself, Ulf pressed the button to release her.

Tayla doubled over, vomiting at their feet. Shakenly, Raine patted Tayla's shuddering back.

"You nearly killed her," Raine accused the man who stared back at her unwaveringly.

"She wouldn't have died. The device wouldn't have allowed her to vomit until the *themoter* is disengaged."

"How would you know?" she raged at him. "Have you ever had to wear one?"

Ulf gave her an affronted look. "No, but I wouldn't have put it on the old woman if I thought she would be hurt."

Old? Raine nearly laughed out loud at the alien's misperception.

"No, you just made it impossible for her to fight you."

"We didn't want to betray our location to the Olggans. We were trying to take you to safety."

She was becoming sick of them saying that. Why were they so determined to get them on their ship? Was it dinnertime?

It was useless to argue with the big jerk when they were surrounded by the other aliens and a severed arm had just landed on her tennis shoe. Gagging, Raine raised her foot to shake the arm off. A dark red smear of blood was left behind.

I guess red blood is universal, she thought inanely, fighting back the tide of hysteria rising within herself.

"Are you okay, Tayla?"

Pale, Tayla nodded as she straightened, unable to talk. Raine couldn't blame her. It was everything she could do not to vomit when an unattached head with sightless eyes went soaring into the air like a macabre volleyball.

Both she and Tayla stood with frozen feet when Ulf started chopping away at the grey and black aliens.

"Move!" Ulf bellowed at them when they didn't immediately hurry through the area he had clear for them.

Stiffly, Raine was able to make her feet move when she saw he had cleared a path to another burnt-out car, next to the one Piper was hiding inside of.

Moving farther away from the fighting between the two groups of aliens, she was tempted to use the chance to escape, but couldn't bring herself to leave Piper in the other car.

Tayla noticed the direction she was staring at and didn't put up any resistance when Ulf forced the car door open to urge them inside.

"When you have the chance, take off. I'll stay with Piper," Raine whispered to Tayla.

"Fuck that!" Refusal was written all over Tayla's features. "I'm not going back without her, either."

The safety of the car was questionable, but anytime one of the grey and black aliens drew close, Ulf would swing his ax, and then he would return to protect the car.

"I thought the other ones were scarier, but the ones with the axes are shredding them to pieces."

Raine had to agree with her. Tayla didn't seem to be

angry at the big alien who had held her electronic device. In fact, Raine caught her staring at him admiringly. *They are a sight to behold*, Raine thought, unable to take her own eyes off Skars.

"The red eyes are spooky, but I'm feeling it."

Raine let her eyes slide away from Skars and back to Tayla. "You're the one who blamed my hormones for wanting to come back," she snapped.

Tayla shrugged. "That was Piper."

"She was repeating you."

"I can't wait until Emma sees them. I'll have to warn her off my He-Man."

"He isn't a He-Man; he isn't even human," Raine reminded her.

"As long he has the body part I'm most interested in, in the same general vicinity, I don't care."

"You'd sleep with one?" Raine couldn't believe what Tayla was saying.

"Hon, I've slept with worse." Tayla lifted an amused eyebrow at her. "Much worse. I don't know why you're looking so shocked. I'm not the one who snuck off and married one of them."

"I didn't marry him," she denied, embarrassed that Tayla had heard Skars call her his wife.

"Pfft," slipped from Tayla lips. "I have a feeling that hunk of burning love thinks you're really married. But if you're not interested, I might give the other guy a pass and focus on your soon-to-be ex."

"How about we worry about getting Piper the hell out of this mess, and ourselves, instead of worrying about whose pants you want to get into?" she snapped.

"Jeez. Jealous much?"

"I'm not jealous. I'm just concerned for Piper."

"Me, too!" Tayla snapped back. "May I remind you that you're the reason we're in this mess? Both Piper and I would still be asleep if you hadn't snuck out. I'm just trying not to freak the fuck out because I'm scared."

Raine felt terrible immediately. "You're right. I'm sorry."

If anything happened to Piper or Tayla, it would be on her shoulders alone. She had to do something other than cower inside the car.

Raising her head, she saw the fighting had gotten much worse.

"You should go help your friends!" Raine encouraged Ulf, who stood close beside the car.

A loud snort came from Ulf, who blocked their only exit out of the car without having the Jaws of Life handy. "They don't need my help. If you are thinking of escaping again, I wouldn't. The Olggans are just playing with us."

Raine moved her head to the side so she could see around Ulf's massive body.

"You mean this could get worse?"

"Já," Ulf replied grimly.

Raine turned over every way they could escape, but with Piper in the other car, it made it much more difficult. If she could convince him to bring Piper to their car, at least that part of their escape would be easier to achieve.

"You should bring our friend over here so you can protect all three of us."

Ulf wasn't biting. "The little one is safe where he is."

They thought Piper was a boy?

Raine saw Tayla give her a satisfied smirk. Tayla, unlike Milly, who kept telling everyone they were going to be eaten, had thought the aliens had other ideas for human women other than food. So, she had helped the women in the vault camouflage their looks, hoping to escape their interest. Raine had been the only one who hadn't bothered with a disguise. If an alien wanted her, it would be a food source. Where looks were concerned, any disguise that Tayla could come up with would only be a step up from where she had started from.

Dammit. With Piper's health challenges, Raine wanted the girl where she could protect her.

The delayed shock of finding the man who she had helped stay alive and was an alien was wearing off, and she started assessing their situation. Then she wished she hadn't. There didn't seem to be a way out this situation, unless the two different aliens miraculously killed each other off. Normally, she wouldn't have a problem with that, but Raine found it hard to fight her protective instinct while watching Skars fight.

Another detail finally clicked into place. They spoke the same language. While theirs were more old-fashioned, they were still easily understood. Now the chance of getting more information about the different alien species overrode her urgent desire to escape.

Sizing up the alien standing close by, she started probing for details that could be useful.

"The grey and black ones are called Olggans?"

"Já." Ulf stared at her as if she had the mental capacity of a child.

Biting back the sarcastic response that she wanted to give him, Raine had to smother it, determined not to be sidetracked from finding out more about the different types of aliens. Especially the ones who would want to put humans on their menu. Knowledge was power, and right now, the aliens had all the power because of the humans' lack of knowledge. She was going to rectify that shit right now.

Raine forced herself to use the same friendly tone of voice when serving a difficult customer. "What are you and your friends called?"

Ulf's chest swelled with pride. "We are Vikings."

Her mouth dropped open. "You're from Earth?" Raine searched the gorgeous face above her own. "You're human?"

"Part human," he corrected her.

Raine really hated to ask, but couldn't stop herself. *No good is going to come from asking,* she cowardly warned herself. The minuscule brave part of her wouldn't leave it alone, though.

"What's the other part?"

"Martian."

I *told you not to ask*, the cowardly part of her sneered as the brave part went fleeing back to nothingness.

"Crap." Tayla's soft mutter echoed her own misgiving.

The situation they were in had just gone from bad to a cross between *Invaders from Mars* to *Vikings*. She had never watched the dark comedy and had been too squeamish to watch *Vikings*. Wishing wholeheartedly she could change the channel and find herself back before the nuclear explosions had happened, blissfully unaware of the hell having headed their way, Raine stared up at the imposing male Viking to continue on her fact-finding mission.

"Your name is Ulf?"

"Ja."

"Ulf, I'm worried about my friend over there. I would feel better if she were here with us."

About to scream a warning when an Olggan tried to sneak up from his side, Raine could only watch in horror as Ulf spun to chop the Olggan's head off with one swing. Not content, the Viking-Martian sliced its legs and arms off, too.

"You didn't have to go in for the overkill." Glaring at

him, Raine tightened her stomach muscles when she heard Tayla retching next to her. "It was already dead." A sudden thought struck her. "Can it regrow body parts like a snake?" If that was the case, he could chop away to his heart's content.

Ulf's red eyes grew darker. "Neinn. I will not take any chances with your welfare. As Skars' wife, you must be protected."

Raine gaped at him. "I'm not his wife! He must have hit his head during the beating. He was unconscious a long time. I didn't even talk to him, much less marry him."

She could tell what she said went in one of his Martian ears and out the other. The human Viking male side of him wasn't listening.

"Believe me; I would remember getting married to a Martian," she snapped. "A woman would remember that sort of thing. At least I would."

Ulf shook his head at her. "No ceremony has been performed. Thorsen won't perform the ceremony until after we leave Earth. Skars does not want to miss out on the raiding."

Raine switched her gaze to her so-called husband, who was blithely butchering any Olggan coming within reach of his ax. "What does being married have to do with his raiding?"

"Married men aren't allowed to raid; too many battles take place during raids, so he would have to stay on the ship. It is more important that he remains on earth and finds more Viking brides."

This had been the fear of all the women in the vault. Raine had worried about it, too, but she was just as worried about getting eaten.

Huffily, Raine gave him a disgusted look. "So," she said

snidely, "you plan on kidnapping and raping us, and then want us to pretend it's okay just because you can say *without our permission* that we're married?"

Ulf's eyes glowed redder, and his skin took on a reddish hue. "Rape? Viking men don't rape women! Skars would not, nor would any Viking, take an unwilling woman. They'd use their own ax on their cock and hands rather than do such a thing."

Stunned at his vehemence, she chose her next words carefully. "I didn't *willingly* marry Skars."

Ulf contemplated her frown. "Skars told us you saved his life. Did you not?"

Not knowing where Ulf going with his question, she told the truth. "I did."

His frown cleared. "Then you're married by Viking law."

"On Earth, we do it differently. The man, or woman, asks them to marry them. Then, after a *long* ..." she drawled out, "while, they get married."

His frown returned, showing his confusion. "Why would Skars have to ask? By saving his life, you showed you're willing to take him to your bed. He accepted by claiming you as wife. All that is left is for Thorsen to perform the ceremony and the bedding."

"That's not all that is left!" Astounded at their belief, Raine looked to Tayla for help and only saw her shrugging at her.

"You're on your own, kid. Makes sense to me. I wouldn't save anyone's life unless I was willing to sleep with them, either."

"That's archaic," Raine sputtered out, not knowing what else to say.

Ulf nodded at her.

"It is an ancient law," he admitted.

"What if the woman doesn't want to be married?"

"Then she divorces him," Ulf explained. "Never heard a tale of anyone divorcing a Viking."

"Well, you will when—"

Tayla put a hand on her, preventing her from saying what she was about to say. "Let's wait on that," Tayla cautioned, her voice low. "At least until we find out the benefits of being married to Skars."

Raine narrowed her eyes on the calculating woman. "There is no *we* here."

Tayla ignored her. "Ulf, as a matter of interest ... would Raine's friends be given the same protection as being married to Skars would?"

"Thorsen offered as much," Ulf confirmed.

"There you go." Tayla became even more calculating. "No Skars, no protection," she warned. "You can't think just about yourself right now." Tayla tilted her head toward the other car.

Raine hated to admit it, but Tayla was right. She would be expected to take one for the team. The problem was that she had never been much of a team player. Not that she hadn't wanted to, but because no one had wanted her on their team. Now, it was finally her opportunity to belong to a team, to make up some of the mishaps that her co-workers blamed her for.

There was another reason much more important to go along with being married to Skars, if for no other reason than Piper. It had been a miracle the young girl had survived this long.

"About the bedding ..." Looking to where Skars was chopping aliens up like he was making a Caesar salad, she asked delicately, "I don't have to actually *bed* him until after the ceremony, do I?"

"Neinn. That is your choice."

Raine gave a sigh of relief. This may be doable.

"Of course, him being a Viking,"—amusement filled his face above the bushy beard—"there is no law preventing him from changing your mind."

CHAPTER 7

RAINE

R aine prayed for divine intervention at the arrogant gloat Ulf gave her. He had every confidence the bedding would happen on Skars' timetable.

"What other responsibilities will Skars have after the ceremony?".

"The married clan members have many responsibilities. The warriors need to be fed, clothed, their quarters maintained. Those who don't raid provide for the warriors. In return, the warriors provide protection and provisions to sustain the clan."

Raine just shook her head at the information she was being given. No wonder Skars wasn't looking forward to nuptial bliss.

"So, Skars was just going to put me on hold while he's out doing his manly fun shit?"

Ulf looked confused. "Manly fun shit?"

"Raiding," she explained.

"Já."

Why was she so angry? It wasn't like they were really married. Because Raine had a feeling of who was going to get the short end of the stick. She didn't see Skars cooking and cleaning.

"Then it's a good thing for him we're not really married," she said with deceptive calmness.

"You are."

Exasperated, she glowered at him. "You just said I wasn't until the ceremony."

"Já, you are. You saved his life."

"So, I'm trying to understand. We're married because I saved his life, yet until the ceremony is preformed, it's kinda like a marriage in name only, meaning he can still live like a single man and also gets to have sex with the woman?"

"Já."

"We have a saying for that on Earth. 'You can't have your cake and eat it, too.'"

Ulf seemed confused then gave an uncaring shrug. "You chose him to be your husband when you saved his life."

"I saved his life because I thought he was human."

"He is human."

"And Martian."

"It doesn't matter. It is our way."

"It isn't mine, so it doesn't count." Raine found herself scooting closer to Tayla when Ulf severed an Olggan into two parts and one half of his body hit the car door.

"Quit arguing with him," Tayla managed to get out between dry heaves. "Who gives a damn if he gets the whole cake? It works for your benefit. Hell, what are you worried about? Afraid you don't have the willpower to resist him?"

"No ..." But she kinda did, not that she was going to confide that tidbit to Tayla.

"I'm going to vomit." A wrenching sound came from

Tayla's throat as the half body seemed to hop before sinking to the ground.

Raine found herself turning on her knees to put as much space as possible between Tayla and herself.

Gritting her teeth, determined not to follow her example, she stared up at Ulf balefully. "Do you think you could kill them more humanely?"

His disgusted snort had her nails clenching on the material of her pants. "Viking women's stomachs aren't so weak."

"Really? Then it's a shame there wasn't one around to save your buddy instead of me when he needed help."

"I'm thinking the same."

Hurt despite herself, Raine almost didn't warn him that more Olggans were running down the street behind him. If she hadn't been concerned for Piper, Tayla, and herself, she would have let them have him.

"There are more of them coming!" Raine warned Ulf, who was already staring in the direction they were coming from.

"I see," he said grimly. "King Jurzed is leading his men. One of them must have sent him a message that they are battling Skars."

Raine stared at the immense amount of Olggans surrounding the Vikings. Her fingers tightened on the burnt car door where she was looking out, feeling a prick of shattered glass prick her skin.

"King Jurzed doesn't normally fight?"

It was easy to see which alien Ulf was referring to as King Jurzed. While all the other Olggans were black and grey, the one standing out from all the others, not only by his arrogant stance, was a deep blue. The two silver bands around his head weren't what caught her eye; it was the thick, blond-white hair falling to his shoulders. Two silver cuffs on each of his arms glinted in the sun as he strode into the fight, carrying a short sword.

"King Jurzed is like Thorsen—both are fierce warriors—but usually, King Jurzed grants General Dartar permission to lead."

"Who is Thorsen?"

"The leader of our clan," Ulf answered without pausing as he hacked an Olggan that had come too close to their car.

Raine didn't let her revolting stomach prevent her from satisfying her curiosity. "Does Thorsen usually lead his men?"

Ulf, unaware she planned to tell every morsel of information to Lucas and the others in the vault, willingly answered her questions. *That is if I ever see them again*, she thought, swallowing the huge lump of fear at seeing the streets filling with Olggans. Raine was seriously beginning to doubt she would. There would be no worry about being bedded by Skars, or any other Viking. There would be none left. For every Olggan the Vikings chopped down, three would replace them.

"No," Ulf answered, still unperturbed about the fierce fighting going on just inches away from him.

"Who leads your clan to battle?" Watching one particular Viking obliterate the Olggans one at time, she was pretty sure of the answer before she asked.

"Skars."

Raine frowned. "Why is King Jurzed leading them, then?"

"He is fighting because Skars killed one of the Olggans' younglings and humiliated one from his household to keep them from capturing you."

Raine bit her lip, remembering the day when she had

left Skars to return to the vault. She had heard sounds behind her, but had been too frightened to look back, afraid she would be captured if she stopped to investigate.

"They want to kill him because of me?"

"Já. As his wife, it was Skars' duty to protect you."

"That's what Skars and you are all doing now?"

"Já, and the woman and the boy with you," he confirmed.

Tayla and she shared a glance at Piper being called a boy again. Because of the disguise Tayla had put together for Piper, they had hoped she would come across as male. That the Vikings were mistaking her for a young boy made it even better.

"He's very young," she lied unrepentantly. "He's very ill."

Ulf briefly took his eyes off the fight he was engaged in to stare down at her. "The boy is sickly?"

"Yes, very sickly." Raine had no problem telling that truth.

"How did he survive the destruction?"

"His brother hid him and all of us."

"It is good that he has a strong clan leader to protect him."

Their attention was caught by Skars, who gave a loud grunt when an Olggan managed to rake merciless claws down his chest.

Well, hell. She couldn't stand and watch the man get killed after he had saved her life, especially if that meant she would have her own personal squad making sure she didn't become alien roadkill. That the others in her group would be afforded the same protection made it a win-win as far as she was concerned, and she could put off having sex until they no longer needed their protection. If not, then how bad could having sex with an alien Viking be? Other than the red eyes, and some of them having an orangish tinge to their skin, they seemed normal.

Her mind refused to go the nether regions of their bodies. She would cross that bridge when she had to. Much later. That was, if her husband survived the goon squad of aliens that were determined to make her a widow.

Seeing a metal rod poking out of the debris of a destroyed building, Raine started to climb out of the window.

"Stay still," Ulf ordered.

Undeterred, she climbed out, taking no notice of her shirt being torn by the metal of the door.

Placing her hands on her hips, she turned to confront the red-eyed alien who surprised her by not touching her to stop or help her climb out. "I'm not trying to run away. I'm going to help if all you're going to do is stand here and watch my husband get killed."

In her mind, she wasn't really married to Skars, but if Ulf and the other Vikings were convinced she had come around to their way of thinking, then maybe they would lower their guard.

"You're not going to try to run away again?" He stared at her dubiously.

"No. What kind of wife would I be if I left my husband when he is in danger?" Trying to come across as sincere, Raine held out hope that Ulf would stop her and step in himself.

"Then you help."

There went that, she thought, glaring at the Viking who should have been called Oaf.

"Thanks," she gritted out between clenched teeth.

Moving to the pile of debris, she managed to yank the

metal rod out. She held the heavy metal rod like a bat as she moved closer to the fighting.

The lump of fear in her throat nearly choked her. Buying time, she looked over at Ulf. She hesitated, still expecting him to stop her. "Aren't you going to help?"

He raised his brows, as if not understanding why she was asking the obvious. "I'll watch the woman and boy."

She had never felt so helpless in her life. All she wanted to do was run screaming in terror and not have to deal with *any* aliens ever again.

Bile from her empty stomach threatened to choke her when yet another headless Olggan fell at her feet. What was with these aliens? Were the Olggans going to rise from the dead? Was that why they kept decapitating them? She had no liking for the Olggans, but there were different ways to kill them beside chopping off their heads.

Lifting her eyes from the bloody ground littered with alien body parts, Raine saw Skars already fighting another one before the one she was staring at hit the dirt while another one was coming up on him with claws extended.

Any fear she held dissolved at the oncoming threat. She needed Skars alive. He could be their only lifeline in a world where humans were on the verge of becoming extinct. Her small group needed the Vikings more than they needed them. She didn't know how their Viking marriages worked, but on Earth, wives protected their husbands.

Holding the metal rod tighter in her grip, Raine closed her eyes and swung at the Olggan about to take her husband out.

At a loud sound, Raine opened her eyes to stare horrorstricken, seeing Skars laid out in the dirt next to the headless corpse.

All the aliens and Vikings stopped fighting to gape at

her. Instead of helping, she had knocked Skars out. Rage filling the Vikings' faces had her debating whether to run or stay. It was the Olggans who made the decision for her.

Using their hesitation to strike out at the one she had been aiming for in the first place, she swung the rod out again, hitting a hand that was pulling out a net hooked to its side. The sucker was going to capture her with the net! Any sympathy she had for the Olggans died.

Coming to the conclusion that it was either do it or die since she had just pissed the Vikings off, she had nothing left to lose. She didn't think the Vikings had cannibalistic tendencies, but the grey and black ones were looking at her like they were starving.

Holding the rod in the middle, she started swishing it around crazily in the air to make the Olggans stay back. Sadly, she couldn't resist the instinct to squeeze her eyes closed again. Then, fighting against the instinct unsuccessfully, her eyes flew open a second after hearing the crunch of bones.

She was so going to die.

CHAPTER 8

RAINE

Why hadn't she kept them closed?

The Olggans' attention was no longer focused on using a net to catch her. Claws were arching toward the portion of her chest where her heart was. Taking a backward step, Raine continued swinging out wildly with the metal rod, trying to avoid getting her chest ripped open.

"Stay back," she warned in a shrill voice. "I don't want to hurt you, but I will if you don't get back."

Unable to understand the words coming from the Olggans, she kept swinging, retreating until she found herself backed up against a crumbled brick wall, drawing them away from a splayed-out, unconscious Skars. The wall like a hard shove would topple it over on her, she tried to edge to the side and found another Olggan blocking her way.

Cornered, she stopped swinging and started poking them with the rod. As frightened as she was, none of the Vikings were close enough to help. Skars had groggily managed to get to his feet and was fighting the one wearing the silver headpiece while trying to move closer to her. The other Vikings, other than Ulf, had their hands full.

Realizing there was no one but herself to save her, she stabbed forward with the rod, aiming for the chest of the Olggan set on repaying her for its injured hand. Raine barely managed to remain in place when she felt herself jerked forward when the darn thing tried to pull the rod away from her.

"Don't let it touch you!" Skars warned.

If she weren't so busy fighting for her life, she would have rolled her eyes at him. Didn't the rod she was using to poke at the black and grey alien already give a big hint that she didn't want to be touched? Regretting not asking Ulf if she could borrow the extra ax hanging from his waist, that might have been a bigger hint when, like the Vikings, she started chopping off body parts. Squeamish, she had to turn her head when Skars dismembered two Olggans while fighting the one Ulf said was their king.

Feeling the rod sinking into flesh, Raine jerked her head back to see the one in front of her bent down with the rod sticking out of its stomach. It took all her willpower to pull the rod back out as red blood spilled out. *Please don't pass out, please don't pass out*, she pleaded with herself.

Fighting back lightheadedness, she reached out to brace herself against the fragile wall.

A brick falling at her feet had her skittishly running forward with the rod. The Olggan must have been stunned at her courageously running at them. They must have become frightened by her skill with the rod, because the aliens leaped to the side, out of her way. They were unaware the only thing that frightened her more than being eaten was being crushed to death.

Hearing more bricks fall, Raine gave a high-pitched

squeal of fright, running past them as they stared at her like she was deranged.

Not knowing what to do to keep herself from getting killed, she ran to Skars' side, knocking one of the Olggans aside that he had been fighting.

"They're going to eat me!" she gasped out.

Giving her a strange look, he jerked the rod away from her. Nearly hysterical, she completely lost it when she realized the other end of the rod was attached to the alien she had knocked aside.

"I'm going to pass out." Grabbing his arm, she fought the swirling darkness.

"No, you're not." Taking her arm firmly, he gave her a shake. "Go back to Ulf."

"No, I have to protect you," she refused, managing to get a hold of herself and stopping the high-pitched screaming coming from her throat.

"Can I have your ax? You can keep the rod," she offered magnanimously.

Somehow, the Olggans must have understood what she had said, and with what she swore were frightened glances, they began distancing themselves from her. All except the king, who was trying to knock Skars' ax out of his hand with a lethal-looking sword.

"Are the others giving up?" she asked hopefully. Surely, Skars would be able to take the king now that it was one on one.

"Neinn, they think you are a witch and will bring bad luck."

She started to tell them that she wasn't a witch then decided being a labeled a witch wasn't such a bad thing if it kept her from getting eaten.

"Ulf!" Skars' harsh shout had her turning in the other

vikings' direction to see the Olggans had discovered Piper's hiding spot, maneuvering themselves so none of the Vikings could reach her in time. Terrified, Piper took off running from her crouched position.

"Don't!" Raine shouted, also noticing Skars and the other Vikings had started swinging their weapons vigorously at the Olggans, trying to make a path toward Piper.

Her warning came too late for Piper.

Raine tried to dart after her, but found herself blocked by the ongoing fight taking place between two other Vikings and a large group of Olggans. Ulf, who was contending with several as he protected Tayla, was unable to reach Piper as well.

Stark fear flooded through Raine when the young girl came to a sudden stop to grab her chest and began to crumple to the ground.

"Piper!" Raine screamed.

Disengaging himself from the fight, Ulf attempted to go to her aid.

Raine felt a woosh of air next to her. Then, out of the corner of her eye, she saw the king spring forward in a leap that put him just inches away from Piper.

"Don't hurt h—" Raine managed to stop herself in time. "Don't hurt him! Leave him alone. He's sick!" she pleaded. "I need to help him."

The king tilted his head to stare at her intently before turning back to Piper lying on the ground like a lifeless doll.

Ulf went to slide his hands under Piper, but before he could, King Jurzed caught Piper in his sinewy arms then took another leap away from the fighting between the Olggans and the Vikings. His army quickly retreated after him, as if they had been sent a silent message to withdraw.

"Let him go!" Raine screamed after them. With the

way clear now, she started sprinting after them, deter-mined not to lose sight of Piper. With her eyes, she tried to keep up with the king until it became difficult to keep track of his position the farther away he got and with the Olggans blocking her view. Raine gave a gasp of frustra-tion when Piper and the king were swallowed out of sight.

Not watching where she was running, she stumbled on the body parts lying on the ground. She would have gone down headfirst if she hadn't been caught from behind and pulled against Skars' chest.

"It's too late," Skars told her. "Jurzed is gone. We won't be able to catch him."

"What do you mean *it's too late*? He couldn't have gotten that far. We have to go after him!" Frantic, Raine tried to throw herself out of Skars' unrelenting hold. "Let me go!" Struggling against him, Raine could only watch helplessly as the Olggans, with the king and Piper with them, disap-peared from eyesight.

Angry, Raine glared furiously at Ulf. "You said you would protect him!"

Affronted, the Viking stared back at her among the bodies he had killed.

Skars turned her around to face him. "King Jurzed will not harm the boy. He was taken for ransom."

Confused, Raine tried to get her fear for Piper under control. "Why? For money?"

"Neinn, for trade."

"*Trade*? What does he want in return? We have no money." Conflicted about telling him that Piper was a woman and not a boy, she kept Skars in the dark.

"King Jurzed wanted me."

"Why does he want you?"

"He would have bargaining power over my brother, Thorsen, who is our clan leader."

Understanding it was a powerplay between the two fractions of aliens didn't ease her fears for Piper.

"Say..." she delicately tried to find out more, "if you were traded for Piper—I'm not saying you will be—*but*, if you were, would he kill you?"

Skars narrowed his red eyes at her, but answered her anyway. "King Jurzed wouldn't kill me. He would bargain for Xioarius if Thorsen finds him first."

Raine was beginning to think she had actually died in the bombing and was living out her afterlife in an alien version of a k-drama.

"Okay ... say ... you're exchanged for Piper, Thorsen finds this dude Xio ... ruiu ..." Raine stopped trying to butcher the name and shortened it. "Xio is given to him, would you be returned?"

"Já."

Raine took that as a yes.

"What would happen to Xio?"

"King Jurzed will kill him."

"Well, that wouldn't be good for him." She bit her lip. Did she care if an unknown alien would die because she had snuck out of the vault? "What would Thorsen do with Xio if he didn't want to trade him for you?"

"Kill him."

That definitely should ease her conscience. The alien would be dead regardless. Unless Xio was good, and that was why the aliens wanted him dead. Maybe he was trying to save the humans on Earth, and that was why the others wanted to kill him. Raine began building an imaginary picture of this hero from another planet, like she had read about in her numerous romance novels.

"What did he do that everyone wants to kill him?" she asked sympathetically.

Skars recognized the compassion in her voice and gave her a disgusted look. "Xioarius is responsible for eradicating our planet from the galaxy. Thousands of lives were taken; many of them our women and children."

CHAPTER 9

RAINE

Her marriage had just departed the honeymoon stage and entered rocky territory. She didn't even have the extra benefit of experiencing a courtship that she had always read about and dreamed of having one day to smooth over the damage she had done.

"I'm sorry," she apologized. "I wasn't aware of the situation." Raine looked up at the bright sky. "Mars blew up?" What she knew about astronomy could be written on the back of a postage stamp, but wouldn't Mars exploding affect Earth's atmosphere?

From the way Skars looked at her, she had dipped lower in his estimation.

"Not Mars, Raum."

"Oh... My mistake," she apologized again. "Ol ..." Raine corrected herself. "Ulf said you were half-Martians. I assumed that Mars was the planet that was destroyed."

Skars' hard expression remained unmoved. "We have not the time for me to explain further. This can be discussed once we are on my ship."

Her husband pressed a hand to his shoulder. At his

movement, Raine heard a short whirling sound that sounded like a hummingbird. She looked up, and her lips parted in a gasp as four objects that looked like some type of motorcycles on the inside were surrounded within a clear circle like a balloon. Each circle hovered next to each of the Vikings.

"What are those?"

"These are our small transport vehicles. They are called nejims."

"We could go after my friend ..." Raine started to suggest excitably.

"The Ferajorin are too close. We must return to our ship." Skars motioned toward where Tayla was getting out of the destroyed car. "Once both of you are safe on board, you can show me where the remainder of your group are hiding, and I will bring them to the ship also."

Raine had two big problems with what he wanted her to do. She wouldn't be able to go after Piper, nor was she willing to show the Vikings where the others were hiding.

Looking pleadingly at Tayla for inspiration on what to do and say, Raine was relieved when the other woman took over.

"We have to get him back. Piper isn't well. He'll become sick without his medicine."

Skars stared her in confusion. "Medicine?"

"Something he needs to take regularly, or he could die," Raine tried to explain as simply as she could.

Piper had been diagnosed with neurally mediated syncope, a malfunction of her heart. She could pass out when triggered by changing positions too quickly, being stressed, or in pain. Finding a big blue alien holding her could be a death sentence to her. She knew it would scare her to death, and Raine didn't have a heart malfunction.

"The Olggans take care of their own. The boy will be put in his household. What he needs will be provided. King Jurzed will make certain he is in good health. The boy will be useless to him dead."

Raine flinched at the callous way he spoke of Piper's death, as if Piper was an inanimate object.

She wasn't about to entrust Piper to a blue dude she didn't know. What if he wasn't nice to her? Piper had been overprotected by her brother, then the group in the vault as they had drawn closer to her. Even Milly liked the girl, and that witch didn't like anyone.

Tayla wasn't any happier than her. "Do the Vikings not protect their household?"

Skars' expression grew thunderous at her question. "We do. The boy does not belong to my clan."

"He does to ours," Tayla spat out. "His brother is the only reason Raine, your *wife*, is still alive. Are you her husband or not?"

"Já, but it is unnecessary to lose the lives of my clan when his return can be accomplished without bloodshed."

"Fine!" Tayla snapped, turning to the Viking who was standing next to Skars. "What is your name?"

"I am Njal."

"Njal, do Vikings divorce each other?"

The Viking didn't immediately answer Tayla's question, looking toward Skars and her.

Raine remained silent, letting Tayla do all the threatening for her. The loan officer was better at it than she was.

Skars' jaw jutted out in irritation.

"My brother will not condone a divorce without cause."

"Why would your brother be given a choice?"

"He is our chieftain."

"So, you'll be given preferential treatment?"

"Preferential?"

"It means, because you're his brother, she won't be able divorce your ass?"

"Neinn, Thorsen will make no difference."

"Good. Then take us to him. Raine wants a divorce."

Skars looked to her questioningly at Tayla's claim.

"He is searching for Xioarius; I cannot take you to him," he refused.

"How convenient." Rudely, Tayla gave a sarcastic snort.

"I do not know what convenient means, but I do not care for your tone." Skars pinned her with his gaze. "Nor that my wife lets you speak for her."

Raine knew she had to speak up. *There goes being on their team*, she thought morosely.

"Excuse us, because we're a little upset that a young boy, who I should have been protecting instead of you, is now in the hands of aliens that have done nothing but kill people since they landed on Earth."

"You are blaming *me* for the boy being taken?"

"No, we're blaming you and"—Tayla gave Ulf a dirty look—"Ulf. Raine only went to help you because he told us that he would protect Piper."

Skars looked toward Ulf. "Why would—"

"I tried to help the boy, yet King Jurzed reached him before me. I didn't expect King Jurzed to take the boy. I could have beaten any others taking her from the distance I was to him. King Jurzed never takes humans into his household, you know that. By the time I realized he was going to take the boy, it was too late," Ulf explained.

Raine frowned. "Why would he have made an exception for Piper?"

"King Jurzed is experienced in battles. He saw you protected me, and I was protecting you. That you cared for the boy was obvious. King Jurzed knew he could use the boy to bargain to get what he truly wants."

Raine looked in the direction the Olggan had taken Piper. The young girl had to be terrified. Lucas had made sure that Piper had been protected since she had been born. Their mother had died shortly after having Piper, their father dying in a car accident shortly before her birth. Lucas had rearranged his whole life to care for the child after his parents' deaths.

"Lucas is going to kill me." Using the sleeve of her shirt, she swiped at the tears she didn't want the Vikings to see.

Skars stared at her uncomfortably. "Who is Lucas?"

"Piper's brother," she mumbled through her shirt sleeve. "I should never have left our hiding spot. If I hadn't been so worried about you, I would have turned back when I saw Piper and Tayla following me."

How was she was supposed to explain to Lucas that the gray and black aliens, who had been the one to claw him, had a blue king who had taken Piper hostage so she could be traded for another alien he really wanted to kill.

A question came to her mind as she tried to come up with the explanation. "Why did King Jurzed look different than the other Olggans?"

Skars brows knitted. "King Jurzed isn't Olggan. He saved their planet when Xioarius almost destroyed it. They rewarded him by making him king."

"King Jurzed isn't from the same planet as the Olggans?"

"Neinn, he is from Neptune."

"So, he is a Neptunian." Raine nodded, as if it made perfect sense when all she wanted to do was sit on the ground and have a good cry.

"Partly."

Raine clenched her jaw. She would bite her tongue before she would ask.

"The other half is Viking," he supplied without her having to ask. "We're cousins."

She really could have lived without knowing that fountain of information.

Tayla's reaction was opposite of hers. While she wanted to cry, the other woman started howling in laughter.

The Vikings gave Tayla wary glances, while it just made Raine want to cry more. Both were at their breaking points. Tayla was just another bit closer than her.

The big, massive Viking closest to Tayla whacked her on the back as if she was choking, sending the woman to her knees.

Raine hadn't moved back when Tayla had started laughing hysterically. She did now.

Tayla abruptly stopped laughing, a bright patch of red highlighting her high cheekbones. Even the other Vikings stared at Ulf in stunned surprise.

"The woman was bewitched," Ulf gave the explanation at seeing their shock. "I knocked the demon out of her." Ulf then extended his hand, as if he was going to assist Tayla back to her feet.

"Be careful ..." Raine started to warn him.

Unmindful of her warning, Ulf bent down to lift Tayla to her feet without her help.

Raine's eyes widened in astonishment as Tayla heaved herself into Ulf's arms to put him in a headlock. Her wrapping her legs around the Viking made Ulf lose his balance.

Raine thought about taking the opportunity to take off, but couldn't bring herself to miss out on what Tayla would do next.

Ulf ended up on the ground as Tayla body-slammed

herself on top of his chest before the Viking could regain air. His head was clenched between Tayla's thighs as she leaned her back against his chest to exert more pressure on his thick neck. She was strangling him while the others remained watching, making no attempt to help.

"King Jurzed wants to trade? Tell him you're willing to trade yourself for Piper. One of you fuckers can take him and bring Piper back here, or I'll kill him," Tayla warned Skars through gritted teeth.

Skars started laughing. "Why would I do that?"

Raucous male laughter filled the air.

"There is no better way to go to Valhalla than meeting death clasped between the thighs of a woman."

CHAPTER 10

RAINE

*I*t may not have been my brightest move to let Tayla take over the discussions with the Vikings, Raine thought ruefully.

Moving to their side, Raine nudged Tayla's thigh with her foot to get her attention. "Stop it. They're laughing."

Tayla pressed her legs harder together. "They won't be laughing," she muttered between clenched teeth, "for long."

It must have clicked in Skars' head that Tayla meant business.

Angrily separating the combatting man and woman, he leaned down and lifted Ulf to his feet, dragging Tayla up also. "Woman, if the Ferajorin arrive before we can depart, we will need Ulf's ax. Release him."

Dropping her legs as they rose, Tayla gave the Vikings a feral grin. "I have a suggestion that should make all of us happy." Tayla's blue-green gaze went to Skars. "Is there a way to talk to each other if you're separated?"

"Já," Skars responded.

"Then you take the other two Vikings and Raine with you to the ship while I can show Ulf where our group is hiding. If Raine thinks it's safe, you can bring more machines to transport us, and we'll come willingly."

Skars seemed to consider the suggestion. "My word isn't enough that none of you will be harmed?"

Raine bit down on her bottom lip. The big Viking seemed hurt that neither Tayla nor she were willing to trust him.

Hesitant, Raine reached out to touch his arm. "I trust you. The problem is, if I'm wrong, several people will pay the price for my mistake. Tayla trusts you, too, don't you?" Raine jiggled her eyes at Tayla to get her to agree.

Tayla tried to appear as if she was agreeing with her, pasting a fake smile on her lips. "A hundred percent," she said, bobbing her head up and down.

Raine wondered if the Vikings would notice if she planted her foot up the other woman's ass.

"How would you know we didn't force her to lie when she talks to you?"

"You can give us a minute alone, and we'll agree on a code only the both of us will know."

Skars frowned. "You want to take Ulf in case we try to betray you?"

"Yes." Raine hated that Skars had put it that way, but it was basically what they wanted.

"Before I agree, you have to tell me how many there are of you."

Dammit, could nothing be simple? She didn't know whether to escalate their numbers or try to make it seem as if there were fewer of them.

Tayla didn't have the same problem opening her mouth to lie before she could. Skars held his hand up, stopping her from speaking.

"My wife will whisper me this number while you whisper to Ulf your answer."

Seeing no way out of doing what she wanted, Raine walked over to Skars. Going to her toes, she whispered the answer as Tayla turned her head to whisper in Ulf's.

"Seven," she whispered huskily as her eyes were caught and held by Skars. Raine felt the heat of embarrassment flood her cheeks. The man must be aware of his impact he had on a woman; she saw it in his eyes and the curl of his sensuous lips.

Amusement filled his face when she hastily took a step backward.

"Ulf doesn't go without his ax."

Raine let Tayla handle that one, keeping her expression blank.

Tayla might have stayed in the ruined car while the Vikings fought the other aliens, but she was able to take care of herself. The woman hadn't been playing around when her legs were around Ulf's neck.

Only working three days at the bank, for enough money to get her new business off the ground, Tayla had spent the other days giving lessons in different fighting styles.

Since the bombing, she had regretted more than once not taking the discount that Tayla had offered her to teach her how to defend herself.

"He can take his ax as long as he leaves that doohickey he threw on us here." Giving Ulf a frosty glare, she agreed to Skars' stipulation.

Skars gave Ulf a nod, and then Ulf reached to his side to remove what appeared to be an old leather bag and tossing it to Skars.

Placing the bag within the folds of his cape, Skars touched the side of the vehicle next to him. The clear outer shell rose upward, leaving Skars room to sling a leg over the side. "You may speak alone to the old woman."

It took Raine a moment for her to figure out that Skars was talking about Tayla. Taking the opportunity, they stepped to the side and out of earshot of the Vikings.

"Congratulations, your disguise worked." Raine eyed Tayla's silver-streaked hair.

"*Pfft*. I told you it would. Men, whatever the species, go by first impressions. They took one look at the color of my hair and the thick makeup to place me in the older-than-hills section." Giving an uncaring eye roll, Tayla gave Ulf a withering glare. "It's not like any of them are geniuses. They probably share the same brain cell. They bought Piper is a boy, and all that took was a baseball hat, short haircut, and boy's clothes." She sniffed disdainfully at the men's gullibility. "Make sure you don't tell stud muffin any different. I don't trust any of them any farther than I can throw them."

Raine didn't agree, but kept silent. She didn't want to waste further time allotted to them.

"What should we use as the code?"

"We aren't going to need a code. I'm going to knock him out as soon as we're out of eyesight and follow Piper. After I get her back, I'll hold Olf"—she deliberately mispronounced his name—"ransom to make them give you back."

Raine wanted to pull her hair out at the mention of ransom. There was going to be a lot of ransoming going on, and she didn't want to be caught out in the cold if her group didn't want her back. She wasn't Ms. Popular in the vault.

"I really don't think that's a good idea."

Tayla pinned her with a level stare. "You want to go back to the vault without Piper?"

"No," she admitted. Lucas could be a little scary where his sister was concerned.

"Fine, we'll go with it. Just in case we should come up with something to show if everything is okay, you could ask what my favorite fruit is. If I answer peaches, you know I'm safe, and if I'm not, I say grapes."

"Works for me."

It was everything she could do not to shake Tayla. The only reason she didn't was because she was afraid Tayla would smash her to smithereens with one of her flying kicks. She thought Tayla was overconfident about her abilities then had to admit the kicks she had taught the whole group before any of them were allowed to go on food searches had proven useful.

"Come." Skars firmly brought an end to their talk, extending his hand toward her as the other Vikings opened their machines.

Raine gave another glance toward Tayla, seeking assurance that they were really going with them.

Giving her a fatalistic shrug, Tayla walked back to Ulf as Raine returned to Skars. Putting off the inevitable, she watched as Tayla ignored the hand Ulf held out to her, getting on behind him. Raine then watched as the shell closed again, enclosing them inside.

Turning her gaze back to Skars then upward, she couldn't make herself take the small step forward.

"Wife, I truly mean you no harm," he said softly, as if trying to calm her.

Raine lowered her gaze back to ground level. "I'm afraid of heights."

"Come here."

His soft command curled her stomach in knots. All the

heroines in her books would have already been sitting behind him.

Hating herself for being such a coward, she was about to take a step back when Skars locked his hand around her wrist and pulled her to him. "Get on."

Forcing herself to lift her leg as Skars steadied her, she climbed on awkwardly, nearly going over the seat when she tripped, not noticing there was a small place for her other foot to go where it would have made it easier for her to do without Skars' help.

Humiliated at the ungainly way she managed to seat herself, she didn't look at the other Vikings to see their reactions.

It was everything she could do not to scream bloody murder when the shell slid down as Ulf and the others' vehicles started rising into the air.

Skars must have sensed how close she was to going into another screaming fit because his soothing voice reached her through the rising tide of hysteria. "Close your eyes and lay your head on my shoulder. Hold on to my waist if you want to, but the side of the nejim will hold you still."

"Okay," she croaked out. "Quick question before you take off. Do you have to have a pilot's license to fly one of these things?" Before he could answer, she was already on to the next question. "Are you *very* experienced flying—"

"Raine..." Skars put his hands behind his back, seeking her hands. Raine didn't resist when he wound them around his waist to press them against his flat abs. "I'm very *experienced* at everything I do."

CHAPTER II
SKARS

Skars felt Raine's hands shaking on his abdomen. Gritting his teeth, he concentrated on the nejim's instruments rather than on the thickening of his cock.

His wife clung to him like the finest whore in Manitorz. The planet Leron was a well-known area in the galaxy where any sexual encounter could be had with any species, at the price of their currency.

Thorsen had stopped there many times during their journeys. Several times, he, too, had gone down to the planet to relieve the sexual frustrations of not having a tru-mate.

Because Reva had foreseen no tru-mate in his future, the vision had guided his acceptance so freely when the opportunity arose to claim the woman holding him now. He was now second-guessing the rash decision.

She didn't trust him. He tried not to blame her for that, but while she ran with the grace of a gazelle, she kicked with the grace of a mule, sounded like a Janree when it was trapped when she was fighting, and fought like a shield-maiden's seamstress.

Not only did she lack any worthy virtues that would make her easily fit into the clan, the only good thing she was good at was lying. The other woman shared the same flaw. Did lies easily fall off all humans' lips? He would warn Thorsen when he reached his ship what he had overheard when the women had spoken alone, unaware the Vikings could easily hear with their acute hearing abilities.

He rose slowly, so as not to alarm Raine into having another screaming fit that had taken all his willpower not to drop to his knees in agony when she had seen she had skewered one of the Olggans. He had only managed to do so because King Jurzed had been watching him and had showed no pain himself. He would have skewered himself on the rod she was holding before showing weakness in front of the fierce warrior.

"Are we almost there?"

His anger decreased at the small whimper he heard in her voice.

"Já. Not long."

He must make allowances for the woman. She was new to the Viking ways and, until a short time ago, humans had no idea aliens even existed.

He would be gentle with her as she learned to be a wife to him. She deserved his gentleness; hadn't she saved his life? Conveniently forgetting it was just a scratch, he snugly docked the nejim into the under-port of his ship. Then he tapped the side of the nejim, and it opened.

"We're here."

Getting off, he held his hand out to her. Her frightened gaze was mixed with curiosity as she looked around the small room where they held the nejims. "That wasn't as bad as I expected."

"I'm happy that you didn't find the trip stressful."

"I thought it would take longer to get to outer space."

Not correcting her mistake, he retained his hold on her hand and ushered her to the metal doorway. As they approached, the door slid open quietly. As it did, her eyes widened at the windows where she could see outside.

"We're not in outer space?"

"Neinn. Have a look."

Raine immediately shook her head. "I'll pass. I get vertigo when I look down from heights."

"Ah … Then it's better you don't look," he agreed, resuming walking forward along the small corridor to another door. Again, the door slid open during their approach to show a small, windowless room. Stepping inside, he tugged Raine into the elevator with him.

Feeling her hand clasp his hand tighter when it started moving, he reassured her. "The elevator is lifting us to the main part of my ship."

"Okay. This is going to take time to get used to."

"Most new experiences do. I've been in your place a few times during my lifetime. When I first started going along with Thorsen to trade with other planets, I was frightened," he lied smoothly.

His wife gave him a searching glance.

Skars couldn't hold back his laughter. "I was nervous," he corrected.

"That I believe." She gave him a smile that had his cock tingling again. "I can't imagine you being frightened of anything."

"You should see me if I come upon a cave of lanree. I'll take off running as if Hades is chasing after me."

The door slid open. Anxiously, he watched for her reaction. They would be spending much of their time in his ship once they left Earth. Many of the furnishings would be moved into the home that he would build for them.

"It's beautiful."

His shoulders straightened with pride at the awe she showed in her soft grey eyes. He also saw the gentleness she used when picking up a fragile vase the size of her palm.

Thinking she wanted to get a better look at the gold the vase was made of, he was surprised when she raised it higher to sniff the tiny flowers.

"What kind of flowers are these?"

"They are snowdrops."

"I love them. I've never seen them before."

"They are from Iaslamire."

Skars considered her while she was focused on the flowers. With the riches he had traded for from other planets, what caught her immediate attention were flowers he had bought with mere change.

"How long do they last?" she asked, gently setting the vase back down.

"They only die if they are exposed to heat."

She tilted her head in curiosity. "The cold doesn't affect them?"

"No. They flourish in cold temperatures."

"Then we need to make sure they don't get hot. They're lovely."

"As are you," he complimented her.

She self-consciously smoothed her hands down to her sides. "Thank you, but I'm aware of the way I look."

He started to argue, but stopped when he noticed her peeking at him through her lowered lashes.

"But I am much more attractive when I'm able to blow out my hair instead of letting it dry naturally. We've had access to a shower where we've been hiding, but we're afraid to use the battery-operated blow dryer Milly found."

Skars reached out to wrap a long brown curl around his finger. "Why not?" he asked, taking a step closer to her.

With wide eyes, she started to take a step then stopped when she realized he wasn't releasing her hair.

"Pardon me. Should I return later?"

Skars didn't turn his head at the sound of a female voice.

"No, come in. I wouldn't have sent for you if I didn't want to talk to you." Unwinding the curl, Skars turned Raine to face the woman who had just entered the room.

"Raine, I want you to meet Reva."

Raine gave Reva a welcoming smile before giving him a searching glance. "I didn't hear you call anyone?"

Skars turned his arm over to show the underside of the sleeve of his shirt. Using the tip of his finger, he showed her the symbols on a small pad. Using the same finger, he casually removed the thin wafer to place it on the sleeve of the shirt she was wearing. Pointing at one symbol, he explained, "Pressing this will notify me you wish to speak to me. I'll teach the others you can contact later."

She frowned up at him. "But what if you need it?"

"I don't plan to leave your side anytime soon. I'll get another when I go to the control room."

Skars turned his attention back to Reva, who was watching them with a patient smile. "My apologies, Seeress. I don't mean to keep you waiting—"

Reva held up her hand. "All is well, Skars. It is understandable she was confused, and as a husband, it is your duty to provide the explanation."

Reva strolled across the plush carpet to stand before Raine. "May I?" Reva held out both of her hands, face up. "I wish to see if the vision of you from several years ago has borne out."

Confusion filled Raine's face.

Skars gave her an encouraging smile.

"Reva is our seeress. Lay your hands directly over hers," he instructed his wife.

Raine did as she was instructed with a glance toward him. "Is she like a psychic?"

Skars let Reva explain.

"Throughout time, we have been called by many names, depending on what planet we are on."

"Oh ... On Earth, we call them psychics," she said helpfully.

He would have to thank Reva later that she hadn't become insulted at Raine's lack of reverence.

The seeress' serene face became expressionless. Even Raine seemed to understand the seriousness of the moment as Reva stared deep into her eyes for long minutes before dropping her hands and walking away, leaving Raine's hands still outstretched.

Skars had never seen Reva act this way.

"Seeress?"

The seeress seemed to shake herself out of whatever vision she'd had to address Raine. "It's my true pleasure to meet you. As wife to Skars, you will be an asset to our clan. Later, when you are more settled, I invite you to my quarters for a meal."

The seeress turned her eyes to address him. "Excuse me, Skars. I must take my leave. I will give Thorsen my permission for the wedding. May the gods bless you with many daughters." Turning on her rose-colored slippers, the seeress glided out of the room, leaving them both staring after her.

"I was hoping, when you complimented me, that compared to other females you had seen on different planets, that at least I could be considered passably pretty. She just blew that out of the water. Your seeress is beautiful."

Reva was indeed beautiful, he acceded dispassionately. Looking toward Raine, he expected to see many emotions—envy, jealousy, and dislike among that had been shown to Reva whenever she was around other women. There were no emotions present on Raine's face but fear.

"There is no need to be fearful of her vision. She likes you. I can tell."

Raine began to look even more upset. "I could tell, too. That's why I'm worried about her inviting me to a meal."

Skars frowned. "And you were displeased with the invitation?" The woman sank lower in his estimation. He could ignore her other lacks, but to not like Reva was …

Raine shook her head. "Not displeased. She seems nice …" She stared at him like she was scared to say something.

"Do not be afraid of me. Do you have a question to put to me?"

"You swear you'll tell the truth?"

His shoulders reared back in insult. "Já," he relied stiffly. He shouldn't have been so harsh with her. The woman appeared as if she wanted to cry. Skars forced himself to gentle his voice. "Ask your question."

"Does she want to share a meal with me, or am I supposed to be the meal?"

CHAPTER 12

SKARS

D umbfounded at the question, Skars could only stare at his wife. He had made a terrible mistake. He must notify Thorsen that no wedding would be taking place.

His eyes dropped to Raine's hands, where she was nervously pulling on her pants.

"The clothes I'm wearing make me look big, but I've lost weight. She wouldn't get as much meat as she thinks. I'm mainly big boned—"

"Reva doesn't want to eat you."

She has the intelligence of a child, he thought bitingly.

Seeing the tears threatening to spill, he thought to soothe her. "Let us go ... I'll take you back to Earth."

Joy filled her face. "You'll take me back?"

"I'll take you. I'll return you to your group, and Ulf and I will leave."

"Thank you so much," she said excitably.

Skars didn't waste time ushering her to the elevator, then inside.

"This is a big relief. I was terrified when your seeress mentioned having a meal with me. Milly warned me about aliens only wanting to come to Earth because we fill their food shortage."

Skars turned his head to see if the woman was joking. She wasn't. She truly believed what she was saying.

"Who is Milly?"

"One of the women in our group," she happily explained. "She was our customer service rep at the bank. Customers complained about her all the time. Lucas finally had to put her in the drive-thru; that way, she didn't have to have much interaction with the customers."

Skars placed his hand on the door, stopping the elevator. Then he slid his hand upward and to the side.

"What are you doing?" she asked curiously.

"You look exhausted. Would you like to shower, change, and rest before I return you to Earth?"

His wife nibbled on her bottom lip. "What about Ulf? Shouldn't he have called before now?"

"I will inform you the moment he does."

The door to the elevator opened, exposing his bedroom.

"Wow. Is this your guest bedroom?"

With a firm hand on the small of her back, Skars escorted her out of the elevator.

"Yes, you are my guest." Unrepentantly, he let his ingenious bride believe the room wasn't his.

"Milly doesn't like you?" he asked, steering their conversation in the direction he wanted.

"How did you know?" Soft grey eyes stared at him curiously. "For an alien, you're very intuitive."

Skars turned the lights on with a wave of his hand then dimmed them by simply lowering his hand until he had the intimate atmosphere he wanted.

"Já, I am." He had arrogantly told Thorsen that many

times over the years. He was much more familiar with women's behavior than his brother.

Skars cynically watched her eyes become worried at her own observation. Then she shook it off and went back to talking about the tispe. During his travels throughout the galaxies, he had met far too many tispe, women who were spiteful toward their own sex to make them subserviate to their demands. They all had one thing in common—they preyed on those they were most jealous of.

"Anyway ... I tried to be friends with Milly, but she has disliked me from the get-go. I've never done anything for her to dislike me, but she does."

Skars knew she was keeping something back from him, despite the innocent look she was giving him.

"What do you think is the reason for her dislike?" he prompted her, giving her a sympathetic glance as he tried to get to the bottom of what she had done.

"She blames me because Lucas—he's our bank manager," she explained, "or, at least he was. The bank is closed since everyone on Earth started bombing each other."

"Raine ..." he prompted her.

"Okay." She took a deep breath before continuing. "One day, I was leaving for break to go to a coffee shop, which was next door. I nicely stopped by her desk, offering to bring something back to her. I always offered to do the same for the others, and I thought it would show I didn't like her if I didn't at least offer to do the same for Milly. I shouldn't have. I didn't see she had a cup next to her keyboard, and I accidentally knocked it over. She was on a call, and she started cursing at me. The customer on the other end believed she was yelling at them." Raine made a face. "It became a big mess. The customer was the owner of a big corporation. They wanted her fired. Lucas was able to save her job, but she had to work the drive-thru. She wasn't happy about switching jobs."

"She is the one who told you the aliens want to eat you?"

Red flooded her cheeks. "She told me, to them, I look like a buffet."

"Buffet?"

"Where more than one can eat," she said with a miserable expression.

"She lied."

"So, when the aliens are capturing the humans, they aren't eating them?"

"No. The only aliens who eat humans haven't made their way to Earth yet."

"That's good to know." Giving a huge sigh of relief, she stared at him quizzically. "Then what are they doing with the humans?"

"Depends on who they are captured by." Determined to switch topics, he went to the side of the room, and as he did, another door opened. "Would you like to shower and get changed?"

Raine gripped her pants tighter around her. "I don't have anything else to change into. I've been searching for more clothes, but I haven't been able to find any."

"I have many. Once you are finished showering, I'll show you."

"That would be wonderful. We were able to wash at the bank, but I would love a shower." Wrinkling her nose at him, she gave him an embarrassed glance. "I'm sure it will make it more bearable for you to be around me."

"Come." He motioned for her to go first into the shower room.

While his bedroom was carpeted in the finest carpet he

could trade for on Uatera, the bed he had crafted by himself to fit his large frame. The three massive ornate chests, he had bought from various planets. They contained gifts meant for the home and wife he hoped to have. However, the room they were entering was as if they had entered another era.

From the ceiling, water fell with a soothing sound to land on the smooth grey stones beneath. The water would be recycled through his ship's filtration system then returned through a series of pipes that would start the whole process over again. To the side was a slated wooden bench that was the only thing in the room other than the plants that covered the walls. It was his sanctuary, the lush greenery displacing the bleak darkness of space and the loneliness of not having a tru-mate.

She stared at the room with the same appreciative gaze she had for the vase. "I may never leave."

"It is yours."

"Thank you. I can't wait to use it." Giving him an expectant glance, she touched her pants, but didn't start to disrobe.

He raised his brows, not understanding why she wasn't readying herself. "Do you require my assistance?"

"No!" She lowered her shrill voice when she noticed his grimace. "I can handle it ... by myself."

He still made no move to leave.

She licked her lips and glanced toward the still open doorway. "I ..." she began nervously. "I like to wash by myself."

"You may do so. I will wait." Skars moved to take a seat on the bench.

"Uh ... I don't feel comfortable washing with you watching."

Frowning at her, he made no effort to get up. "You are my wife—we have no secrets. Would you feel more comfortable if I undressed?" He started to rise from the bench.

"No!"

He flinched. Her shrill was making his skull ache.

"I thought we weren't truly married until your brother completed the ceremony?"

"True."

"Then let's save you watching me shower until after the ceremony. It will give us something else to look forward to."

"I prefer not to wait," he stated arrogantly.

"I prefer to wait, and what I want matters more than what you want where it concerns anything with me being naked." Her eyes narrowed to mean little slits.

Thorsen had warned him being married came with compromises. Unfortunately for his little bride, she wasn't married to his brother. He viewed compromises as a sign of weakness. He hadn't become the best trader in the galaxy by not getting what he was determined to have.

"Very well." He rose from the bench, pretending to look around, as if something was hiding within the room. "If you see my pet okrakratus hanging around, don't scream. He is afraid of loud noises." Striding to the door, he didn't spare her another glance.

"Wait!" she whisper-screamed.

Skars turned back to her, keeping his face expressionless.

"What is an okrakratus?"

"There is no way for me to explain what he looks like. Earth doesn't have any creatures that are similar."

Raine warily searched around the room while she stood rooted to the same spot. "Does he bite?" she whispered.

"No, he has no teeth."

"Oh ... Okay ... You can lea—"

"They latch on and suck," he told her helpfully.

Her hand flew to her neck. Skars wondered what she was imagining.

"Perhaps it would be better for me to wait until Tayla. I mean, until Ulf calls."

Skars wrinkled his nose at her. "If you insist."

She clenched her teeth at him. "Fine. You can sit on the bench. Just be a gentleman and keep your back turned."

"If you insist." Skars resumed his seat on the bench, with his back turned toward her, listening intently as she began removing her clothes.

"Human women are very modest," she instructed him.

"Truly?"

"Very," she insisted. "We don't believe in being naked in front of men until after they are married at least thirty days."

Skars was happy his back was to his lying bride.

"I was unaware of that knowledge from my ancestors."

"Earth has changed since your ancestors were taken."

"How so?"

"Well, like after a couple is married, they wait six months before they sleep together, then another six months before they actually have sex."

"Times have not changed for the better. If a husband is allowed to see his bride naked after thirty days, why does he have to wait six months to share the marriage bed?"

Skars' eyes went to the small mirrored tile that he could easily see between hanging plants. Naked Raine had moved underneath the ceiling waterfall. Her body was exquisite, from breasts that hung like mouth-watering fwetasip fruit with red berry tips to curvy hips that a warrior could hold on to and not lose his grip. Her body had his lust rising.

"Oh ..."

Skars rolled his eyes at her trying to work herself out of that lie.

"Oh ... That's to build anticipation."

"Why would I need to build anticipation when I already want you?"

Seeing the shock on her face, Skars wanted to shake his head at the human males. How could this beautiful woman doubt her desirability?

"You're attracted to me?"

"I find you very desirable."

Her hand went to her stomach with a worried frown. "That's only because you haven't seen me compared to other women. I'm overweight compared to other women."

Skars gave a snort. "Fragile women who would run rather than fight an Olggan?"

Her frown cleared at the compliment. "You know, you're right. I didn't run."

Noticing she was looking around for something, he questioned her. "You have a need?"

"I don't see any soap?"

"Pluck one of the red or pink flowers from the plants near you," he instructed.

Watching the mirror, Skars saw her pluck the pink one and started rubbing it on her skin to make a lather.

"This smells fantastic. Can I take some of these with me when you take me to Earth? We're starting to run low on soap."

"Já," he easily lied in kind.

When started washing her hair, he had to quell himself from joining her under the water. The movement was making her breasts jut out, as if begging him to suckle on one.

"I expected the water to be cold," she said inanely. "It's the perfect temperature."

"The rocks at your feet automatically set a comfortable temperature for whoever is using it."

"Wow, and Earth thinks they're advanced. I'm finished. Where are the towels?"

"You don't need one. Step off the rocks onto the wood next to you."

Skars watched as she did as instructed. She started trembling as air blew upward and downward from the vents. Her berry nipples turned a deeper shade of red. The sight had him partially rising from the bench, about to make Raine his bride in fact when a transmission came in from Bjorn.

Pressing a button on his shoulder, he listened to the message. Then, abruptly rising, he went to the doorway, ignoring Raine's startled squeak of outrage.

Going into his bedroom, he came back with a thin covering, which was usually used on the bed. Returning to Raine, he averted his gaze, handing her the cover. "You may use this to cover yourself. Come with me, and we'll find garments to fit you."

"You could have told me where this was, and I could have gotten it for myself."

Skars turned as she wound the covering around herself. "The nejim that Tayla and Ulf were in crashed ..."

His wife went pale as he began explaining his urgency.

"Before Bjorn could land to get them, they were taken captive."

"By the Olggans?"

"No, by the Volzon."

"What are we going to do?"

"Nothing."

"We have to do something," she argued, tightening the cover around her.

"We have to wait."

"For what?"

"Their ransom demand."

CHAPTER 13

RAINE

"You may choose which garments you prefer."

Raine pulled the satin sheet tighter around her breasts. How was she supposed to choose? When Skars had started opening the three chests along the wall of the guest room, she hadn't expected him to take out the myriad of clothes that made it impossible to choose from.

Spreading the clothes out on a bed that Raine estimated was the size of a California king and a queen that took up most of the room, she could only stare in indecision.

"Would you prefer for me to choose for you?"

Raine quickly shook her head. "No, thank you." Hesitantly touching the soft material of a pair of peach pants, she stared wistfully at the matching blouse. She would never be able to fit in the outfit.

"You choose the ..."

Raine shook her head. "It won't fit." Embarrassed, she looked toward Skars. "None of these will."

Skars' brow knitted in a frown. "How do you know if you don't try them on?"

"I just do." Raine waved her hand over the clothes on

the bed then waved it downward over her body. "I wouldn't be able to get the zipper closed on the pants."

Confusion filled his face. "Zipper?"

"You know the part ..." Raine started to explain then thought it would be easier just to show him. "I'll be right back." Returning to the Garden of Eden bathroom, Raine couldn't help but give it another appreciative glance.

The room was beautiful. It was how she had always imagined the Garden of Eden to look. Lush greenery covered the walls and the floor, except where the water was trinkling from the ceiling. There, it had something that appeared like AstroTurf, but wasn't. It had the feel of real grass on her bare feet, but the texture was different.

Picking up her clothes, she reluctantly went back into the other room, despite wanting to toss the sheet and step back under the water just so she would be able to experience the body drier again. Whoever had invented that bad boy deserved the trophy for inventor of the year. Raine personally thought it was a shame Earth didn't have any. They could have brought world peace.

Mortified now that she was clean, she uncomfortably showed him the zipper and how it worked, aware of how dirty and shabby the clothes were.

"There isn't one on these clothes."

Before she could react, Skars plucked the dirty clothes out of her hands and strode to the wall. Raine could only watch helplessly as the clothes were sucked from his hands and into a hole that she hadn't noticed before.

"I need those back." Raine rushed to the hole. "Make them come back."

"I cannot. They have already been shredded and sent to the waste room."

Raine glared at him. "Those were mine."

"They are where they belong." Skars arrogantly strode to the bed. "Choose, or I will choose for you."

"None will fit!" she yelled at him, almost in tears. The last thing she wanted to do was try on clothes that wouldn't fit in front of a man who was as attractive as Skars.

Raine looked away when his eyes caught hers, not wanting him to see how upset she was. She had no one to blame but herself that she was overweight. She had the willpower of a flea when it came to lattes, takeout, and about anything that tasted good. There wasn't anything better than reading a good book, drinking a latte, and having a box of your favorite chocolates as a stand-in for a hot man who wouldn't give her a second glance if she were being robbed in broad daylight.

Skars picked up the peach pants. "Reva is an excellent seamstress. She sews her own clothes. If they don't fit, she will make the necessary adjustments."

"Unless she has another yard of the same material, she won't be able to. Perhaps Ulf has an extra pair of pants and shirts I can borrow ..."

His face filled with bewilderment. "You believe you are the same size as Ulf?"

Raine felt herself blushing in humiliation. Was she bigger than she thought? Was she bigger than Ulf?

"Almost. He's taller, and I can roll the pants—"

"Put my arms the distance apart that you think you are." Standing in front of her, Skars stretched his arms.

She had never been so embarrassed in her life, and there had been many embarrassments. There had been a time she had thought a worker at her favorite coffee shop had been flirting with her. She had then heard the cackling of laughter when she had moved away. In the reflection of the door, she had seen him blowing out his cheeks and using a squirt bottle to mimic her being a whale. Or the one time that still gave her nightmares. The time she had been invited to go to a birthday party by one of her coworkers, only to find out the reason she had been invited was the birthday boy had a fetish for overweight women and her coworker thought they would click, unbeknown to her. Believing she had finally found the man of her dreams at the attention she was receiving from him, when she had left to go to the restroom and came back, the birthday boy had been showering his attention on another woman and was sitting at another table. Hurt, she couldn't understand what she had done to put him off. She had asked her coworker until she finally confessed why she had been invited, and while the birthday boy had a thing for over-weight women, he wanted them pretty, too.

"Skars, I know you mean well, but I know which clothes will fit me."

He didn't lower his arms, his frown becoming ferocious. He moved his arms farther apart himself. "Do you believe you can fit between my arms?"

Raine gauged the length. "No."

His face went expressionless. "More or less?"

"More."

Skars moved them farther apart. "Now?"

"More."

He moved his arms wider. "Now?"

"A little more."

Skars moved his arms until they were spread out to twice the size of his body.

"There." Raine told him before he could ask.

"You believe yourself to be this size?"

"Yes." Miserable, she decided the next time they

rationed out food, she would give her portion to someone else in the vault.

Skars' expression remained inscrutable. "Then if I do this"—he moved his arms closer together until they were just a little wider than his body—"you shouldn't be able to walk into my arms without my arms touching you."

Raine nodded her agreement. "No."

"Let us see. Walk into my arms."

"Fine!" she snapped. "This is ridiculous. Don't you understand this is embarrassing?"

God, why did You have to make me love lattes so much? Complaining to God in her head, she took a step forward, easily walking between his arms. She stopped when she didn't feel his arms at her sides.

"You moved your arms!"

"I did not." He closed his arms around her to pull her closer to his hard chest. "You are my wife. You are a Viking wife." Imperious, red eyes blazed down at her. "Vikings were taken from Earth because we're strong, hearty, and we can survive what the weak cannot. We overpowered our captors, stole a ship, found a planet which we could survive on, then went to other planets to free the Vikings who Martians had traded or sold our people to."

"Neptune. Ulf said that was where King Jurzed was from." Raine tried to slide the sheet higher around her breasts, but Skars was holding her too tightly.

"It was before Jurzed's time. It was his grandfather and many like him who were rescued from Neptune. As it was my great-grandfather who had started the revolt on Mars, and who had found the planet we called home. My great-grandfather offered the Vikings from Neptune land on Raum because their species required extreme cold. We required warmer climates, so we stayed on the same planet yet led different lives. It was the same with the Vikings who my grandfather rescued from Saturn. They needed extreme heat that not even we could survive. They made it their home.

"The first few years we lived on Raum, it became contentious between us. Forced to stay in the areas designated to us because of our physical differences, we began to resent each other because food was more plentiful in our area while the water was in the other, and the metals we needed to trade with other planets were in another.

My great-grandfather was able to come to an agreement to supply the others what they needed, and the rest would be traded to other planets, and all three of the Viking cousins would share in the bounty. Raum flourished, and so did each the Viking cousins. My great-grandfather was a great man. My grandfather took over overseeing the agreement when he died.

"We lived in harmony and grew wealthy so much that other planets grew jealous. Our wealth and the technology we could trade for made us nearly invincible.

"My grandfather gifted Thorsen with a ship of his own, as he had our father before him. Our grandfather gave Thorsen permission to take his ship out on his first trading mission without our father's guidance. Most of our men wanted to go along for the journey. A large quantity of Neptune Vikings had been called on for help in dealing with the Sorn that were destroying the Olggans' planets. The Saturn male Vikings celebrated a festival, and many of the males had gone to take part of the competition in which they crown the victor as the High Archuru.

"We arrogantly left Raum undefended. We had put faith in our security measures. They were broken by the betrayal of a Viking woman from Jurzed's household, who had lowered the shields to allow her lover inside while Jurzed and his warriors were gone."

"Xio." Raine pressed her lips together tightly to stop them from trembling. Heartache was plainly visible on Skars' face.

Skars nodded grimly. "Xioarius was allowed to land his ship to wait for Jurzed's arrival. He told the woman he wanted his permission to marry her. Minutes before his arrival, Xioarius snuck away in a light ship when the shields were again lowered for Jurzed, Thorsen's, and the high chieftain of Archuru.

"Xioarius miscalculated the explosion. The bomb went off, destroying every man, woman, and child on Raum. What he didn't count on was that our three ships carrying the majority of our warriors hadn't docked. We've been chasing him from planet to planet, until now. Xioarius came to Earth before the war hit. He hasn't been able to escape, and he won't be allowed to this time," he swore grimly.

"That's why you, your brother, and King Jurzed are here? Not to take control of Earth? Not to raid like Ulf said you wanted to do?"

"There is nothing left on Earth I desire ..." He tightened his arms around her until she was standing on her tiptoes. "Except you."

CHAPTER 14
RAINE

Raine felt her insides melt as if she were a marshmallow set under a broiler. She had never expected a man to look at her the way Skars was looking at her now ... unless she was on the dinner menu.

Still unable to get Milly's warnings out of her head, she looked up at Skars warily. "Uh ... Skars"—the last thing she wanted was him getting angry like the last time she had asked, but the fear wouldn't go away—"you swear you aren't thinking about eating me?"

His gaze scorched her, but not in anger. "It isn't wise to ask a Viking male if they're thinking about eating you. The answer will be já every time."

From the way Skars was looking at her, she didn't need to go under a broiler. His eyes were lighting her on fire from the inside out. Even in her wildest imaginings, she had never dreamed a man would look at her the way he was, and certainly not one who looked like Skars.

As her breathing escalated, the sheet knotted around her breasts started slipping down. She wiggled her hands to adjust it. Skars gave a hungry growl, which froze her.

"Um ... Skars?"

Whatever she was about to say was blasted from her mind when his mouth landed on the cleft between her breasts as if he was starving. Stiffening, she waited for his teeth to start tearing into her flesh.

A startled whimper escaped her. She was about to die. None of the defensive maneuvers Tayla had taught them kicked in to push him away. She wasn't ready to die, but God, there were worse ways to go other than being beneath this man's mouth.

Expecting to feel a harsh bite of pain, Raine stood stiffly until she felt the tip of his tongue licking over the curve of her breast. Was he tasting her to see if she tasted good?

Nuzzling the sheet lower, Skars covered the exposed nipple of one breast with his mouth.

Finally, it dawned on her. He was making out with her. Having never experienced this type of male attention before, it took a while for her to relax in his hold.

It wasn't bad. In fact, it was pretty good. Not only was she experiencing tingles in her breasts, but she felt a tightening in her groin, making her wiggle against him.

Embarrassed when she felt the hardness against her belly, she forced her hips to stay still. Then Raine nearly jumped out of his arms when a large hand landed on her bottom to bring her hips back to his.

Managing to slide her arms from between them, she cautiously raised them over his shoulders, expecting him to pull out of her embrace at any second. When his arms closed tighter around her, she gave a sigh. This was the closest she had ever been to a man.

As he switched his mouth to the other breast with another growl, brain fog began swirling, making it impossible to focus on anything other than the gentle way he was licking and caressing her nipples.

Piper, Tayla, Lucas, and the others in the vault, all her worries disappeared into the fog. A new world was opening to her, one in which there was unbelievable heat and desire that she had only read about in books.

When she arched closer to Skars, he clenched his hand on her bottom, the action parting the sheet and leaving the front of her body completely naked. Raising his head, he released his grip, letting the sheet fall to the plush carpet. Without a word, Skars went to his knees to nudge her thighs apart.

"You are a gift from the gods."

Being called a gift from the gods had the fog completely engulfing her. Lost in the sensations he was arousing, she never wanted to be found. Having a man like Skars on his knees happened to other women. Never, ever to her.

Two thick fingers went to her groin to swirl then rub in a motion that had her grabbing his shoulders to prevent herself from falling to the floor.

Raine bit down on her lip, not wanting to distract him, terrified he would look up at her and change his mind about what he was doing.

His red eyes did look up as he withdrew his fingers to bring them to his mouth.

"Do you know what you taste like?"

"N-no," she stuttered out.

"You taste like a fruit I had once on Xeturn." Skars sidled closer to her on his knees. "I traded a whole case of our finest mead for a small amount of them. I savored each" —Skars' mouth went to her crotch, sliding his tongue forward to take the place of his finger—"and every one until they were gone," he muttered between her thighs.

Her thigh muscles started trembling when his tongue entered her to search her depths. His mouth plastered itself to her as if he was determined to devour her until there was nothing left.

As if the breath she just sucked in would be her last, no book she had read could describe the feelings she was experiencing. She urgently lowered herself onto his mouth, wanting the tongue exploring her to reach higher, to fill the ache that was turning the fog in her head into a vortex of liquid fire, the same shade of the eyes that were watching every expression she made.

The heated warmth of his tongue arose the sensation of lava licking at her until her slight tremors exploded until her legs were unable to support her any longer and she started to fall.

In one fluid move, Skars caught her as he rose to his feet. Easily carrying her to the bed, he laid her down.

Raine felt as if her eyelids weighed a thousand pounds, so she didn't want to lift them. Preferring to give in to the sleep rather than to raise them to find that what she had just experienced was nothing but a dream, or worse, that he was staring at her with regret that he had touched her at all.

Had her refusal to try on the clothes made him do that out of pity? She knew if they had sex, it would be a pity fuck. Was there a term for performing oral sex out of pity?

Her tired thoughts drew a blank. She would worry about it when she woke, if she did. Maybe it wasn't a pity whatever-the-term-was, and it was just to see if she was palpable before he slaughtered her the way he had the Olggans.

Curling on her side, she felt a warm blanket placed on

top of her. Aw ... That was nice of him. Her Viking husband was a gentleman.

CHAPTER 15
SKARS

Skars stared down at his sleeping bride. The dark shadows under her eyes showed the exhaustion she must have been battling since Earth had been overtaken.

He headed to the bathing room and quickly washed then changed from his uniform into the soft, supple leather pants he preferred. Striding from his sleeping room as he snapped silver cuffs around each of his wrists, Skars glanced toward the bed to make sure she was still sleeping. The woman hadn't moved.

Wanting to be back in his room before she woke, he immediately went into the elevator to lift him to the flight room. Directly above the main room, he went into the navigation room.

Bjorn, Njal, and Arne were already there, waiting for him. He had sent for them before he had bathed.

Pulling up the maps on the tall, round table that was downloaded to his computers, the other warriors gathered around.

"My wife said they were hiding in a vault. She also mentioned working at a bank. That explains how they survived and how we spent days searching and couldn't find her."

He commanded the computer to search for banks within the vicinity where they had found the women today, and a laser light projected a map over the table.

"There is only one."

Skars' commanding gaze went to Bjorn. "There are seven of them. I want them found and brought back here. I will message Thorsen to send more men to assist you. I don't want them hurt. If Reva reveals they will be of no use to us, I'll find a place for them to stay safely on Earth before we leave."

Arne gave him a disbelieving grunt. "How are we supposed to get them to come if they refuse? Ulf was taken because the old woman attacked him."

"Tell them Raine told you where they were, that you are there to take them to her, and if they want to see the other two again, they have to come with you. That our only wish is to find them a place where they will be safe."

"What if one is a Viking descendent?" Bjorn spoke up, his yearning visible.

"Then my woman won't be the only human leaving with us." His woman would be furious, but Skars had no doubt he could manage her. He had found his bride; he wouldn't deny the other clan members from finding theirs because of any interference Raine might want to give. Ultimately, it would be out of his hands. The people brought back to the ship were Thorsen's responsibility, not his.

"Send me a transmission when you have found them. Make sure you take enough themoters to control them if there is no other way to bring them in. I don't want any mistakes."

The three warriors left to follow his orders.

121

Pressing a button on the table, he contacted Thorsen.

"Brother." His brother's voice filled the computer room.

Skars filled him in on what had happened on Earth and afterward with Ulf and the other woman being taken.

Thorsen's curses had Skars taking one of the chairs to wait it out until his brother's temper cooled.

Thorsen's words finally calmed, but Skars could still hear the temper beneath the surface. "I will make contact with King Jurzed. He is not getting Xioarius, no matter what value your bride puts on the boy."

"The boy is not a boy," Skars informed him. "They disguised the woman to make her appear to be one. I heard them talking. They were unaware I could hear. She has blonde hair. Reva told us in her vision that I would find one in the area that I landed on."

Thorsen resumed cursing. Only the fact it was a woman would change Thorsen's mind about trading Xioarius to King Jurzed.

"We can only pray to the gods that King Jurzed doesn't find out before we can come to an agreement to make a trade. One which doesn't include me forgoing my oath to kill the one responsible for killing our mother and father."

Those weren't the only ones he was to exact revenge for. Thorsen wanted to make sure Xioarius died numerous times over for the death of his wives and three sons.

He could remember every detail of that day. Their grandfather had gifted Thorsen a ship, which he could take on his own trading missions to new planets while their father would continue with the ones already established.

The ship was a beauty, and their grandfather hadn't spared any expense to outfit the ship to his expectations. The main ship could easily hold sixty warriors, twice as much if they doubled up, hundreds if they used the cargo holds meant to hold the goods they wanted to trade.

Not only was the main ship capable of anything Thorsen could desire, underneath, there were four dock pads where smaller spaceships were carried. When all four ships were docked, a walkway provided access to the main ship. Thorsen had gifted one to him, and the other three had been gifted to Ulf, Bjorn, and Njal.

To celebrate the maiden journey, all the clan members who had wanted to had gone along. Thorsen had asked Grandfather for Reva to come also, wanting rather than taking an older, more experience one, knowing unlike the other married seeresses, she wouldn't have a husband on board and spoil the fun they were determined to have.

Reva had repeatedly refused, wanting her sister to go, only complying when their grandfather had given her no choice. So, with her sister's encouragement, Reva had boarded the ship.

Spending weeks traveling from planet to planet that they had never visited before, with the cargo holds full, a transmission had been sent for them to return to Raum.

Wanting to enjoy their last night of freedom, the warriors had spent the night drinking and had still been deep in their cups when they came within eyesight of home.

"That's enough, brother." Skars had taken the cup that was filled with a gold and glittering liquid that had cost him two pouches of silver from Thorson. "We're almost home. I don't want a repeat of the last time you drank too much and crashed Father's ship on Leron."

"Be thankful I did." Thorsen raised his chalice at him. "Grandfather wouldn't have gifted us our ships if I hadn't.

You especially with your own ship, we no longer have to live under Father's roof."

Unable to disagree, Skars had downed the contents of the cup, regretting spending good coins on what tasted like sparkly piss.

"I say we give this glittery piss to the women and kids as souvenirs," Ulf said, sprawling his giant body out on the long bench that curved around one of three walls of the main room. The bench was so padded that Ulf's ass sank until it could no longer be seen, with a soft, creamy material that a handprint could be seen when lifted.

Skars raised a brow at the boots on the expensive table that his mother had commissioned as a gift for Thorsen.

At his glower, Ulf lowered his boots back to the floor.

"Já," Bjorn, Njal, and Arne all chorused together. Their agreement on the quality of the drink in their cups didn't stop any of them from tipping up their chalices to finish them.

"Ulf, your wife would drink her own piss before she'd drink this shit." Skars, unable to finish his own, moved to dispose of it. Moving to the wall of the ship, he was tipped his cup so the suction from the disposer would suck it inside. He then went to the cabinet where the liquor was kept and took out one he had made for himself. It didn't sparkle, but at least it was palatable.

All the men on the ship howled with laughter.

"Já, she would," Ulf said, touching his chest, but the moment he did, he screamed out in pain. He practically ripped his shirt open to reveal the chest tattoo.

Dismayed at his actions, they all started to go to his aid. Bjorn and Arne jerked Ulf's arms back so they could better see what was happening. Helpless, they all watched as the black ink under the skin slowly started to burn. The putrid smoke wafted out of his chest, the smell gagging them so badly that it brought tears to their eyes. It left a freshly raised scar where all ink used to be.

A bellow of excruciating pain escaped Ulf, dragging out his throat at the never-ending grief he would have to carry until his dying day.

Each of the warriors knew what it meant for the tattoo to disappear, as all of them carried a distinctive one on their own chest. Still stunned at what had happened, they slid their gazes to the doorway as Reva ran into the room, clutching her chest, blood seeping through her fingers.

"My sister ..." She was pale as death as her eyes flew around the room, looking for Ulf. Rushing toward him, she stared at the open wound where the tattoo used to be.

Before anything else could be said or done, the ship gave a sudden jerk as glowing red lights started blinking from inside, showing the alarm system had been activated.

Helping Thorsen to his feet, Skars and the rest threw themselves toward the closest window so they could see what had caused the alert. The other warriors were doing the same when another blast came from the planet they called home.

They were hundreds of miles away, but the ship felt the blast.

Thorsen slapped the wall. "Thane!" he shouted the warrior's name responsible for navigating the ship.

The warrior didn't reply. Like Skars, he was being forced to watch Raum disintegrate in the distance, his own chest burning with the same putrid smell, as if the tattoo had been removed with the heat of a branding iron. Even though he already knew what was going to be there, he still ripped the shirt open to look at the wound, which drops of blood coursing down to his stomach. The tattoo that covered his chest above his heart was disappearing into smoke, just like Ulf's had moments ago.

All Raumulean Vikings were born with their own beautifully intricate tattoo of an encircled tree. Faint at birth, the tattoo would grow darker, the roots spreading upward into a tree with branches as the child aged until the Viking reached adulthood. Each branch contained leaves with a pattern that was unique to each Viking family member, to represent their living members—mother, father, sisters; later, wives and children—as more lines would appear as they entered your life. With death, their lines would disappear, leaving behind a small scar to represent the pain of their loss.

Skars gazed down unbelievably at his chest as his entire tattoo disappeared, leaving a large patch of scarred flesh behind. His entire family had just been killed, as were his men's as they all cried out in anguish.

The only remaining survivors of their planet were those on board the ship, or the two other ships scheduled to return.

The room was filled with shouts of rage and grief. Warriors that Skars once would have sworn were unbeatable had now lost everything in a second. They had no home, no women, no families.

Thane's hoarse voice finally came through the communication system found in every room on the ship.

"Where should ...?" Thane's voice cracked. "I don't know what to key in for our destination?"

Thorsen tore his shirt apart, bunching the remains on his wound as he walked to stand over Reva, who was on her knees on the carpeted floor. "Did you know?"

Reva raised tear-stained cheeks to meet Thorsen's demanding glare. "Já."

Thorsen grabbed Reva, staring at her threateningly. Skars pulled him away from her.

"Why didn't you tell us?" he yelled.

"Hilda wouldn't let me. As your grandfather's seeress, she told him of our visions and what they foretold."

"Grandfather? He knew, and he let my wives and children die?" Thorsen shouted as he started throwing anything he could touch in a berserker rage.

Skars, Arne, and Ulf launched themselves at Thorsen, taking him to the floor. They kept their chieftain pinned under them until he lay quietly, and all they could hear were sobs of grief coming from him.

Waiting until he no longer made any sounds, they climbed off him.

Thorsen's face was stark and bleak when he rose from the floor.

"I wanted to tell you, Thorsen. I begged your grandfather and Hilda to tell you. They swore me to secrecy. Still, the night before we set to leave, I decided I was going to tell you the morning when I woke. That night, I had a vision. A vision of the future after I told you. You wouldn't have been able to save Raum or the ones we will mourn, as everyone on board this ship, and the two others that were late arriving home, would be gone. No trace of our existence would have been left."

The full enormity of the decision that their grandfather, Hilda, and Reva must have brought Thorsen to the reality that he was now facing him as their new chieftain.

Skars looked over Reva's shoulders to the window at her back as the last of the burning debris disappeared from sight, unable to bear the sight of the warriors lost in their own personal grief. He had lost his grandfather, mother, and father, two sisters by marriage, and three nephews.

His grief didn't compare to what they must be experiencing.

These warriors had followed him blindly on trading missions. While many had gone well, just as many had them battling for their lives to get on certain planets.

Most had lost not only parents, but wives and children. Whole families destroyed in less time than it would take to fill a chalice with wine, and with the destruction of their planet, they were even denied any chance of rebuilding that vital structure that would enable them to heal, to rebuild. Whoever had done this had effectively destroyed their race.

Thorsen's voice dragged his eyes from the window.

"We do what we always do." Thorsen looked each man in their eyes, giving them the words they needed. "We take our revenge. Whoever is responsible will die."

Thorsen sweeping gaze landed on Reva. "Who?"

"Xioarius."

The familiar name had Skars thanking the gods that Thorsen's ax was in his room, or nothing would have been left unmarred in the room that his grandfather and mother had made.

"This is my penance for not taking his life when I had the chance," Thorsen snarled in self-recrimination. "I swear, as chieftain, I will never make that mistake again. I give my word that I will not stop until Xioarius and those who gave him aid with the destruction of Raum die by torture. They will know the pain of each life taken on their flesh, as we felt it on ours. This, I swear to you."

CHAPTER 16
SKARS

S kars dragged his thoughts away from the past to the conversation with his brother to contemplate the dilemma that Thorsen found himself in. If Thorsen found Xioarius first, no amount of possible Viking mates for his warriors would be considered for a trade. Thorsen had sworn an oath that he intended to fulfill. There could be another option, which the chieftain would consider. That was if she was still with him and was still alive.

"Xioarius didn't destroy Raum on his own and hasn't been able to hide from so many without help. Those could be used for trade when we capture them."

"Too true," Thorsen said from the computer in the wall. "Those, I may be willing to bargain with. I will give it deep consideration when I find Xioarius and those who I find with him."

Unexpected relief allowed him to breathe easier.

"If you're not far, I sent Bjorn, Arne, and Njal to the others in my wife's group. I gave instructions that I didn't want them hurt. Are you in the vicinity...?" Skars hesitated to ask.

Thorsen picked up on his concern. "I will send more men. It may dissuade them from acting too rashly when they are confronted."

"My thoughts also." Skars rubbed his temples, growing tired. If he hadn't needed to be available to his warriors if there was trouble, he would be asleep next to his new bride. "Any luck in your search for Xioarius, or someone to work the computer?" Skars asked, forgetting about his duties.

"None. The humans have become adept at hiding before we arrive. Erik has yet to find how to work the sensors to search for the underground cities that Reva describes from her visions."

"You didn't sacrifice Erik?" Skars taunted his brother at the irritation he could hear from Thorsen.

A disgusted snort came from the wall. "The gods would have punished us for sending Erik their way. We need to appease them, not anger them further."

Since his brother refused to sacrifice Erik, Skars had one he would enjoy sending their way.

"I have a worthy sacrifice in mind. I will send word when it has been completed."

"Keep me informed."

"As always."

Skars ended the communication and began pacing the room. Moving to the table, he pressed a button for a screen to appear. "Show me my sleeping room."

Skars stopped pacing long enough to see Raine was still sleeping, the clothes he had wanted her to wear in a clump at the foot of the bed.

Anger arose anew at how she had maintained that none of the clothes would fit her, comparing her size to Ulf. Were the human males that the Martians had left on Earth blind as well as weak-willed and frail?

Raine was a tall, buxom beauty who drew many appreciative gazes from *all* the Viking males, along with the Olggans. He wouldn't be surprised if Jurzed offered to trade her for the frail woman he had stolen, even if she was the descendent Reva had seen in her vision.

He wished he could be there when Jurzed found out he had captured a woman. He had already violated their law just by the mere act of touching her. The Viking males in Jurzed's clan wouldn't care that he hadn't been aware the boy was a woman. Unlike Thorsen, Jurzed didn't have the benefit of having a seeress.

He was still watching his Raine sleep when Bjorn sent a communication that he had found the group. He refrained from instructing him again not to take aggressive tactics against them.

It wasn't his un-confidence in Bjorn that had him resuming his pacing; it was the unpredictable humans which worried him.

Growing concern filled him as time passed without another word from Bjorn. His worry eased when the message came they were loaded and were coming to the ship.

After sending a transmission to Thorsen, Skars left the navigation room to go down to the main greeting room.

Feeling the slight bump of Bjorn's spaceship docking to his, Skars clasped his hands behind his back to stand commandingly within eyesight as Bjorn brought them out of the lift.

Keeping his expression neutral, he surveyed the group of survivors that filed out. All of them appeared unharmed and without the restraining devices he had ordered Bjorn to use only in case of an emergency, but one. The lone male. The device on his chest showed he had tried to fight.

When they saw him, the quiet room broke into rapid shrieking chatter, which the translation tool in his ear had trouble keeping up with.

Skars raised an imperious hand to silence the noise. Why were female humans all so loud and made that same obnoxious sound when they talked?

"Quiet." Snapping out the order immediately silenced the females, but provided the male an opportunity to ask his questions once they were silenced.

"Where is my brother?"

"You are Lucas?"

The man narrowed his eyes on him. "Yes."

"I am Skars," he introduced himself, much like he had on his trading missions.

"I don't give a fuck what your name is. I want to see my brother immediately."

The antagonistic male stood straight and tall as he tried to take control of the situation. Skars could sympathize, but he couldn't let the human have the control he desired. He had lost any power over his life the moment humans had decided to use instruments of mass destruction against themselves.

"I will talk, you will listen," Skars sharply told the six women and lone human male in the room. As he spoke, the elevator slid open, and Reva glided out.

The humans' eyes widened as Reva came forward to stand next to his side. She had the same effect on them as she'd had on Raine. The midnight-blue gown and cape threaded with gold were modest yet highlighted the perfection of Reva's beauty.

It was unsurprising that the human male's eyes lingered on her before he returned his expression of anger to him.

Knowing silence would be short-lived, Skars began his explanation at what had happened on Earth and how both the boy—Skars kept it to himself that he was aware of the woman's deception—and that Tayla, as well as one of his men, were now prisoners of King Jurzed and the Vozen.

"I have hopes I will be able to negotiate a trade for them. My chieftain, Thorsen, and I are as unhappy at their being taken as you. It was beyond our control. We tried to leave the area before the Olggan and King Jurzed arrived, but as we tried to convince them, the boy would not have been taken prisoner, nor..." Skars' voice became lethal as he continued, "would my clan member have been taken captive if Tayla hadn't fought him, causing his vehicle to crash."

"We know who is responsible for this."

Skars' gaze went to the woman standing militarily in front on him. She appeared to be the same age as Raine, but the ugly expression on her face and eyes showed she had none of Raine's gentleness of spirit.

"They wouldn't have been out there at all if they hadn't snuck out after Raine. Where's she at? I bet she wasn't taken. The big jinx always manages to come out smelling like a rose while everyone else has to deal with the consequences."

Skars tightened his lips in disapproval. When he pinned her with his gaze, the woman took a step back to hide behind the male.

"Where is Raine?" Lucas gave the woman the same menacing glare when she went past him before swinging his gaze back to him.

"She is resting. You no longer need to be concerned about her welfare," he bluntly told them. "She is my concern now. And know this, I will not have my bride disparaged within my hearing again."

Turning slightly to his left, he rose a questioning brow at Reva, silently asking her the question he wanted answered before he said anything further to the humans.

Slowly shaking her head, she told him there were no tru-mates among them.

From the sudden slumping of the shoulders of his clan members, their disappointment placed a heavy load on his heart. He had hoped for the impossible for them, but he was resolute that he wouldn't stop until every crevice and hiding place was discovered before he would give up hope for his clan's happiness. For them to have the happiness they had on Raum, they needed a tru-mate.

"Did you say *bride*?" Lucas didn't back off his questioning despite the decree Skars had just handed down.

"Oh my God, he sounds like a vampire claiming his bride," a hysterical voice of condemnation came from behind Lucas' back.

"You're called Milly, aren't you?" Skars asked.

"She told you about me, didn't she? The jinx has tried to ruin my life since I met her—"

"Silence!" Skars shouted. The translation tool had implanted the term and definition into his brain.

Vikings were suspicious people. The other Vikings in the room had the same tool he had implanted. The jealous woman could become dangerous to Raine's welfare if the Vikings gained this knowledge and became spooked.

"Raine chose me as her husband. She will tell you this when she wakes and after you all have been fed and rested. Make sure you give her thanks, because only for her are you under my chieftain's protection. You will be treated as guests until we are able to find a safe place for you to live.

Bjorn told me you have a wound on your back which needs treatment. My brother will send his healer to tend to you and the rest of you if you have a need. We are not normally so welcoming to our visitors; only your friendship with Raine allows the privileges I'm granting you. Those who aren't willing to show the due respect for my bride, Bjorn will immediately escort you back to Earth where you were located."

Skars walked over to Lucas and removed the restraining device, his eyes daring him to strike out at him. Lucas pursed his lips at the unspoken challenge.

"You are the only hope of getting my brother back. I'm staying." Lucas turned to look at the rest of the women, including the one behind his back, before turning his head back to him.

"We're all staying."

CHAPTER 17
RAINE

"The color makes your skin glow."

Startled at Skars' silent entrance, Raine spun around in the peach outfit that she could no longer resist trying on to see if it fit.

"I was just getting ready to come look for you." Flushing at the compliment, she gave him a shy glance. "I didn't want to go wandering through your ship without any clothes on." She unconsciously rubbed her hand on the opposite sleeve, appreciating the sensuous feeling of the slinky material.

Seeing him for the first time since the intimate moment when he had given her ecstasy that she had never experience before, Raine timidly watched as he walked across the room toward her. She had never been so nervous in her whole life. How was she was supposed to act? Being that it was her first time to be in this awkward position, she wanted to play it cool and not embarrass herself, but on the other side of the coin, she didn't want to come across as blasé. Or should she? Was he going to pretend it never happened?

Skars solved the problem for her.

Taking her by her upper arms, he pulled her into an embrace. "Good morning, wife."

The sense of rightness at being called his wife calmed her mounting anxiety like nothing else could have.

"Good morning." She was lost in the surge of happiness at being close to Skars and the tender way he had greeted her; it then registered in her mind what he had just told her. "Morning?" Frowning, she jerked out of his arms. "How long was I asleep?"

Frowning, Skars pulled her back. "Two of your days."

Raine started futilely wiggling away. "Lucas and the others will be worried sick. You have to take me back to Earth. How could I have slept so long? I'm a terrible person."

"Wife, there is no need to upset yourself. All is well."

"How can all be well? Lucas has to be frantic about his si—brother! I hav—"

Two fingers were placed over her lips. "Shh ... I will explain if you give me the chance. While you were sleeping, I sent my clan to find your friends. They were brought aboard, fed, and rested. I will take you to them once you have eaten."

Raine put her hand on his wrist to pull his fingers away from her mouth. "How did you find them? They must think I told you where they were! They probably hate me now even though I didn't."

"I told them that areas close to where I found you were searched. It didn't take much time before Bjorn found them."

"So, they know I didn't give up our hiding place?" she asked to make sure.

"Já."

137

"Whew, that's a huge relief. I didn't want them to think I told you their location before they could decide they wanted me to. We make decisions that affect our group together. I don't want them to think I went behind their backs."

The discerning look Skars was giving her made her wonder what he was thinking.

"You're very concerned about all their feelings and welfare, yet only one in your group expressed the same concern for you."

She didn't need to ask which one. Lucas took all their safety seriously, despite no longer having a bank to manage.

"That's probably because they're scared to death," Raine rushed to make excuses for them. "Did you tell them they wouldn't be raped or eaten?"

Skars' brows lifted to his hairline. "No ... I didn't think it needed to be said."

"Of course, it needed to be said," she argued heatedly, trying to draw his focus away from the lack of caring for her that they had probably showed. "They've been worried sick about it ..."

His cheekbones started to turn crimson. Raine didn't think it was a reaction to becoming embarrassed. She was accidentally making him angry. For some reason, people around her tended to become irritated without any good reason that she could ever figure out.

"That's what they spent time being frightened about?"

Raine thought about telling him scowling wasn't a good look for him. In fact, it was a bit frightening. She would wait until the crimson color on his cheeks wasn't signaling her to shut up.

"None of your friends seem frightened that they would

get eaten or raped. One did seem frightened you may be married to a vampire."

"That would be Milly. She has a few irrational fears." Raine ignored the pointed glare he was giving her to go on with her explanation. "She loves to read horror and science fiction during her lunch breaks. I told her she should switch to romance novels; she would be a much happier person," she confided to him.

"She is like Loki," he said with flaring nostrils. "Her happiness is brought by watching someone else's misery."

Raine hated to agree with Skars' assessment of Milly, but she had been coming to the same conclusion the longer they had been forced to stay in the vault together. Milly must have made an impression on Skars, because his cheekbones were like watching live coals flicking under his skin.

"Her clothes were much cleaner than yours or any of the others'. She made everyone else give her the first choice of sleeping rooms, and when they were fed, she was first in line. Why is she allowed to act this way? The other women are much older than her; she should be more respectful to them. Three of the women are very frail. Reva is seeing to their needs until Thorsen arrives with our clan healer this evening."

"That's wonderful news. I've been worried sick about them. Silvia, Kaz, and Kennedy were living in the retirement village where the bank is located. When they came in to get their money before the bombs landed, Lucas knew they lived on their own, so he convinced them to stay with us. Emma and Karina aren't in much better shape. They were both just waiting for their retirement date to be approved. Don't tell Brinn I told you, but she is around the same age as them, but she pretends to be years younger. I pretend I don't know her real age," she confided in a low voice, even though they were the only two in the room. "I felt terrible when her fiancé ditched her before the bombs landed. He's much younger. She thinks he was just concerned about his parents and that's why he didn't come and get her." Her voice dipped even lower. "But, just between me and you, I think he never had any intention of coming for her."

Did he just roll his red eyes at her?

"That still doesn't explain why you allow Milly to behave the way she does?"

Raine stared at him in confusion. "It doesn't? I thought it did. We're all afraid of her. Most of them are too scared, depressed, or hungry to take her on. Piper was too sweet to say anything, and Tayla didn't because she was worried she would put her in a half nelson if they got in an argument and didn't want to make the older ladies frightened of her. Tayla doesn't mind if dudes are afraid of her, but she feels bad if older women are."

Skars gave her a dark glower. "Viking brides are not afraid of trying on clothes, nor of other women, and they do not scream like a howling lanree when they make a kill. We are the ones to be feared."

"When I said afraid, I didn't mean in a physical sense. I meant, I'm kind of sensitive, and I try to avoid having my feelings hurt if I can. The only reason I'm telling you this is because you're kind of hurting my feelings now." Raine curled her toes in the carpet, unable to take the disappointed expression on his face. She wished she were a braver person. Her father had told her once that she was a coward at heart when her mother had flown off on one of her rages, but that it was okay if she was, because he was one, too.

A loud sigh came from him that caused the top she was wearing to billow against her skin.

"Do you want a divorce?"

Skars gave her a gentle shake. "No. I do not want a divorce. I want you to listen to my words and take them to heart. You are a Viking bride; others *fear* you."

"I'm a Viking bride; others *fear* me."

She must have sounded surer than she was when he gave a pleased smile as a reward.

"Já, that is what I want! Come eat. I want my bride's stomach to be full before I take you to your friends. I will not have your appetite destroyed by their inaccurate fears."

She really didn't want her appetite spoiled, either. She was starving, and she wanted to enjoy their first meal together. Technically, it would be the first date she had ever gone on.

"Wait." Raine pulled back when he would have led her to the elevator. "I don't have any shoes. You threw them away."

"Sit," Skars ordered, moving to a wooden chest he hadn't opened when he had taken the clothes out of the other two.

She loved the feel of the slinky outfit as she moved; the clothing made her feel pretty and sexy. The top skimmed over her breasts to delicately flow around her waist. The loose pants were the perfect length, down to her ankles, and had a slit from the ankle to just below the knee, which would open and close as she walked. She wished she had one in every color of the rainbow. She loved the clothes so much.

Skars turned back to her from the chest and must have caught the gist of what she had been thinking. "You like the clothes I gifted you with?"

Raine ran her hand down the pant leg. "I love them. I've never worn anything so pretty," she answered truthfully.

Skars knelt down in front of her to take one of her feet. Raine watched as he pulled a peach-colored, soft-soled slipper with a red rose embroidered on the front onto her foot.

"It fits." She raised disbelieving eyes to his.

"You are pleased?"

"Very." She nodded as he placed the other one on. "Thank you, Skars. I'll try not to get them dirty. I can even wash them before I give them back."

"Why would you give them back? They are yours. All the clothes are my wedding gifts to you."

"I ... don't understand. You bought women's clothing? Were you planning to marry someone else when you bought them?" Raine didn't know how to respond to the generous gift.

"Neinn."

Raine lost sight of his face when he rose to stand and took her hand, beginning to tug her toward the elevator.

"It is my duty to trade for the clan's wants and needs. When I see something I want, I have learned to purchase it rather than regret the loss afterward. It can take months to travel to planets. Some wouldn't be worth the time or expense to return."

"Which makes sense. It's not like you can beam yourself from one planet to another." She gave a small laugh as they entered the elevator. Then she couldn't help herself as the doors closed, giving him a curious glance. "Or can you?"

Raine wished she hadn't asked when his glower returned.

"Neinn."

"I was just asking. There is no need to get so testy. Don't

142

you want me to ask questions when I'm curious about something?"

"Já. You can ask Ulf."

Joy filled her at the information. "Ulf? You managed to get him and Tayla back while I was sleeping?"

"Neinn."

"Then how am I ...?" She broke off as it dawned on her why he had chosen Ulf to answer any question she wanted answered. "That's just plain rude."

"I'm a Viking husband; get used to it."

CHAPTER 18

SKARS

"Wait!"

Skars halted, about to usher Raine out the elevator at her hissed exclamation.

Suddenly on the alert, he stared around the galley. Seeing no danger, he cast her a questioning glance.

"Are any of my friends here?" she whispered, edging behind him. "Were they given clean clothes, too? I don't want them to think I'm getting preferential treatment."

Now that he understood there wasn't any danger lurking to pounce on them, his hands clenched to prevent himself from returning to their room, to punish her for scaring him badly enough that any potential offspring he might have would refuse to make their journey to be housed in their mother's womb, who would be constantly making the scraping noises which put every hair on his body on edge.

Unclenching his hand, Skars hauled her out from behind his back to march them into the galley. "There is no one here but us," he gritted out. "I wanted us to share our first meal together alone." Another decision he was regretting. One of a long list of mistakes he had made since his arrival on Earth.

"Have a seat. I will get your food."

Without waiting to for her to take a chair at the long table that at least fifteen could sit at easily, he went to the compartments on the wall to choose a variety of foods for Raine to taste. Choosing several for himself, he loaded the offerings onto a tray.

Sitting down across from her in the middle of the table, he placed several dishes in front of her. "Our food is different from what you're used to. I chose some which should be similar, if not plain. We like our foods spicy, so those are unseasoned until you are adapted to our taste." Skars pointed at one dish. "This should taste like a beef steak to you."

From her guarded expression, he guessed the computer was wrong.

"How did the others like it?"

Skars leaned across the table to cut a small bite, spearing it with a utensil then raising it to her lips. "Vikings do not show fear," he reminded her.

Giving her a pleased look when she opened her mouth, he waited for her reaction.

"It's actually really good."

He cut several more pieces for her before moving to the next dish to spear a purple vegetable. "This should taste like your potatoes."

Raine opened her mouth, this time without his prompting. Chewing the food, she raised her thumb in the air.

"Does that mean it is acceptable?"

"Very." She grinned at him.

Feeding her from each of the remaining dishes, he gave the utensil to her so he could eat his own meal.

"These purple things are really good."

"They are called doths. The meat is trippe." Indicating the other dishes, he gave her the names of the remaining ones on the table.

"Ulf told Tayla and me that you and your men could speak and understand our language because of a translator device in your ear."

"Já. The device takes in what you say and gives me some different options of what to say based on my way of thinking."

Her eyes widened. "You have an AI device in your head?"

"AI?"

"Artificial intelligence."

Skars didn't care what term the humans used. It was obvious they didn't have the capabilities of much more advanced species.

"Scientists have been trying to develop it on Earth, like medical breakthroughs, robots, and self-driving cars."

"They would have been better trying to concentrate on how not to destroy themselves," he commented sarcastically.

"You don't think much of humans, do you?"

Skars looked up from his food. "Are you not angry at the wasteland Earth has become?"

Mournful, grey eyes had him setting his utensil down.

"Not all the damage done to Earth was caused by the bombs. Las Vegas wasn't. All the damage you can see for miles around here wasn't caused by humans. Don't get me wrong. I am angry. I miss being able to buy my books, watch television, buy what I want to without leaving my apartment. But, in reality, what I miss the most wasn't caused by the bombs."

"If the humans hadn't been so determined to destroy each other, none of us would have come here."

"I can't fight against your logic, which is true." Raine's head tilted to the side. "But the same could be said against your people. Your people lost their planet, which should have given the different species of Vikings reason to band together, but it seems to me it's driven you apart."

"Já, but not against each other. King Jurzed wasn't fighting to kill me any more than I was fighting to kill him. Nor did he lift a sword to hurt any other Viking. Each Viking species has vowed to serve their own brand of justice to Xioarius. Thorsen wants his revenge for his family, and for our clan," he explained.

"And King Jurzed? Did he have a family? A wife and children?"

Skars moved his food away, his appetite gone. "Neinn. Jurzed's family consisted of Ziea, his sister, and his clan members. Jurzed and his clan weren't on Raum when it exploded. They were given the task by my father and several other rulers in power from other planets to become Guardians to track and bring to justice to those who violated laws on their planets and had fled to escape justice. They were rarely on Raum. They were scheduled to return that day. They had been delayed when word had reached them that an outcast had been spotted."

"We had somewhat similar organizations on Earth. United States Marshalls, FBI, CIA, and Interpol."

"Jurzed and his warriors were tracking exiled Ozions who were planet skipping, leaving numerous victims behind, when Raum was destroyed. He and other clan members blame themselves that they weren't home."

"They shouldn't blame themselves. Maybe they would have died also."

"I cannot agree, nor would any other Viking clan. Jurzed being there would have made a difference."

"I don't understand how he could have made a difference?"

"The shields would never have been lowered for Xioarius. Jurzed had made the petition to bring him to justice for the crimes he had committed on other planets where he had blamed others to cover his crimes."

"Has the petition been granted since Raum was destroyed?"

"Já, but Jurzed is not tracking Xioarius nor those who helped him as a guardian; handing them over for their crimes isn't something he's willing to do. This time, Jurzed wants to carry out justice by his own hand."

Raine stacked the empty dishes on the trays. "So, it's not only Xio that King Jurzed wants to kill?"

"Neinn, there are others who are just as responsible."

A thoughtful expression crossed her face then cleared. "The person who lowered your planet's shields."

"Já."

Raine seemed hesitant to ask then seemed unable to help herself. "Who?"

"King Jurzed's sister."

CHAPTER 19
SKARS

"If you're finished, I will take you to your friends." Skars rose from the table, carrying the tray. He placed it on the conveyer belt, which would start moving once the tray was set down. The belt would automatically take the dishes and tray to a cleaning machine that would clean and sanitize the items for their next use.

Raine was waiting by the elevator when he turned. He could see the anxiety in her expression. He couldn't understand why his wife was so anxious of the reaction that the group of humans would have toward her.

"All will be well." He sought to reassure her as they went into the elevator.

"I don't know why I'm so nervous." She made a face of self-reproach at herself. "I'm just not much of a confrontational person. And please don't tell me Vikings aren't afraid of anything. I get that." Raine expelled a shuddering breath. "Believe me; I get you're not, but I am. My father used to call me raindrop. He said I would dry up the moment someone made me uncomfortable. I guess he was right."

Giving a self-recriminating shrug, Raine lowered her gaze from his to the slippers peeking from her pants.

Where was the courage he had seen her exhibit when she had rescued him the day he had arrived? She had shown extreme courage when she had jumped out of the vehicle when she had felt they were being outnumbered by the Olggans. Yet now, she was practically cowering in fear before seeing her friends who had no weapons to raise against her.

To him, the misplaced fear was irrational, and he had no idea how to combat it other than to return the humans to Earth without her seeing them. That was the direction he would prefer to take and would take if Raine wasn't treated with respect.

Letting Raine go first when the door opened, Skars gave the gathered group a warning glance behind her back, intimidating them and letting them know that he would not allow any rude behavior.

The older women in the group gave squeals of delight at seeing Raine. Slowly, they rose from their sitting positions on the lounger and hurried to her to take turns hugging her.

"We've been so worried about you," one said.

"I'm fine, Silvia."

Skars watched as Raine hugged the blue-haired old woman.

The others took their time hugging her, their frail arms shaking when it was their turn.

Their reaction confused Skars even more. Love and concern for Raine was evident by the elderly women's reaction to seeing her.

Giving them space, Skars bypassed them to go talk with Bjorn.

"Thorsen will be here in a few hours to get them off our hands. Any problem?" Skars asked.

Bjorn indicated with a slight movement of his head to the two who remained seated.

"She seeks to cause trouble."

"How so?"

"She kept whispering to the others."

The woman must have sensed they were talking about her, because she swiftly went to Raine. She made no effort to hug her like the older women, and it was easy to see that she was complaining to Raine.

"Would you like me to return her to Earth?" Bjorn muttered.

Njal crossed the room to be included in their discussion and gave a low, disgusted snort. "I can save Bjorn the time. Let me release the docking door, and I'll throw her out."

Bjorn's disgusted expression became interested. "Would the human survive the fall?"

"Neinn. She will be Thorsen's to deal with when he arrives."

From the pleased smiles on Bjorn and Njal, Skars had no doubt they would try to convince Thorsen to choose the speediest method to rid himself of the woman.

Ignoring their complaints, Skars listened as Raine talked to the group, assuring them that she was safe and what had happened on Earth.

"Is there any more news on Piper?" Lucas asked.

Skars strode forward. "Our chieftain will speak to you when he arrives. Thorsen has been told of your brother's health condition and has conveyed our willingness to make a trade for him."

"What if King Jurzed refuses?"

A flicker of respect grew for the human male. Lucas was

showing his main priority was the concern for his family member while acknowledging he had no power over what the two Vikings decided.

"There will be an agreement made. The what and when are up to Thorsen and King Jurzed. He will be able to address your concerns much better than I."

Lucas shoved his hands in the pockets of his pants in a frustrated movement. "Can you at least tell your chieftain that, if he can't come to an agreement for Piper, then use me to trade for something else? I want to be with my brother."

If he wasn't aware of Piper being a woman, the woman called Milly would have given it away. Raine and the rest of the women maintained their facial countenance.

Skars gave him a curt nod. "I will make your wishes known."

Having had enough of Milly, he decided it would be best if he left. "I will see to that duty now. Wife, do you wish to stay here or return to your room?"

"I'll ... wait here."

He didn't miss the slight pause she had made. Irritated that Raine did not take the opportunity he was giving her, Skars gave his men meaningful glances before stalking off.

In the elevator, he slid his hand on the wall to take him to the upper level to the computer room.

Taking one look at his face, Arne stood from behind the bank of computers. "Unless you need me, I'll take my evening meal early."

Still irritated, Skars waved him away without watching him go. Walking to the wall closest to him, he placed his hand on a panel. Instantly, the wall changed to show a clear view of the outside.

His acute hearing picked up the almost silent opening

of the door and the soft footsteps of the woman who had just entered.

"Go away," he ordered without turning around.

"I felt your anger from my room."

"Then you shouldn't have come. I don't want to talk right now, especially with you."

"You are blaming me for your frustration with your wife?"

"No one else is responsible."

Undeterred, Reva moved closer to his side. "What are you most angry about? Having to make adjustments to your behavior to please your woman, or are you displeased with the woman herself?"

"She isn't as I expected her to be," he complained.

"You have been raised since birth to expect the changes that would occur when you found your tru-mate. You are searching and becoming disappointed that such isn't happening with your bride. I warned you of this when you reached manhood, and I told you a Viking tru-mate wasn't in your future. The Martian half of you is instinctively seeking a closer tru-bond, which will never be there, while your Viking half thinks you will never be content if the Martian isn't.

"My sister would laugh often after many husbands came to her and told her that they had been given the wrong tru-mate. Viking males don't lightly take the loss of their freedom or emotions. It is the Martian side of them, which makes them settle on a particular mate. One grounds the other. Because you will never have a tru-mate, the Viking part of you will never be content; the Martian side of you is."

Reva's voice took on a mocking tone. "*What if the seeress is wrong*?" She mimicked the words that had been going around in his mind constantly. "What if I chose wrong? That is the true cause of your distress, not your soft-hearted, gentle bride. You don't trust in me or yourself."

"She isn't as I expected her to be."

"I don't suppose you're her ideal mate, either." Giving a small laugh, Reva moved to stand in front of him. "Raine is important to the future of the clan." She imploringly stared into his eyes, as if she could share some vision with him. "My loyalty will always belong to our clan, but the other clans need the path that Raine will clear for them so we can live as before Xioarius tried to destroy us. Most importantly, whether you're willing to admit it or not, you need her. Deep down, you think the gods are punishing you for not giving you a tru-mate. They aren't. Raine is your gift from them ... to all Vikings. She will lead us to whom is destined to accomplish what even your father wasn't able to achieve. She will make us whole."

When her impassioned plea didn't get the response from him that she wanted, she exasperatedly gave him her back. "If you truly feel as if I've made a mistake in my vision, then I will confide my vision to the chieftain. He will make Raine his bride, and mayhap my vision will still come to be."

Skars turned toward her abruptly. "Raine is mine."

Reva didn't attempt to hide her gloating expression. "Then what are we arguing about?"

Skars tiredly rubbed his temple at being outmaneuvered by the seeress. "Nothing. But could you at least try teaching my wife not to be so softhearted?"

"Aw ... I cannot." Laughter shone in her eyes. "Her soft heart is the only way she will fall in love with her Viking husband."

CHAPTER 20
RAINE

Raine uncomfortably watched Skars leave. Why hadn't she taken advantage of leaving when he had given it to her?

Milly's pinched expression spoke volumes that she was holding back.

The elevator door had barely closed behind Skars when Milly's eyes traveled down every inch of her body. Rudely, Milly shoved Silvia aside to interrupt Brinn's telling her how nice they were all being treated.

"Some of us are clearly being treated better than others." While making sure she spoke low enough that those who were standing next to her could hear, Milly also made sure, from the position she was standing, they would be unable to see the jealous way she was looking at her.

Licking suddenly dry lips at the hateful way Milly was acting, Raine took in the clothes the others were wearing. They were clearly human clothes. The women had been provided with jeans or loose cloth pants with a mixture of different types of either long- or short-sleeved tops. Lucas had been provided a pair of jeans and a long-sleeved T-shirt. Dropping her gaze, she saw they had all been given new shoes as well. In fact, all the clothes appeared new.

If she had found the clothes while out searching for supplies, she would have thought she had found the holy grail. They would have been ecstatic if she had brought the finds back with her. None of the others seemed discontent with what they had been provided with except for Milly.

Raine already knew what had Milly so upset. It wasn't that her clothes were different from the others'. What had her angry was that she had something Milly didn't. Every member of their group had learned to keep harmony by giving Milly the first choice of anything.

"I'm sure, if you ask for some like mine, they would give you what you ask for." Raine gave the suggestion. "I'm sure the only reason mine are different is because of the size. I'm taller than any of you—"

Milly tugged on the waistband of her pants. "Wider, too."

Raine twisted her hips away from Milly's grasp.

"I was about to say that." Raine forced a small laugh from her throat, not wanting the older women, or Milly, to see how hurt she was at the comment. While Raine didn't care how Milly treated her, she had learned that the older women would also face the repercussions of Milly's dissatisfaction.

None of the elderly women had the medications they had been on before the bombings and, while none of them had a medical crisis so far, Raine lived in fear that Milly would cause one by the derogatory way they would be treated because of something she hadn't done or given to Milly.

"Stop it, Milly." Lucas furiously stepped in sideways between them. "You might be used to ignoring me about how you treat Raine, but God help you if you do anything to jeopardize me getting Piper back. Not even that fucking vault will prevent me from tearing you apart."

Lucas' threat didn't have Milly backing down. "Perhaps Raine is right. I'll wait until I get to know them better before I ask. Exactly how close have you become with Skars? Or is that too embarrassing for you to answer?"

She desperately tried not to blush at Milly's intrusiveness. "I have my room," Raine tried to skirt through revealing how intimate she and Skars had been. "And we just ate before he brought me here. He told me I have been asleep for two days, so you all have probably spent more time with him than I have. Have you all eaten?"

Hoping the other women would help her change the focus of the conversation, she gave them a beseeching look.

It was Lucas who came to her aide.

"They made sure we've been fed anytime we ask. The food is good, just different."

Raine nodded in agreement. "I had to make myself stop from asking for more of the trippe, and the purple doths that tasted like potatoes were really good also."

Too late, she realized she had screwed up for going into details about what she had eaten. From their expressions, they had been given something different.

It only took Milly a heartbeat to voice her dissatisfaction. "Must be nice. Our food consists of smoothies, or our choice of three different types of soups. Lucas, you should make them aware you and I have our own teeth, and we can chew our food."

Raine's anger soared when Brinn had to blink back her hurt tears.

"That was needlessly cruel of you. When Skars comes back, I'll make sure to tell him that you aren't happy with what you've been given, Milly, and the others aren't the ones complaining to me about anything."

Biting down on her bottom lip to keep it from trembling, she glared at Milly until the woman grabbed Lucas' arm, pretending to be frightened of her.

Familiar with Milly's tactics of manipulation, she didn't let it faze her this time. Everyone in the group was aware of Brinn's inability to eat certain foods because the dentures she wore required adhesive, and it wasn't like they could run to the store and get it for the woman. Raine had searched fruitlessly herself to find the adhesive in places that none of the others had the stomach to search.

"Already trying to start some shit, aren't you?" Milly snapped out like a stinging whip. "Do you want to get us in trouble? Anytime something good happens to us, you can't stop until you shit on it and make it useless to everyone else."

"I'm the troublemaker?" Raine could only stare at Milly in consternation. Well, at least she was taking a break from being called a jinx. At least that one she was more deserving of.

If not for leaving the other women and Lucas, who seemed about to blow a gasket, she would have asked for one of the Vikings to take her back to her room.

Linking her hand with Brinn and Silvia, she walked them back to where they had been sitting before she had arrived. "How is your room?"

Silvia gave Brinn a heartening smile. "Brinn and I are sharing one, Lucas and Milly each have their own, and the rest are sharing. Skars told us this morning when his brother arrives tonight, we'll be moved onto his ship."

Seeing the worry, Raine sought to reassure her. "Did Skars tell you he's only doing it because his brother has healers? He's worried about you." She might have over-exaggerated Skars' concern, Raine thought guiltily, but it was for a good cause. Actually, two good causes. One to reassure the women, and the other was to ruin the rest of Milly's day.

Lucas waited until the women had settled back down and were at ease before he asked Brinn to switch places with him. "Are you really okay?" he asked once they had traded spots.

"Yes. It's a little nerve-racking being in a new environment. I imagine it's the same for all of us."

Lucas leaned forward until her head would block them from seeing his. "Not quite. None of the aliens are claiming to be married to one of us."

"I can explain."

"You don't have to; Skars told us. To tell the truth, I don't give a flying fuck what happened. Nothing can be changed, and right now, my concern is Piper. We both know that it was a matter of days before the vault was found or another one of us was killed. Him deciding to call you his wife is a lifesaver for the rest of us, if they are being on the up and up and not pulling the wool over our eyes. I just want to"—Lucas leaned forward even more—"make sure you're not expected to do anything you don't want to."

"I'm not. Skars has been very kind to me, other than I think I'm a disappointment to him."

Lucas frowned. "Because you don't want to be intimate?"

"No, I think it's because I don't act like Viking women do." Raine leaned her head forward, her lips barely moving. "I don't think he likes Milly."

Lucas rolled his eyes at her. "He can join the fucking club. We tolerate that bitch. There hasn't been a day that has gone by when I haven't regretted taking Dobbs that day and had Milly go with me."

Raine had to pretend to cough to smother a laugh.

"I think that's why she refused to go out with anyone other than me. She knows the rest of them would have given the aliens a lighter to light a fire to cook her on if they caught her."

She had to smother another spurt of laughter when Lucas didn't bother covering his. God, how long had it been since she'd had a good laugh? Raine couldn't remember. She didn't know if the humans would ever have a new normal, but Skars had made it possible so every moment wasn't spent in fear.

Wiping a tear of laughter away, she peered at Lucas critically.

"How's your wound?"

"Much better. I was given a salve, and it seems to have done the trick at healing the infection."

Raine placed a hand on his arm. "I'm glad. I was worried at how sick you were becoming. Next time you go hunting, take Milly and a lighter," she teased, bringing a smile to his lips.

Lucas' hand had just covered hers as they laughed, when he casually glanced to their side. Turning her head, she saw Skars staring at them from outside the elevator. He must have been standing there for some time when they had been joking about Milly.

Her smile died at the outraged, possessive glare he was giving her.

"Come, Raine; Thorsen has arrived."

Not liking the way he spoke to her, or the possessive way he was staring at her, Raine didn't immediately rise to her feet. "What about my friends? Shouldn't they come, too?"

Skars' nostrils flared at her delay. "Bjorn will escort them as they gather the belongings they brought with them, and the ones I gifted them with. You will see each other during the evening meal, which Thorsen has invited them to."

"Oh, okay." Standing, she gave each of them a reassuring smile, even managing a slight one for Milly before going to Skars' side.

As they entered the elevator, Raine felt a decidedly chill attitude emanating from him. Squaring her shoulders, she chose not to ignore his unmistakable anger.

"What did I do wrong this time?"

"Have you bedded Lucas?"

It was the last thing she had expected Skars to say. "No! Are you kidding me?" Indignant, she flew her hand out to poke Skars in his chest. "Lucas is the only reason those women and I are still breathing. He could have just been concerned for Piper and himself after the bombing and the aliens started attacking everyone. I've seen him go hungry numerous times to make sure we all had something to eat. I respect him as much as my father. Never once would it have occurred to Lucas to take advantage of the situation we've been in. He's just not that type of man. What you saw was us being able to do something we haven't been able to do in a long time—share a flipping joke! Which, if you had at least one human funny bone in that body of yours, I would have shared with you, but since you don't"—she gave him another hard poke—"I won't."

"Tell me."

Raine stubbornly crossed her arms over her chest. "No. It was a good joke. You don't deserve to be able to laugh.

I'm too mad at you right now. And just so you know, I was a pain in Lucas' butt when he was my manager at the bank, and since we've been locked up in the vault together, he would take a running jump off this spaceship rather than be in a relationship with me."

His stiff posture started to ease out his rigid frame. "I apologize. My jealousy overtook my judgment."

"Yes, it did." Raine wasn't ready to kiss and make up.

She was extremely proud of herself for standing up to Skars. *It's a brand-new you*, she complimented herself as she stepped out of the elevator with Skars.

"And I'll tell you something else ..." Querulously, she turned her head to give him hell about hurting her feelings yet again, but Raine didn't recognize this portion of Skars' ship as being one she had been seen before.

"Uh ... Skars, is ... that ... Earth?"

CHAPTER 21

SKARS

S kars turned his head to see what Raine was gaping at. Through the clear protective walls of the walkway, which led to Thorsen's ship, he saw Earth orbiting below.

"Yes."

He turned his head back to her, and his eyes widened when he saw Raine lying on the floor. Kneeling next to her, he couldn't understand what had happened to his wife. One moment, she was standing there, giving him hell, and the next, she was splayed out on the connecting walkway. Had he not given her enough to drink for her human body?

Bending his head down to make sure she was still breathing, he jerked his head upright again at hearing a startled scream.

"I told you he was a vampire!"

If he weren't so concerned about his wife, he would strangle the female woman screeching at the top of her lungs from within the elevator filled with the other humans and Bjorn and Njal.

Before he could get the ringing in his ears to stop, Lucas

shouldered his way out of the elevator to kneel down next to Raine. "What happened to her?"

"I do not know. She was talking to me, and then she was on the floor."

Accusatory steel-blue eyes glared at him. "You must have ..."

Skars saw his head turn to the side, his eyes widening.

"Are we in outer space?"

Skars nodded. "I told you Thorsen had arrived. His ship is much larger than mine. We felt his ship would be too big a target to remain in Earth's atmosphere."

"You might have made that much clearer before letting Raine walk out on what looks like a glass floor."

"It is not glass. The material is made from the strongest—"

"I do not care," Lucas bluntly stopped him from completing his explanation. "And I don't think Raine will, either. She is terrified of heights. We have to get here out of here before she comes to."

When Lucas started to lift Raine, Skars pushed him away. "I will carry my wife."

Taking Raine into his arms, he started striding down the corridor as the others hurried after him. Reaching Thorsen's elevator, Skars was forced to wait for the rest to cram inside before the door would close.

"Didn't Raine tell you she is afraid of heights?" the female with blue hair ventured to ask.

"She did. I forgot."

Unable to escape the mixture of emotions on the faces around him, Skars ignored those who were staring at him in irritation and glared at Milly, who had called him a vampire and seemed pleased at the condition Raine was in.

Then he managed to give Bjorn and Njal an accusatory look for the one of sympathy they were giving him.

They feel sorry for him! The chieftain's deputy! They saw Raine as weak, and they were giving him sympathy for taking a weakling for a bride.

Concern for his wife prevented him from smashing his friends to the floor.

"Move," he commanded when the door opened.

His hurt pride was soothed when everyone practically ran over each other to get out.

Carrying Raine into Thorsen's greeting room, Skars maneuvered through the waiting clan members.

"Who ...?" Thorsen started to ask as he pushed by his brother without stopping.

"My wife." Placing Raine down on the soft cushion of the seating bench, Skars hovered over her.

"Trygve," Skars called out for the healer.

"I am here. Move aside."

Reluctantly, Skars stood to give Trygve space enough to care for Raine.

Thorsen peered over Trygve to look at Raine in interest. "Is she breathing?"

Skars wanted nothing more than to grab the closest chalice of mead to ease the pounding in his head. "I think so." Skars had to link his hands behind his back to prevent himself from shaking Raine awake to make sure she was alright.

The brothers watched as Trygve took a small vial out of his pouch. Opening the pouch, he started to wave it under Raine's nose.

"Wait!"

Lucas' shout had all the Vikings in the room reaching for their weapons. Skars had to close his eyes as the pain in his head increased when the women started screaming in terror at his clansmen's actions.

"Halt," Skars managed to get out through gritted teeth. "They react that way when they are frightened," he explained to Thorsen, who appeared ready to chop off Milly's head.

Skars instantly regretted not waiting until the deed was done. He could have gotten rid of Milly and would have been able to place the blame on Thorsen. He wouldn't make that mistake again, Skars promised himself.

"I didn't mean to shout." Lucas moved to stand in front of the frightened women. "I just didn't want Raine to get hysterical and pass out again when she can still see outside. Are there any coverings we can cover the walls with so she won't see we're no longer on Earth?"

Under the watchful eyes of his clansmen, Skars went to the wall and changed the visage from the view of the outside to opaque.

"Thank you," Lucas said while still keeping a wary gaze on the Vikings surrounding him.

Feeling a heated flush under his beard as he went back to Thorsen's side, Skars motioned for him to put his ax away, speaking to him in their old language. "They aren't aware their loud voices hurt our ears."

Thorsen wasn't appeased. "Then I will tell them."

"You will give them a weapon to use against us," Skars warned.

"I will tell them, then kill them."

"My bride would blame me."

"I blame you." Thorsen was so angry that his beard was jutting out. "They can go back to your ship. I do not want them."

"They have to stay here."

"Why?"

Skars drew a blank. As he looked around for a chance to give himself time to come up with an idea, his gaze spotted a familiar face.

"Have you found anyone to help with the computer?"

From the death glare Thorsen was giving him, Skars had his answer.

"Neinn."

"We need to find out more about them. Perhaps one of them can."

"Then we kill them."

"Then you can have them returned to Earth safely."

"My way is quicker."

"Chieftain, they will be useless to us dead. On Earth, we can watch them. They could lead us to more humans."

"I will allow them to stay only until I find if they are useful. But you need to find a way to explain why there has to be no more instances of loud noises coming from them."

"I will."

How he was supposed to manage that without alerting them to their weakness, he had no idea, but he decided to check on his wife rather than argue with a riled Thorsen.

Raine was being helped up into a sitting position on the bench when he turned back to her.

"You are better?" he demanded, switching back to the language she could understand.

"Yes. I don't know what happened." His wife shyly blushed with everyone watching them. Sliding her legs to the floor, she started to stand.

"Stay seated."

"I'm fine." Ignoring his order, she rose to stand next to him. "Are we on your brother's ship?"

Skars shot his brother a pleading glance. "We are."

Placing a protective arm around her shoulder, Skars drew her closer to him. "Thorsen, my bride, Raine."

Thorsen's eyes narrowed on his before his gaze switched to Raine.

Taking a chalice that Bjorn was holding from his grasp, Skars gave it to Raine, feeling her trembling under his arm.

Raine took a drink. Expecting her to take a small drink, he was surprised when she finished the chalice then handed it back to him. "I was thirsty. Thank you."

A proud grin came to Thorsen's lips. "Would you like more mead?"

Raine gave Thorson a shy grin. "Maybe later. Thank you."

Unexpectedly, Thorsen pulled Raine out from Skars' protective arm to lead her to where food and drink had been set out for a meal.

"Come, sit next to me."

Skars nodded in approval when she glanced his way.

Skars poured himself a chalice after taking the seat next to her on the bench.

Thorsen placed a large portion of hithea on her platter.

"It's like your chicken," Skars told her.

Skars gave his brother a pleased grin for honoring his wife by giving her the food meant for him.

"What about the others?" Raine asked as the clan began taking their seats now that Thorsen and he were seated.

"Bjorn, take them to their rooms," Thorsen offhandedly commanded while filling his platter from the banquet that had been laid out on the massive table.

"Oh ... They won't be joining us? I should go with them, so I know which room is mine ..."

Skars placed a hand on her shoulder when she started

to get up. "They can eat with us, and then Bjorn will take them to their rooms."

Thorsen's eyes dueled with his when he invited them to sit. Skars thanked the gods that the remaining seats were toward the opposite end. With so many clansmen taking their places, the humans were out of view. He hoped out of earshot, too. He doubted his ability to hold Thorsen back if any of them made their grating sound again.

"Skars told me that you and your friends survived by hiding in an underground vault?"

Skars filled his platter as he listened to Thorsen talk to Raine.

"We did."

"Are there many vaults like yours on Earth?"

Raine took a small bite of her meat before replying. "I'm sure dozens of them would be similar, but none quite like ours. Our bank was older. In fact, our bank was due to be closed in a couple of months because it was so out of date. The previous bank manager, who had been there for sixty years before he retired, had a fear of being locked in the vault. Don't ask me why, but it did come out later after he died that one of the tellers had been locked in overnight. So, after that, he had a safety system installed."

"How did so many of you manage not to be captured or killed?"

Raine's sad expression had them all pausing in eating.

"One of us was—Dobbs. He was killed the first day Lucas and Dobbs went out to check and see if it was safe for the rest of us to go out."

"I see this saddens you." Thorsen filled her chalice from the gold pitcher.

"He was a very sweet man." Blinking back tears, Raine reached for her chalice.

169

Skars' brows rose when his wife finished the drink off in one swallow. He wasn't the only one. The whole clan was filled with amusement while watching Raine toss back her drink as if it were water. Despite his mirth, Thorsen wasn't diverted from his questions.

"You all went to this vault for shelter?"

"Some of them did." Raine nodded toward the end of the table where her friends were eating. "Some of us worked there."

"Doing what?"

"I was a teller. Lucas managed the bank. Milly was … she was a customer service representative."

"Did this place have computers?"

"Yes, it did. All our work involved using computers."

The information bought her a beaming smile from Thorsen.

"You know how to use a computer?"

"Very well," she bragged, helping herself to the pitcher to refill the chalice.

Out of the corner of his eye, he noticed Lucas and the women's expressions as Raine bragged. Milly's face had gone so purple that he began to think she was choking to death. Not intervening in the hopes it was Oden's gift to him, he returned his attention to Raine and Thorsen.

"My ship has a computer. Do you think you would be able to work it?"

"I don't know." Her confidence seemed to be replaced with doubt.

Thorsen refilled her empty chalice.

"I'm sure I could if whoever is in charge of the computer teaches me how."

That wasn't the answer Thorsen wanted. "You would have to be taught?"

Raine kept them waiting for her answer as she downed her third drink.

"Oh, yes ... Running a computer is difficult. I'm sure your computer runs on a different language and commands than what I'm used to."

"Would any human be able to use our computer without being taught?"

Raine turned her head to the end of the table again. "Lucas would know better than me. What do you think, Lucas?"

Lucas was staring at Raine the way he imagined he had stared at Milly when she was choking. Lucas did not want to share the information Raine was asking for. He wasn't the only one who noticed it, either.

Thorsen cast Lucas a look that let him know he expected an answer.

"I wouldn't know of anyone personally ..."

The human was lying.

Rubbing his knuckles over his lip, Skars cocked his head to the side, as if thinking. "What gift would you give to the person who told you of someone capable of working our computer, Chieftain?"

"Depends on the value of what he wanted for the information?" Thorsen's glance went to the same man who his was still resting on.

Resolve crossed Lucas' features. "You already know what I want."

"Your brother," Thorsen stated.

"Yes."

"Who is this person, then?"

"I'll give you the name when I get my brother back, not before."

"I give you my word your brother will be returned."

171

Lucas was unaware of what Thorsen was offering.

Skars couldn't help himself from going rigid. King Jurzed had demanded what he wanted for Piper's trade. Thorsen's word was his bond. He had never broken it, nor would he ever. By offering Lucas his word, Thorsen meant to keep it, which meant he would have to meet King Jurzed for Xioarius. His brother had already sworn a vow to kill Xioarius. How was he going to now fulfill Lucas' demand, and then his own vow to the clan?

An unamused smile came to Thorsen's lips. "I will gain your brother's release, but be aware, if the person you say can work our computer fails and isn't up to my expectations, you will wish he had remained with King Jurzed."

"Are you saying you'll kill Piper?"

"Would you be happy with our bargain if only half of your brother was returned?"

"No." Lucas turned a sickly pale.

Thorsen shrugged. "I expect to be just as happy when our bargain is met."

"You will be."

"I'm sure I will be." Thorsen raised his chalice. "Everyone fill their chalices! Skars, your woman meets with my approval. I will instruct Reva to prepare for a wedding ceremony. I will make a sacrifice as my gift to you so Odin can share in the festivities."

"Sacrifice?" Raine choked out.

Skars helpfully patted her on the back.

"Já!" Thorsen bellowed.

Skars echoed the bellow, "Já!"

Appalled, Raine whispered to him, "I don't want your brother killing animals at our wedding."

Thorsen beat him to reassuring her. "Animals?" Thorsen frowned. "Do you think us barbaric? My brother is getting wed; only the best will be sacrificed for his happiness!" Thorsen used his chalice to point down the table. "I will allow you to choose which one to send to live in Odin's domain." Thorsen tilted his head to Raine's to mutter aside, "Please pick the young one. You can choose whichever, but Skars and I prefer the other one."

Skars managed to give a look of pretended innocence, while giving his brother a withering glare when Raine turned her head away to assure Milly that Thorsen was joking.

His brother made a face back, silently communicating why he wasn't taking the opportunity to rid themselves of the screamer. They were still dueling each other when Raine turned back and caught the faces they were making.

"Aren't there any other choices other than my friends? For example, what are the aliens called that are green and mushy?"

"Mushy?" Skars asked uncomprehendingly.

"Their faces look as if they're smushed." Raine loudly clapped her hands together, causing all the Vikings to jerk in startlement. Rubbing her palms together in a twisting motion, she said, "You know, mushy."

"They are called bruulls," Skars supplied helpfully.

"Yeah, those." Raine nodded happily. "I wouldn't be opposed to you sacrificing as many bruulls as you want to. As long as I don't have to watch." Giving a wave of permission toward Thorsen, she said, "You can have at it."

Skars felt his cock stirring at this bloodthirsty side of Raine. He wasn't the only one. Appreciative stares directed at her had him frowning heavily at his clan members.

He would speak to Reva to hurry the wedding ceremony. While by ancient law, he considered himself married to Raine, he didn't trust any of them not to sway her mind toward them.

If a few of them didn't stop staring at her so covetously, he was going to come up with a few suggestions for sacrifices himself.

CHAPTER 22
RAINE

"What's the rush?" Raine tried to pull away from Skars' hand on her arm as he attempted to steer her toward the elevator. "I was enjoying the talk I was having with Bjorn. He was tell—"

"I have heard the story before. He stole it from me."

Raine arched her brows at the jealous tinge in his voice. "Bjorn could have showed me to my new room when he took the others to theirs."

"You're staying in the same room on my ship. Your friends are staying on Thorsen's."

"When will the healer see them?" she asked worriedly. "Silvia and Brinn looked so tired when they left, and Lucas' wound needs to be checked."

"Trygve is with them now. He will take good care of them."

"I noticed how sweet he was to Brinn when he sat next to her at the table."

Brinn had been so despondent lately, preferring to stay in her little corner of the vault and growing increasingly isolated from the rest of the group. She was part of the

175

reason why Raine had done everything possible to keep Milly from picking on the depressed woman.

After the huge meal and the countless cups of the wine she had drunk, she became sleepy, but found herself startled out of her sleepiness when Skars turned her to face the back of the elevator as the door started to open.

"Wha—"

"Wait here."

Raine felt the movement next to her as Skars left the elevator then returned a second later to take her hand. As she walked out into the corridor, she gazed around the passageway.

"Is this where I passed out?"

"Já."

"Aw ... That's why I don't remember it. I still can't understand why I passed out. Usually, the only thing that fazes me is heights. I have to admit I'm a coward where that is concerned."

Raine practically had to run to keep up with Skars because he was walking so fast. She was almost out of breath before they were again enclosed in the other elevator.

"Were you frightened of heights as a child?"

Terrifying images assailed her of long-ago memories she never let herself dwell on.

"Nothing beyond the range of normal childhood fears. How about you? Are you afraid of anything?"

"No, not anymore."

Other than giving him a questioning glance, she didn't pry. She didn't want to divulge what had created her fear.

As she got out of the elevator, Raine noticed something different about the bedroom from when she had left. "Where did the window go?"

"It's still there. I prefer it darkened at night."

"That makes sense. Your ship can be hidden in the day within the clouds, and at night, they would be seen."

"Já."

Had she caught a caustic edge in his response to her? She was probably just tired and imagined it.

"Thank you for walking me to my room. Good ..." Raine broke off. "What are you doing?"

"Going to sleep." Skars continued to strip himself of his clothes.

"Naked?" she croaked out.

"Já."

Raine tried to avert her gaze, but it was almost impossible to look away as the Viking revealed more of his body. "But this is my room."

"Mine as well."

"You slept here with me for the last two nights?"

"Já."

"Why are you just telling me this now?"

He shrugged. "Because I'm preparing to go to bed."

"What's to prepare? You're getting naked! Stop it!"

Should she turn around? She was torn between wanting to look and turning away, but her curiosity about his body won out over the scandalized part of her.

"You are my wife. Viking men and women sleep naked. Clothes are for when you are up and about. Do humans not sleep naked?"

"No," she lied, partly. "We sleep fully clothed. We have day clothes and nighttime clothes."

"We will sleep the Viking way. It is much better."

"I prefer to sleep clothed."

"You may do so if you wish." In no uncertain terms, he

was letting her know he was going to be sleeping naked regardless.

Her courage failed when, after he had taken off his boots, he started unbuttoning his pants. About to spin on her heels, she dropped her eyes onto what he had uncovered.

"What the—"

"What's wrong?"

"Your—" Her eyes grew wide at what she was staring at, unable to find her words to express the strangeness of his cock.

Noticing what her eyes were staring at, he smiled devilishly. "Do the human males pale in comparison?"

"Uh ... Well, it certainly looks a bit different." While the base wasn't much different than what she had seen in pictures, which usually showed huge penises, something she had always been skeptical about, his had a bulbous head with strange lines going down it to meet at the sacs. "The head is ... different, for sure." She uncomfortably tried to make the sensible portion of her brain start to function again, knowing he wanted to know what exactly was different about it.

"Ah ..." he said, somehow understanding what she was too shy to get out. "Stroke it."

"What? No!" She backed up a bit toward the elevator.

"Come on. Are you scared?" Skars practically dared her while raising a brow. "You know I won't hurt you."

"It's not that," she said, taking another step back. "It's just ... I've never touched one before."

She became even more embarrassed when he stared at her in wonder.

"Human or male?"

"Neither."

"Are you an innocent, Raine?"

The gentle way he was speaking to her started to loosen her reserve.

"Já."

Her heart skipped a beat when he gave her a beautiful smile because she had used his language.

"Why?" he asked simply as he took off his shirt to place it atop one of his wooden chests, giving her a stunning view of his butt.

Distracted, she answered honestly. "No one wanted me."

"I want you." Skars walked forward until he was within reaching distance. "Touch me."

Raine didn't know what possessed her, but she found her hand moving toward him, as if it belonged to another woman.

At first, she just touched the silky flesh. Then she spread her fingers around the thick length. She felt awkward and excited at the new experience as it started growing harder and longer under her touch.

"More, Raine. I want more."

"I don't think it can handle getting much bigger," she said half-jokingly, while the other half was saying, *Hell nah*.

"Já, it can." Giving her a lecherous grin, he surrounded her hand with his own, showing her the movement he wanted from her. "This is what I like. Start slow, then go faster.

After clasping her fingers tighter around his penis, he released her hand to put his on her upper arms to pivot them in the other direction. Slowly, he edged her toward the huge bed until she could feel the soft covering behind her.

179

Stroking his penis, she became fascinated as his arousal heightened, turning it an angry red.

"Are you sure it won't explode?" she asked hesitantly.

"Já." He laughed. "At least, not yet."

With a gentle push, Raine found herself seated on the bed, bringing her eye level with his protruding cock. From this viewpoint, she could see, with the movements of her hand, there was something expanding from the slit at the top. Skars' penis didn't have the smooth bulbous human males had; his was more cylindrical. As her hand moved on his length, the skin started to flower out like a rose blooming.

The lines on the head started to change to a different texture, and the longer she stroked, the redder his penis grew, the slits thickening and turning those areas of his rougher. While it was a bit freaky at first that it was reacting that way, she thought it was beautiful.

"I don't think we're meant to fit together," she said nervously.

Skars' hands went to her top to pull it tenderly over her head.

"On some of the planets I've traded on, there live small creatures which have become highly prized pets. They are extremely rare, and those that are sold must be extremely well cared for. They are extremely gentle, with beautiful grey eyes and affectionate natures. Without special care, they don't live long." Skars stroked his knuckles gently across her cheek. "You have the same-colored eyes as a crinda, and the same gentle spirit. I have never called another woman wife, and I will never, other than you. I have flown through galaxies to find you, Raine. We're meant to fit together."

She had never dreamed a man, neither human nor

alien, would ever say anything so romantic to her. Despite wanting to give in to the emotions Skars had soaring through her, though, so many misgivings were holding her back.

One being, while this would be her first time having sex, she was pretty damn sure it wouldn't be his. Skars was too sexually confident. He had said he had been to several planets to trade. How many women had he said the same romantic phrase to? She was willing to bet more than one.

The thought of him having several honeys waiting for his return trips brought a screeching halt to what she had been about to give him.

She reached for the top he had taken off and covered her breasts.

"Human women don't have sex before they've been married for six months. We've already broken the rule for you seeing me naked. Don't your people have rules they stick to before getting married?"

"Neinn." Skars' eyes crinkled at the corners. "You would take my clan's way of doing things in consideration?"

"Of course. It would only be fair." She saw no harm giving him that point.

Taking her by her upper arms, he moved her away from the bed.

Clutching her top, she watched, confused, as he pulled the mattress with the covering off the platform it was on to drop it to the floor. Lying down on the bed, he held his hand out to her.

The sensual way he was looking at her left no doubt at what was on his mind.

"My people count time differently than humans do. By our time, we have been married over a year."

Did she really want to argue and win this argument?

181

No, she did not. Her feet were already moving closer to the bed before her brain had said it was okay. Then she was crawling over the mattress until she was on her knees beside his hips.

"If it doesn't fit, I'm going to say what all human men hate to hear."

"What is that?"

"I told you so."

He grabbed the back of her neck to pull her mouth close to his. "Do human women hate to hear it also?"

"Even more."

"Then I won't say it," he gloated.

"I would wait until it actually fits before you start bragging about it."

Skars bracketed her jaw with hard fingers as his shoulders rose to press her down on the mattress. As he leaned over her, his fingers held her as he angled his mouth onto hers.

He pried her lips open with his tongue to thrust inside in a voracious kiss filled with mind-numbing lust; Raine couldn't believe it was meant for her.

Releasing her jaw, he jerked the top away from her to crush her underneath him. All her misgivings were vanquished at the onslaught of Skars' lovemaking.

He clung to her as his hands roamed and explored her body as his tongue did to her mouth. At his impatient tug at her pants, Raine willingly lifted her hips to help him finish undressing her.

When his fingers dipped between her thighs, she opened them wider, wanting to feel his hands on the most intimate portion of her body. Her body dampened under his touch, remembering the ecstasy he had given her before, wanting it again, and again.

Raine started to grab him back when he reared back onto his knees, breaking her hold on his shoulders. Afraid he had changed his mind, she was about to beg him when she saw what Skars was doing.

Holding his penis in his hand, he placed the tip on her vulva. She managed to hold back a scream when the skin at the top started to bloom and spread out to latch on to her.

Unimaginable pleasure took her senses on a joyride that Raine didn't think the female body was meant to experience. Her neck arched back, and she would have sworn her eyes rolled backward at the overwhelming pleasure.

Skars returned his mouth to hers to lick at her lips.

"You are finding pleasure, já?"

Raine couldn't have moved her vocal cords if an Olggan suddenly appeared in the bedroom.

"Raine?" Skars tried to coax her.

"How can it feel so good when you're not even inside of me?"

Devilishly, he gloated at her, "It gets better."

Raine almost asked how he knew, but she decided that was one question she never wanted answered.

"Watch." Raising his head, still sitting on his knees, Skars positioned each of her knees over his until she was open to both of their gazes.

"Maybe it might be better if I don't look the first couple of times ..."

The unusual sight would have probably sent her running out of the bedroom, if not for the sensations his penis was creating. It felt as if the skin that had latched on to her was massaging her with erotic bursts of electric shocks.

"Do you feel them, too?"

Skars stared at her in confusion. "What?"

183

"It feels like static shock."

Seeing he was becoming even more confused, she explained, "Like a sting of electricity. Is that normal?"

A strange look crossed his face at her description. "Já, it is for your pleasure."

Raine had the peculiar feeling Skars wasn't telling her something. She was about to press him when Skars used his fingers to detach the flap of skin that had been sucking on her vulva and moved it lower to her opening.

When he placed it at her opening, Raine braced herself for him to thrust it inside of her. There was always a lot of thrusting going on in the romance books she had read.

If she had thought her eyes had rolled back in her head when his penis had latched on to her vulva, it didn't compare to the feel of him entering her. His penis changing back to the shape of a bud of flower as it slid through her opening, Raine could have sworn the head became malleable to easily glide inside. As it went in, she felt the sense of fullness she had expected to feel with how wide his penis was. Like a balloon, he was expanding inside of her body.

Raine moved her hands to Skars' shoulders to hold on as his hands went under her knees to pull her hips closer to his.

"Lie back."

He didn't have to ask twice. She was incapable of doing anything other than follow his lead. There was nothing but a pleasure so intense that she wondered if human women would be able to live through making love with a Martian even if he had DNA from their ancestors on Earth.

It also felt as if it had latched on to ...

She was unable to hold back her screams of fulfillment

when the ecstatic shudders struck her like a lightning bolt when he found her G-spot.

Skars' mouth landed on hers, effectively fusing their mouths together. If she had been capable of speech, she would have thanked him. She would have died of embarrassment if Reva's room was close to theirs and heard her screams.

Her pelvis thrashed against his, their lovemaking becoming frenzied. The climatic shudders didn't stop until Raine was afraid she would never be able to survive another climax. Just as she was about to start hitting his shoulders to make Skars aware that her death was imminent, the climax stopped, and she once again felt him burrowing higher inside of her to latch on to another part.

"I told you we would fit."

Barely left with enough strength to lift one eyelid, much less argue, she let him gloat, especially when he started doing all the thrusting she had read about in her books. Action was always better than the written word.

His body moved over hers as he moved her into the positions he wanted until she found herself lying face down on the mattress with him plunging into her from behind. His body was like a piston that didn't have an off-switch.

Just when she was about to confess she didn't have a Martian woman's stamina, she felt him grasp her hips in a tight grip as his mouth caressed her neck.

Skars must have become worried he had killed her when she remained unmoving, so he rolled her onto her back. When she didn't say anything and remained still, she felt him lift one of her eyelids.

Raine swatted his hand away. "Skars, there is something I forgot to tell you about married couples."

Amusement filled his eyes at her exhaustion.

"Married couples only have sex every"—Raine tried to focus her brain as to how long it was going to take to recover from tonight and came up with a conservative figure—"twelve years."

"Our time is much different ..."

She wasn't going to fall that for a second time. "I already took that into account. The twelve years was in alien years."

Teasingly, Skars caressed the tip of her breast. "No exceptions?"

Raine swatted it away. She wasn't going to take any chances about stirring his wayward penis.

"Is there any way not to use that latchy thing?"

"No."

"Then no exceptions."

CHAPTER 23

RAINE

"Are they going to let us remain on their ships, or are the Vikings going to find a place to settle on Earth?"

"I have no idea, Silvia." Raine wanted the answer to that question herself.

When Skars had finally arranged for her friends to come for a visit, she had known they would have questions that she herself wanted answers for. What was unexpected were the long awkward silences after she couldn't answer them.

"Skars really hasn't told me anything," Raine told them truthfully. Skars would leave early in the morning and remain gone throughout the day, often returning when she was sitting down for an evening meal.

"It's been two weeks. Skars hasn't told you if Thorsen is getting any closer to getting Piper released?"

Raine put her hands out, showing Lucas she was just as in the dark as he was.

"Every time I ask, Skars says King Jurzed is refusing to trade for Piper until Thorsen has Xio; then the king would be willing.

"Did Thorsen try to trade me to King Jurzed so I can be with Piper?"

"King Jurzed refused to trade anything for you."

"Then give me to him for free."

Raine pressed her dry lips together. She had hoped to keep Lucas in ignorance about that request. "He didn't want you." Nor did he want Milly, which Thorsen had offered to give him as well as two barrels of their wine. Raine kept that fact a secret, not wanting to hurt Milly's feelings.

Glancing toward Milly in the new clothes she had just given her to wear, Raine started twisting her hands nervously. The woman was too happy with herself for Raine not to know she had screwed up.

Skars had agreed to let them come to his ship to share their evening meal tonight because there was some type of clan meeting on Thorsen's ship. During their dinner, Milly had spilt a glass of wine on her clothes, and she had made her go into the chest that Skars had given her for her clothes to find another outfit she could wear. Milly had snatched a matching sea-blue top and pants to change into.

Bjorn, who had remained with them after escorting them to her room, had given her a warning stare she shouldn't. Raine pretended she hadn't seen it, not wanting to argue with Milly.

"Maybe the meeting they're holding tonight is to decide what they are going to do with us, and that's why we came here?"

Brinn's query drew her thoughts away from Milly, who was making her feel uncomfortable with the passive-aggressive way she kept staring at her.

"I'll ask when he comes back."

"What if he doesn't come until we're gone?" Milly's

pinched lips showed the politeness she had been exhibiting so far was fading fast. "Will it take another two weeks before her highness sees us again?"

"Milly,"—Silvia cast Bjorn a worried glance—"he can hear you."

"How was what I said bad?" Milly's face became just as pinched as her lips. "Calling her highness shows she's better than us."

"I don't think I'm better than any of you."

"You don't? My mistake."

Standing by the elevator, Bjorn moved to take a position further into the room, playing idly with the ax hanging from his side.

Milly slunk back in her seat.

"I'll ask Skars if his brother can answer any of the questions you're worried about."

"Please don't."

Raine saw Brinn's hand shake on the drinking glass she was holding when she looked toward her at her quiet plea.

"We really don't want to make trouble. We can wait until you invite us back."

"How are you feeling, Brinn?" Raine reached out to take Brinn's free hand lying in her lap.

"Almost back to normal, considering I live on a spaceship. Chieftain Thorsen has given us each a room, and Trygve comes and checks on me daily."

"That's a relief. I've been worried about you all."

"Don't be. They are taking good care of us." Sylvia gave Brinn a wink. "Especially Brinn. I think Trygve has a huge crush on her."

Brinn's cheeks turned crimson. "He does not. He's just been concerned over my blood pressure. They don't have medicine like we used to have. They treat most of their ailments with medicinal herbs. He doesn't want to give me what they would take because their bodies are different."

"I'm glad he's being cautious."

"He also told me Chieftain Thorsen has ordered all his men to find any medicines when they go through buildings."

"They are going through buildings?" Raine asked. "What are they looking for?"

Brinn shrugged. "I imagine what everyone else is looking for—food and supplies. With so many people on board, we really don't know how they are fixed for supplies."

Disquiet, Raine saw the expression on Lucas' face. Remaining silent, aware of Bjorn listening to their conversation, she placed the question on the mental list she was going to ask Skars later tonight.

Releasing Brinn's hand, Raine picked up her glass to take a drink. This drink was different from what they had drunk on Thorsen's ship. It was glittery, and the taste was weaker, yet on her third glass, it was headier the more she drank.

Reva stepping off the elevator was a welcomed distraction of having Milly's eyes drilling holes into every movement she made.

Raine smiled at the woman. They had shared lunch a couple of times. Several times, Raine had made attempts to see her when she had grown bored with her own company, but each time, she had been told Reva was busy. She had asked several times if there was anything she could help out with on the ship and had been refused.

"Bjorn, you may escort Raine's company back to their rooms."

Wondering why Skars or Thorsen hadn't just

messaged Bjorn, Raine didn't protest their leaving. As much as she disliked being bored, Milly put a cloud over any enjoyment she might have with the rest of her friends whom she had grown close to when they had lived in the vault.

Hugging each goodbye, even Milly, who pulled away when she made the attempt, Raine waited until the elevator had closed behind them to say anything.

"It's good to see you again," Raine said sincerely. She genuinely like Reva. She even thought they would become close friends, if given the opportunity to spend more time together.

The beautiful woman gave her a smile. "I didn't interrupt?"

"No. I'm afraid they spent most of the time wanting to get answers from me when I know just as much as them."

"What questions would you liked answered?"

Reva went to the low table to pour herself a glass of the glittery wine. "Is your clan planning to stay on the ships, or will you eventually find a place to make a home on Earth."

"I had hoped to answer some of your questions. This one, I think it be best if I let Skars answer for you."

"Your clan has no plans to make Earth a home, do you?"

"Very little places on Earth are habitable. The soil is filled with contaminations. Some of the weapons that humans used against each other weren't meant to destroy lives on impact, but to makes it impossible to grow anything, which would sustain those who did survive."

At the reality of what Reva was telling her sank in, Raine also sank down onto a padded bench.

"Our clan is mainly made of farmers and traders. There is no benefit for us to stay, especially since many of our lives would be lost trying to stake a claim when there are so many coming from other planets to ravage what little is left."

Raine trailed a finger over the rim of her glass.

"Where will your clan go once you left Earth?"

"We don't know. We are searching for planets which are habitable for our needs."

"If Earth weren't destroyed, would it be habitable for your needs?"

Reva made a face after taking a sip of her drink. "I should go. Chieftain Thorsen is waiting to speak with me." Reva set her drink down on the table.

"Raine, when you request visits from your friends, please tell Skars not to include Milly. There is no need to subject yourself to her hatred."

Unhappily, Raine looked away from Reva's gaze. "It's pretty obvious she dislikes me, isn't it?"

"She doesn't dislike you; her feelings go much deeper. You shouldn't have given her any of your clothes. Skars won't allow her to keep them."

"She only needed to borrow them because she spilled her drink on hers," Raine quickly explained.

Reva stared at her quizzically. "You are afraid of her."

Raine wiped her clammy hands on the sides of her pants. "Já."

Reva gave a small smile of approval at her using their language. Then her quiet footsteps crossed the distance separating them to come sit beside her.

"I don't understand. Skars told me how brave you were when you fought the Olggans when you thought he was outnumbered."

"He was."

Reva wouldn't let her off the hook.

"Why do you tolerate her behavior around you?"

Raine emptied the glass of wine to refill it again. She had a slight buzz going on. Otherwise, she would never have dropped her guard enough to confide in Reva.

Raine turned her head from side to side to make sure everyone had left, even though she had seen them leave just minutes before. "Milly reminds me of my mother."

Reva's mouth dropped open. "You were afraid of your mother?"

"My mother was schizophrenic. Do you know what that means?"

Raine guessed Reva's translator in her ear told her.

"Your mother had a mental illness?"

"Yes. When I was a child, I was too young to understand why my mother was different from other parents. She even acted differently when my half-brother would come for visits once a month. One day, she would be fine; then the next, she would be burning my toys in the backyard, or I would find all my clothes in the bathtub."

Raine lifted her hand to her hair, becoming lost in the memories of her childhood. "My father tried to make sure she stayed on her medicine, but she got good at pretending to take them then hide them. Her behavior became increasingly erratic, so much so that my father became afraid of me being left alone with her.

"When he came home from work one day, she had shaved both our heads. He sent her to a hospital so she could get the help she needed. She stayed there for several months until my mother begged to see me, saying she missed me. He planned a special day out for us and got permission to take her out for lunch, and he promised not to leave me alone with her."

Raine was unaware her hands were jerkily rubbing up down on her thighs. "Both of my parents got out of the car, but when Dad went to open the back door for me, Mom shoved him to the ground and started stabbing him. The hospital wasn't aware she had found a knife, but Mom had. She used it to stab him twenty-four times before taking the car keys from him to drive off with me in the back seat.

"I kept crying for her to take me back to Dad. I was only five years old, but I knew he was hurt badly. She didn't listen; she just kept screaming at me that we'd never be separated again. When the police started trying to get her to pull over, she stopped the car on a bridge and dragged me out of the back seat. Holding me, she climbed over the rail ..." Raine closed her eyes tightly, remembering how terrifyingly high the bridge had been.

"Raine." Reva's gentle voice brought her back to reality. "What happened?"

"She jumped. I was fortunate that a boater was just yards away, and he was able to get to me quickly. I had two broken legs and a fractured clavicle, but I survived."

"Your father?"

"He recovered, somewhat. He was confined to a wheel-chair for the rest of his life."

"Did your brother survive the war?"

"I don't know. There isn't a way for me to contact him. He lived in a different part of the United States."

"Perhaps Skars can help you find him," Reva suggested.

"We weren't that close." Raine evaded any more questions by refilling her glass from the last of the bottle. "You don't like the wine?"

"Neinn." Reva rose from the bench to give her an amused look. "I have a bottle in my room. You may have it if you wish."

"Thank you. It's my favorite so far." Raine stared down

into the wine. How could any woman not like the sparkly wine?

As Reva moved away, Raine remembered a question she had wanted to ask her then had forgotten.

"Reva ..."

Reva paused. "Já?"

"Was Earth habitable to the Viking clans before it was destroyed?"

"Já."

"Could it be fixed with your clan's help?"

"Neinn."

Disappointment filled her. There was no way she was going to go planet hopping until they found a new home planet.

"It would take more than our clan. It would take all of the Viking clans. We are farmers, builders, miners, and guardians. If all the Viking clans could be convinced to work together once again, Earth may stand a chance."

From what Skars had told her, the different clans couldn't even agree on who was going to be given the privilege of killing their enemy.

"From what I've learned in the short time I've gotten to know your clan, I'd have more luck convincing them to drink this wine."

"Do you know why Skars bought that wine without tasting it?"

"Neinn."

"Because it reminded him of liquid gold. From a Viking male's first breath to their last, they can't resist the lure of precious metals, whatever form it takes."

Raine placed a hand over her mouth to cover a hiccupping giggle. "Skars got taken in by fool's gold?"

Reva nodded. "I wouldn't say it to him, but já. He's still not happy by how bad it tastes."

"Then he can give it to me. I'll take it all."

"That's because you were never blinded by the wine's looks, so you didn't have high expectations that couldn't be met. Strain the wine and put in a chalice, then ask if he likes it or not. If Skars gives his approval, then all the men will start drinking it as well."

Perceptively, Raine stared at Reva. "You weren't blinded by the glitter, and you didn't like it."

"Only because I dislike wine, regardless if it's sparky or not."

"If I do as you're suggesting, would you tell them the wine was the sparkly kind after I strain it?"

Raine and Reva shared a feminine smile.

"From a Viking female's first breath to her last, we can't resist the lure of pulling the wool over our men's eyes, whatever form it takes."

CHAPTER 24

RAINE

Raine knew Skars was furious with her the moment he stepped into their bedroom. After Reva had left, she had showered and was sitting on the mattress on the floor as she brushed out her hair.

"Why did you give one of the presents that I gave you to Milly?"

"Her clothes were wet from spilled wine, and since they had been brought to your ship to prevent them from finding out what your clan was discussing, I thought it prudent not to send her back for fresh clothes."

"She could have remained in her wet clothes." He angrily brought his hands to his hips as he gave her the other alternative.

"I was being a good hostess. Next time, I won't be."

"There won't be a next time," he snapped. "Bjorn told me of her behavior toward you. In the morning, I will send for the clothes. Those are Viking clothes, meant for my Viking bride. When I get them back, they will be destroyed."

"Those are one of my favorites. I'll wash them—"

197

"I saw her in the clothes when she returned. I will not see you wearing the same as her."

"But—"

"If you had given me a gift, I would not have parted with it so easily."

Raine felt terrible. She had unintentionally hurt his feelings.

Reaching for his hand, she tugged him down on the mattress to remove his boots. "I'm sorry, Skars. I was wrong." Raine hugged his boots to her belly, angry at herself for letting Milly manipulate her. Deep down, she knew Milly had deliberately spilled the wine on herself just to get some of her clothes. "I'm such a coward where she is concerned. I won't even try to get you to reconsider changing your mind about her not visiting me again."

He gave her a curt nod. "I will not be changing my mind."

"Of course not," she soothed. "I wouldn't expect you to."

Setting his boots aside, she gave him a hard shove to push him back and lean over him. "Did you miss me today?"

"Did you miss me today?" he countered.

"Já. Very much," she promptly answered, rubbing her cheek against his briskly beard and curling up next to him like a kitten. "How did your meeting go?"

Raine felt him stiffening under her hands.

"Well."

"Has Thorsen gotten any more information about Piper? Lucas is really worried. Do you think Thorsen could give him an update on what is going on?" She rolled the litany of questions at him before she forgot. "And could he talk to the women? They are wondering if your clan plans to stay on Earth. And, if you do stay, would you just plan to live on your ships, or—"

Skars placed a hand over her mouth. "I will take Thorsen with me in the morning. Both of us will answer what questions they have."

Raine nudged his hand from her mouth. "Can I go, too?"

"Neinn," he said inflexibly.

"Why not?"

"Because, if Milly says one word to you, I won't wait until our wedding to sacrifice her."

Raine giggled and rose onto her knees to start unbuttoning his pants. Scooting down to his feet, she started pulling them off.

Skars sat up on his elbows to give her a suspicious look. "You've been in my wine again."

"I'm bored. Can I go to Earth with you tomorrow after you talk to my friends?"

"Neinn. I don't want to have to worry for your safety while we're there."

"Has it become worse since I came here?"

"Já," he answered shortly.

"Have you come across any survivors?" He lay back down on the bed, and she started massaging one of his feet.

"A few."

"What did you do with them? You didn't kill them, did you?"

"Neinn, we don't seek to kill those who don't try to kill us. So far, those we have found have been too starved and frightened to put up a fight."

Raine blinked back tears, imagining how hard things had become since she had left.

"Thorsen brought them to his ship. He will feed them and have Trygve check them out."

Raine remembered what Ulf had told them when Skars had been fighting the Olggans. She had broached the subject each time he had told her he was going to Earth, yet Raine couldn't help but seek reassurance once again.

"Skars, I know you're searching for items which can be used for trade on other planets, but you promise you're not looking for women to make brides out of them the way you did me?"

Skars' expression grew chilly.

"I have explained to you how our law permitted me to take you as my wife. Such a situation is rare. I admit I did take advantage of the opportunity." His facial features became gentler as he sought to reassure her. "How could I not want such a rare creature who save my life?"

Raine blushed at his gentle tone.

"I'm sorry to keep doubting you," she apologized. "I just wanted to make sure. The thought of any woman being made to do anything they're unwilling to do makes me sick to my stomach..."

"Have I treated you with anything other than respect? Asked you to do anything you're unwilling to do?"

"No," she answered honestly.

"Then I promise to extend the same courtesy to any women we find."

"Thank you, Skars, for relieving my worry. Is there anything I can do to help? I can talk to them and reassure them that you won't harm them."

"Neinn, because they won't be staying. Once we make sure they are healthy, we will find them a safe place to stay where they won't be in any danger."

"That's so nice of Thorsen." Seeing the strange look he was giving her, Raine hurried to correct her blunder. "And you, too, of course."

Bending her neck, she traced the tip of her tongue over his big toe. Holding his ankle with one hand, she started playing with his toes. Then, moving her mouth to his ankle, she ran her tongue over the hickey she had left there the night before. She had found out one night, when she wanted to find out if he was ticklish—he wasn't—that, to her delight, his feet were a highly erotic area to him.

She had made a lot of new discoveries about herself after the first night she and Skars had made love. She was the sex fiend in the relationship, not him. Breaking the twelve-year rule had been her decision, not his, even though he had been sucking on one of her nipples when she had come to the decision.

Leaving his ankle behind, she nibbled her way up his leg to bypass his penis and kiss her way up to his chest. She unbuttoned his shirt and splayed the two sides apart to ogle the hard planes and lines of his physique.

Gliding her tongue over one of his tattoos on the side of his chest, she splayed her hand over one on his biceps.

Curious, for the umpteenth time, she noticed the massive scar over his heart. Usually by this time, she was in the heat of the moment and had more important things on her mind than to ask about his scar that was the size of the palm of her hand.

"How did you get burnt so badly?" Raine ran the pad of her thumb over the scarred flesh.

"It was my birth tattoo. Each Viking male and female has one which shows the lineage of their immediate family. It resembles Yggdrasil, the tree of life in Norse mythology. Have you ever seen pictures of it?"

Raine shook her head.

Skars scooted away from her to rise from the bed. He moved to a wooden trunk and carefully shifted objects she couldn't see before taking out an overlarge book. Carrying it back to the bed, he sat down next to her and solemnly opened the book to flip through the pages.

"My great-grandfather made this book so our clan wouldn't forget our history." Skars pointed at a picture. "This is a drawing of Yggdrasil. He drew this from memory."

Raine stared down at the page. The drawing was of one large circle with a tree that had as large of roots as it did branches inside it.

"It's beautiful."

Skars nodded. "Our tattoos were similar. Our grandfather believed that it was the gods' way for us to never forget our origins, regardless of how many species we mated with, so we would not lose sight and always find our way back to our family."

"It would have been cool to have seen what your tattoo looked like to see the difference."

Setting the book aside, Skars got up again to go to his chest, this time taking out a smaller chest. He set it on the bed and opened it to take out drawings.

Raine shifted into a cross-legged position and, fighting back tears, she slowly went through them. To say the drawings were beautiful didn't do them justice.

"Who drew these?"

"The newer ones were done by Astrid, Reva's sister. The others were done by other seeresses from earlier times."

The pictures must have taken hours to complete with the level of details they showed. Raine pointed at several pictures where there were odd-colored, weird-shaped trees. In the background, mountains and lakes, and people smilingly posing for the artist.

"Where were these drawn?"

"Raum."

Her breath caught in her throat at the thought that such stark beauty had been destroyed. Then her mind went to the beauty which had been wiped out on Earth. Evil knew no boundaries, or it seemed, no solar system.

"I'm glad these weren't destroyed."

"The book is supposed to stay with our elder seeress. Astrid gave the book to Reva when we left Raum to go on a trading mission. It was Thorsen's first one in the ship our grandfather had gifted him."

"If Thorsen hadn't been given the ship, would you and the others have been on Raum when it was destroyed?"

"Já."

Rain pressed her trembling fingertips to her forehead at the realization how close she had gotten to never meeting Skars.

"If this book was supposed to stay with the elder seeress, how do you have it?"

"On each trading mission, a seeress goes along for protection to make sure nothing goes wrong. Astrid gave Reva the book to carry with her."

Raine supposed the seeress was the Vikings' version of psychics. She had never believed psychics could see into the future or into the afterlife, but she could see Skars did. She did have to admit that it did give her pause that the book wasn't left on Raum to be destroyed.

"Do you think Astrid knew?"

Skars nodded. "Both Astrid and Reva were prewarned. At first, Reva refused to go, but after Astrid and my grandfather commanded her, she went."

If that was true, it must have been a heartbreaking decision for Reva.

"Did any of you know?"

203

"No, Reva wasn't allowed to tell. It would have destroyed the future both Astrid and Reva saw for our clan."

"Wow, I'm glad I don't have that gift. I'd never be able to keep from warning them."

"That is why the gift is only given to those who can use it wisely."

"So, why isn't the book in Reva's belongings?"

Skars shook his head. "I don't know. Reva asked me to keep it. Perhaps the memories are too strong for her to bear they are gone."

"You think she blames herself?"

He nodded. "Já."

Raine didn't think she would want a reminder in her possession every day that she could have stopped a catastrophe from happening.

Slowly, she pulled out another drawing, and her breath caught in her throat.

The picture was of Thorsen, Skars, and an older version of Thorsen—their father. The three men were shirtless, their tattoos similar yet different. Seeing the tattoo in the drawing gave her a better perception about how they had once been where the scarred flesh was now. The tattoo was very similar to the drawing which Skars' grandfather had drawn of the Yggdrasil. In the inner circle was a tree with sprawling branches growing from a trunk. Underneath the trunk were roots. On the limbs were leaves. The tree sizes varied between the three men. Skars had the smallest tree with the least amount of leaves, Thorsen's tree was larger in height and size, and his had less leaves than his father's and more than Skars'.

"Why didn't Thorsen have the same amount of leaves as you? Your dad has more leaves than either of you? Why don't you have any leaves on your lowest limb?"

"I don't have children. Thorsen had three."

Sadness arched between them when she looked up from the picture.

"Thorsen had children?"

"Já."

"He lost his wife, too?"

"Wives. He had two."

She pierced him with her eyes. "How many—"

"I was unmarried."

"How many wives are you allowed to have?"

Skars slid his hand behind her neck to pull her to his sensual mouth. "It seems just one."

She grabbed his hair to put more distance between their mouths. "Do Vikings have premarital contracts?"

"Neinn."

"They do now. I want it in writing that you're only allowed one."

Skars arched a brow at her. "Then I get to write something into this contract."

"I only want one husband. I couldn't handle two Vikings. I barely have enough stamina for one."

Skars laughed. "Viking women aren't allowed more than one husband."

Raine made a face at him. "Of course not," she scoffed. "I see Martian men are the same as human ones. Okay, so what do you want written into our contract?"

"You can't divorce me."

Damn. He was asking for a biggie, but she was kind of asking for a biggie, too. If she were a man, who wouldn't want two women to cater to him?

"All right, fine. But you better not make me regret my decision."

"I won't." Ignoring her hand in his hair, he gave her a

kiss that spun what they had been talking about right out of her head.

Breaking the kiss, Skars placed the drawing back in the chest then carried it to his bigger chest. Plopping down next to her, he rolled on top of her.

"You make me very happy that you agree not to divorce me."

"You made me hella happy you won't be marrying another woman."

Her hand went back to his tattoo, seeing a small detail that had escaped her before. The barely perceptual symbol would have been missed if she weren't so close to it.

"I can see a symbol next to your scar."

"Thorsen's symbol," Skars explained.

Twining her arms around his neck as her legs circled his hips, Raine lifted her lips up to his. "There's no hiding when you're connected to someone, is there?"

"No, there isn't. Our tattoos will show the connection the moment we are touched."

Raine's head fell back to the pillow in surprise. "What do you mean, *when we are touched*? Do you mean when we have a child and you hold him, the mark will appear?"

"No, the mark will appear when *she* is conceived."

"I take it you want a girl." The man was full of surprises tonight. She would have thought all Viking males would desire a son.

Skars dipped his head to nuzzle her neck. "I want her to have your eyes."

Every bone in her body melted, wanting nothing more than to feel the heat of Skars inside of her as something nibbled at the back of her mind to ask.

"What did you mean a symbol will appear when you're touched if you weren't referring to children?"

"When we touch … the ones we are meant to love"— Skars continued to nuzzle her neck—"our wives or our husbands, the symbols of their names will appear on both of them, marking that they belong to the other."

Raine arched her neck back on the pillow, becoming afraid of losing him. "What if you touch someone after you marry me and her name appears on your chest?"

"It won't."

"But … what if it does?"

"The woman would have to be Viking for it to be appear, and there aren't many left. Reva told me long ago that I would marry a human woman."

Raine relaxed back on the bed. "I like Reva."

"She likes you as well." Humor filled his voice.

Luxuriating being under Skars, she rubbed her breasts against his chest as she teasingly dragged her fingertips over his cheekbones and beard. "Is there anything else you want to include in our contract? I'm willing to bargain."

Skars went to his side to prop his head on his hand. "Depends on what you're thinking about. Is there something else you want me to promise you?"

"I'm afraid of heights …" she began. "Do you really see me being able to go into outer space without going into cardiac arrest?"

"The heart stopping is bad."

Skars took her hands by the wrists to raise her into a sitting position and remove the loose shirt she had swiped from him. Cupping the breast closest to her heart, Skars lifted the nipple to his lips, his tongue coming out to lick the tip.

"I could find a safe place on Earth, and you could fly back every night from your adventures in outer space," she reasoned, running her hands over his sleek shoulders. "I miss having ground under my feet."

Skars used his chest to push her back down to the soft mattress. "You will have ground under your feet again when we find another planet we can call home," he promised.

Lowering her lashes, she didn't argue. His mind was made up, and she was sure so were the rest of the Viking men. She had no confidence in ever being able to change his mind, much less anyone else's in the clan.

Not for the first time, she wished she were the type of woman who, when men were in love with them, they were willing to move mountains for. While she thought Skars liked her, enjoyed the time they spent together, and definitely reveled in having sex with her, Raine didn't think any of it would be enough of an incentive to stay on Earth with her, much less move a mountain.

"Well, at least I have several months to prepare myself." Lifting her pelvis to his, she made it obvious what she wanted from him.

A long sigh escaped her when the head on his penis latched on. The twin sensations of having her vulva and nipple sucked at the same time did provide a glimpse of what it would be like to go to outer space. Skars could make her feel as if she never wanted to go back to Earth. The problem was, every time she went up, she could never quite escape the eerie feeling that, one day, she was going to crash and burn.

CHAPTER 25

RAINE

S tanding with her hands on her hips, Raine stared at the immaculate room she had just finished cleaning. She was bored to tears.

Leaving their bedroom, she went to the main room, only to find it was just as clean as she had left it yesterday. Returning to the elevator, Raine was bored enough to do something she had never done before. She moved her hand on the panel next to the door in a different direction than Skars had showed her.

When the door slid open, she didn't recognize the area. She stepped out and started walking down the small hall-way, coming to a door that Raine experimentally put her hand on to see if it would open. Disappointment didn't prevent her from continuing down the hall, coming to another door. There were only two others left farther down. She was already becoming pessimistic that none of them would open.

Her heart lurched in fright when it did open. Should she leave and ask Skars about it when he returned tonight before entering?

Boredom had her disregarding that sound piece of advice.

She came to standstill at what was inside the room. Several minutes passed before she could make her feet move.

The room had been made into a conservatory. Plants of every color and size were growing, some reaching high toward the ceiling. Cautiously, she remained where she was with visions of several horror films playing out in her mind. Could one be capable of eating a human like the Venus flytrap on Earth?

Her eyes widened when they came to the far wall, and she saw several plants she recognized. Homesickness had her hand going to her belly to settle the ache.

Leaving the room, Raine went to the two other rooms to find even more plants and trees. The last room held trees that had what she assumed were different varieties of fruit when she recognized lemon, lime, and apple trees from Earth.

She wondered if this was how the Vikings were able to feed themselves between planets, or would they have to depend on the planet food supply?

Promising herself a fresh squeezed glass of lemonade tomorrow after she was able to get Skars' permission to pluck some lemons, she excitedly entered the elevator.

Feeling like she was becoming a pro, she slapped her hand on the panel.

Her smile froze when she came face to face with Milly. The woman looked as if she was freaked out that she was in the elevator.

"What's wrong? Has something happened?" Raine asked, getting a sick feeling in her stomach. "How are you alone ...?"

"I knocked out Bjorn when he came to take me to eat!"

"Milly, you shouldn't have done that. They'll be angry—"

"I don't give a fuck if they are!" she yelled. "I'm trying to find my way off this ship before they sell me like the other women your husband has been bringing on board."

"He's trying to help them, and the men—"

"They aren't helping the men; they send them back once Reva looks them over. I guess none of the men are healthy enough to sell, but the women, they don't care. They sell them anyway."

"You have to be mistaken."

"I'm not mistaken. I just saw it myself. When I left my room, I managed to get on another floor. I was able to hide before they saw me, and I saw it all. They just left. If I can find the right floor, I might be able to sneak onto the ship that is taking the men back to Earth. Help me! We have to get off this ship!"

"I'll help you, but I can't leave the others behind. I have to—"

"I don't give a fuck what you do! Just get me off!"

Raine raised her hands helplessly. "I don't know where to take you? I've never been in this area before, nor where to go ... wait, I think I do." Skars must have met up with Thorsen, and Milly was on the floor which connected Skars and Thorsen's ship together. All she had to do was stay on Skars' elevator and go from there.

Raine reached out to take Milly's hand. Milly jerked her hand away before she could touch her and ran onto the elevator.

Raine remembered that when Skars had first brought her here, he had brought her in the elevator from the lowest level, so she slid the palm of her hand downward as far as it could go. The elevator door closed, and it began moving.

"It sickens me that I need your help," Milly snarled. "I told the others they were too good to be true. I bet you knew all along and were just keeping us in the dark!"

Aghast, Raine stared at the woman who was making no pretense of the hatred she felt for her.

Once the door opened, Milly sprang out, leaving her behind before Raine could stop her. Trying to catch with up with her, Raine nearly tripped over her feet when she saw the view outside the window.

Sheer terror had her going to the floor.

On her knees, Raine searched for something to hold on to, as if she were on an adventure park ride. Hearing the stride of footsteps, she looked up to see Skars bearing toward her, with a grim Arne following behind holding a struggling Milly.

Reaching her, Skars bent down.

"Don't touch me." She was too terrified to even scream at him.

Going to her bottom, she circled her knees with her arms and started rocking herself.

"Let me carry you to our room," Skars pleaded.

Raine lifted her head to meet his eyes. "Is what she told me the truth?"

"What did she tell you?" Skars went down to his knees beside her.

Raine crawled farther away from him before going back to her bottom.

"I told her what I just saw!" Milly screeched.

"Lower your voice. I won't be yelled at," Skars warned coldly.

Milly lowered her voice. "I told her that I heard you and Thor—"

"You are not allowed to say his name so familiarly," Skars issued her another warning.

"I overheard the chieftain and you discussing selling off the women you just had on board and sending the men back to Earth."

"Is that the truth?" Raine asked.

"Partially."

Tears started sliding out of her eyes at his admission. "You've been lying to me the whole time I've been on board."

"Já."

"Where are the women now?"

"They just left."

"Did you sell them?"

"Neinn."

"Then where they did you send them?"

"They were given to King Jurzed."

"Will they be set free?"

"Neinn."

Her hand went to her mouth to stifle a broken sob.

"If you would just let me explain—"

"I don't want to hear any more lies from you. What I do want is for you to get my friends and take us back to Earth," she sobbed out, her heart breaking in two. "I'll never be able to trust you again."

"Very well. I will take you and Milly, but the rest of them will remain here. The women are in fragile health; they won't survive on Earth. To take them would be to send them to their deaths."

Swallowing back her sobs, Raine nodded.

"Go back to our room, and I will send for you once we are back on Earth," he instructed her.

"Why? You didn't have any problem letting the men leave, or did you? Did you just dump them in space?" Horror-stricken, Raine started to get to her feet, miscalculating how close she was to the window.

"I need to dispatch my ship from Thorsen's. We are no longer in the area I found you. If I sent you to the same area as the men, you wouldn't even be able to speak the same language."

Turning her head from the sight of Earth, she came face to face with Skars, whose face was filled with rage.

Raine didn't even try to fight the darkness, sinking into its warm, welcoming embrace.

CHAPTER 26
SKARS

Skars watched as his woman snuck inside yet another building in a futile search for food. He clenched the stone wall of the building he was hiding in. From his experience, he was safe from being spotted by Raine.

Shaking his head at her making no effort to look up toward the rooftops, he was tempted to climb down just to shake some sense into her.

Hearing a sound, Skars spun to see King Jurzed coming up behind him.

"What are you doing here?"

"I could ask the same from you." Jurzed looked downward. "Ah ... I see you're watching your woman. I would never allow my woman to behave this way."

"At one time, I didn't think I would either."

Jurzed eyed him sharply. "You love the woman?"

"Já. I didn't want to, but I do. Reva told me she was my gift from the gods, and she is."

The two stood in silence, watching as Raine came out of the building, only to move to the side to climb inside a window.

Jurzed gave a low laugh. "Your woman is very determined."

"Já. Too much for her own good."

Skars raised his ax so the sun would glint off the metal, signaling Bjorn to watch her from his viewpoint.

"Did you and Thorsen come to agreement?" Earlier in the day, his brother had messaged him that they were to meet.

"Neinn. I will keep the *boy* for a while longer."

"Why?"

Curiously, Skars saw the smile on his lips.

"He amuses me. He has tried to escape seven times. The last time, he nearly succeeded."

"Thorsen won't be pleased if he escapes you or is harmed."

"No one escapes me." Jurzed would use any method to get the person he was chasing. Once he had them, they didn't escape his custody until he was ready to release them.

Becoming worried at Raine's prolonged time inside the building, Skars readied himself to climb down the building.

Jurzed placed a hand on his arm, halting him. "She's coming out."

Relaxing, Skars watched her move in another direction.

"Were any of the women I sent tru-mates?"

"Neinn. My men are losing hope."

From the expression on Jurzed's face, his men weren't the only one losing hope.

Skars gave a sad nod of agreement. "Ours, too. We've had two more who ended their lives since Thane."

As Thorsen's deputy, Skars understood the weight that both Thorsen and Jurzed felt at the loss of their men.

"If we could find just one, it would give them a spark of

hope," Jurzed said musingly, his attention becoming distracted.

Skars turned his eyes in the direction that Jurzed's was, failing to see anything. Not seeing anything, Skars turned his attention back to watching out for Raine.

"Já, all we can do is keep searching."

Skars had missed the long talks he used to share with Jurzed. Their property had bordered his father's. Jurzed, Thorsen, and he had snuck out many times to get drunk and torment their fathers with their misadventures. On one occasion, they had snuck onto Jurzed's father's ship and taken it out to visit a planet their fathers had banned them from visiting. When they had returned, Thorsen and he had walked away, leaving Jurzed to face his father's wrath alone.

"Is she how you expected her to be?"

Jurzed's mind must have been on the same memory.

"Neinn. Raine is too tender-hearted, terrified of heights, and believes every misconception about those coming from other planets."

"How so?"

Skars was almost too embarrassed to tell him. "She believed we wanted to eat her."

Jurzed shoulders shook in laughter. "One does."

Skars laughed back, shaking his head. "I don't mean that way. I mean she *really* thought we wanted to eat her."

Their shared laughter was a respite they desperately had needed.

"I regret you will not be coming to our wedding."

Jurzed's expression turned serious. "I as well."

"Thorsen won't break his vow to the clan."

"Nor will I break mine," Jurzed countered.

217

"You fighting with Thorsen will be needless if High Archuru catches Xioarius."

"Then we need to catch him first."

Skars knew that was what both men were counting on, while he knew the High Archuru better than either Thorsen or Jurzed. Skars understood what they didn't, that the High Archuru wouldn't stop. In some ways, he was more lethal than either of them combined. With the emotionless side of his alien nature, he would stop at nothing to achieve his goal.

Deigning not to argue any further, Jurzed gave him an amused smile. "Tell me, was it worth my punishment for us to visit here?"

"Já," Skars admitted without embarrassment. "But don't forget you benefited from our trip as well."

After Reva had told him that he would marry a human, it had been a constant worry of his that he wouldn't know how to make love to her. Confessing to Thorsen and Jurzed during one of their drunken bouts, they had devised a way for him to get the experience he needed to please a human wife. They searched for any knowledge they could find about Earth, and what they had found out was there was no way for them to go unnoticed. Jurzed had been the one who had found a holiday that a portion of Earth celebrated in which they could blend in—Halloween—and the best place where he could find success of having sex in the short time he would be able to spend there—Las Vegas.

Both men looked out over the destruction of the city.

"I wasn't surprised to find the bombs the humans used against each other weren't targeted here."

"Neither were we." Dismally, Skars remembered the once massive structures now broken to pieces. "Pity those who came to attack Earth didn't have the same day we had."

"Or night," Jurzed drawled out in amusement then grew serious when they saw Raine climb out of the window. "She is straying farther away from her hiding spot."

Skars' lips tightened in a grim line. "I have left her human food where it can be easily found, yet she never searches where I place it for her to *find*." Skars shook his head at the haphazard way Raine would pick which building to search.

"You have more willpower than I. I would have dragged her back to my ship by now."

"Two more days, and I will." Skars clenched his jaw when Raine tumbled down a pile of debris she had tried to climb to reach the entrance of a building.

"Tradition or not, I would have broken the rule of not being able to see or speak to her for a week before your marriage."

"She is angry at me. It will give her time to cool her temper."

"So would a sound spanking."

"I want to win her trust."

"Trust me; she would learn not to endanger her life if she were mine."

"That's easy for you to say. Wait until you try to win a woman's heart—" Skars cut off the end of his sentence, seeing Jurzed was no longer listening. He had moved away to the corner of the building to look in the direction where he had been staring when he had first arrived.

"Do you see …?"

Jurzed stiffened then turned to him. "Order Bjorn to get

your woman; he is closer," he told him, already running to the doorway which led downstairs.

Skars ran after him, his hand going to his suit to message Bjorn.

"What did you see?" Skars shouted at Jurzed as they ran.

"Grones!"

CHAPTER 27
SKARS

R unning out of the building, Skars saw Bjorn already fighting off several grones. Arne, farther away, was engaged with two of the vicious aliens and wasn't doing well.

Seeing Jurzed running in Arne's direction to help, Skars frantically searched for Raine. He had lost sight of her when he had run down the stairs.

"Raine?" Bellowing at the top of his lungs, Skars surveyed the area for her.

"Here!"

Hearing her voice, he saw her climbing onto a broken piece of concrete, which had been a massive statue the size of a towering building that had crashed to the ground when the aliens had attacked. Three grones were on her heels as she climbed.

Reaching the block, Skars used his ax to chop a dangling leg off one the grones who hadn't managed to completely hoist his short body up. The high-pitched squeal had him wincing. Using his ax to sever the ugly head from the body stopped the painful sound, to his profound relief. Next time, he would chop their heads off before they could make the noise that pierced his brain like a spike.

As he climbed onto the block, he saw Raine was continuing to climb higher on the tilted statue using twisted metal which used to be a roller coaster. Aware of how frightened she must be to be scaling the statue, he controlled his instincts to climb in the same direction. Instead, he swung his body to the side and managed to catch a metal cord hanging from inside the statue. He could reach her quicker. The drawback was, if the grones reached her before him, he was leaving her defenseless.

Putting the handle of his ax in his mouth, he started pulling himself upward. From the corner of his eye, he saw Raine kick the grone closest to her in the face. The resulting squeal had him pushing past the pain to heaving his body up the cord.

Scrambling onto the shoulder of the statue, he spotted Raine jumping up to reach a prong on the crown of statue. Holding on, she wrapped her legs around it to scooch along the length until she reached the concrete crown.

Skars didn't think Raine was aware just how high she had gone up the lopsided statue. Sliding on his ass, he maneuvered himself to the jawline. He was getting closer to her, about to climb up the ear of the statue, when he saw one of the grones try to grab the pack from Raine's back.

"Odin's piss!" Skars grunted out, releasing his hold on the ear. Landing with a hard bump, his body started sliding downward. He was barely managing to catch himself, but was able to heave his body in the direction of the grone.

Bracing himself for the sound the alien was about to make, he leveled his ax at the grone's legs. His ax severed them in one swipe, sending it spiraling downward. The last one left paused to glare at him with slitted eyes.

Changing trajectory, the alien started making its way toward him.

Relieved that Raine was no longer the grone's focus, he still worried when she continued moving upward, unaware she was no longer being chased.

Loosening his grip on the handhold, he had to stop his body's momentum. Hoisting himself up would give the advantage to the grone, but Skars didn't care, too concerned Raine would fall when she realized how high she was.

When Raine had still been on the ship, Bjorn had messaged him about how Milly behaved toward Raine. Activating the system, he had started listening, and as soon as Reva's duties were completed, he had sent her to his ship until he was able to leave.

Listening to Raine describe her childhood to Reva had brought an understanding as to why she tolerated Milly. Raine believed herself a coward where Milly was concerned, yet Skars disagreed with her. He thought her self-protective instincts were sensing Milly meant to do her harm.

When he had gone to escort her and Milly to Earth, he had taken Raine to the vault where they had been living in. Milly had been taken to a location farther away, where it would take days for them to reach each other on foot. Ignoring her protests when Raine had found out Milly wouldn't be with her, he had stridden away uncaringly.

He would kill the woman himself before he would let Milly near her again. The only reason he had let her live was because he was sure one of the numerous species on Earth would kill her, and he wouldn't have her blood on his hands if Raine were to ask.

The grone used its tail to slap at his hands as it stood

over him. Skars felt his body start to slip again. Taking his ax out of his mouth, he swung at the grone, swearing when he missed and the grone snapped its tail back to jerk the ax from his hand. Odin's balls, he was in trouble.

The grone had the advantage, standing over him, and had his weapon.

Meeting the slitted eyes, Skars didn't flinch when the tail curled back, preparing to deliver a killing strike.

Suddenly, the grone started squealing out in pain as it plummeted toward the ground.

Jurzed's face appeared over the side as he leaned over to offer his hand. Skars swung his free hand up, catching it in his as Jurzed pulled him up.

"How many are there?" he asked as he searched for Raine.

"Not many. They were on a scouting mission. My men will escort them back to their ship and send a message to the others waiting for their return that they would have to fight Thorsen if they want to come back."

Skars didn't respond. He didn't have enough air in his lungs when he saw the predicament Raine had put herself in.

"Skitr!" Jurzed swore.

"Quiet," Skars snarled, raising a shaky hand to begin climbing to where Raine was standing on a deck, which was drooping crookedly as she stared down, transfixed and frozen in place.

They both started climbing. It took them heaving the other up to keep one from falling to their death.

"How did she manage to get so high?" Jurzed asked, plastered to the side of the statue.

"My woman is high strung." Clinging to the stone of the

statue with a death grip, he tried to explain his wife's mad behavior.

"You said she was afraid of heights?" Jurzed's lips were just as colorless in terror as Skars was sure his were.

"Já, but she must have been more afraid of the grones."

Finally managing to reach a spot just below her, he was about to climb on the deck when Jurzed stopped him.

"Neinn, it cannot hold both of you."

Jurzed's calm voice had him looking at the deck. He was right; the deck wouldn't hold both.

"Raine ..." Keeping his voice soft, Skars attempted to pull her out of her terror-filled haze.

She didn't react. Her eyes were glazed, as if she was gazing inward.

He gritted his teeth at what he would have to do to pull her out of the childhood memory that she was unable to escape on her own.

"Wife! Hear me!" His strident order had her blinking.

"Skars?" Tremblingly, she clutched part of the broken railing. "What are you doing here?"

"I never left you. You have been within Bjorn's, Arne's, or my eyesight since I left your side."

"I have?" she asked tremulously.

"Já. I did not travel galaxies to lose you because you do not understand our ways."

"The Viking way sucks!"

Neither man could prevent their amusement from showing at Raine's insult while she appeared ready to pass out in a faint.

"Já. We can discuss it back on my ship."

"I'm scared I'm going to die." She whimpered when the rail started making grating sounds.

"I cannot climb to you; you'll have to climb down to me.

I sent Bjorn for a transport, but I'm afraid the rail will give out before he can get here. If you climb down, I will hold you until he arrives," he promised.

"I can't climb down. I'm too afraid," she whimpered.

"Wife, I will not let you fall. I swear."

"I can't." Tears rolled down her cheeks.

"Wife, look at me. I have something I want you to see." Holding his position on the statue, with his free hand, he started to unbutton his shirt until his shirt lay exposed. "Can you see from there?"

"I can't." She narrowed her eyes on him. Then it must have dawned on her what he was trying to show her. "Am I pregnant?"

"You are carrying my child, wife. You have to be brave and climb down. Please, Raine, I'm begging you to come to me. If you do, I swear I won't let you fall."

"How should I climb down?"

"Get down on your stomach and scoot over the edge. I will be able to reach you."

Heartbreaking cries came from her as she followed his instruction.

Getting in position underneath her, Skars grabbed her by the top of her thighs while Jurzed held him steady from behind as he lowered her into his arms. Turning her in his arms, he sat down with her in his lap.

He wanted to cry tears of his own when she burst into tears of relief. She raised her head, and he felt her hand smooth over a spot on his chest.

"I'm really pregnant?" she asked in an awestruck voice.

"I wouldn't have lied to you about—" Skars stopped at her disbelieving look. "I may have been willing to lie to get you off the deck, but before the night was over, you would have been, anyway."

A whirring sound had him carefully rising, with Jurzed's help, to place Raine in the nejim Arne was driving.

"What about you …?" Raine gave Jurzed a shy smile. "King Jurzed?"

"Bjorn is coming also. I won't be far behind," he promised, giving Arne the go-ahead once the door was closed.

Once the nejim was heading away to his ship, Skars turned toward Jurzed. "I owe you my gratitude. I will repay my debt to you for your help this day."

"That's two debts you owe me. I'm keeping count." Jurzed held his hand out for him to clasp.

A smile came to Skars' lips. He was sure of that fact. One day, there would come a reckoning for the debts he owed Jurzed, but today wasn't that day. Jurzed was smart enough to hold the debts over his head until he would benefit from them the most.

"The cost of the first debt shouldn't be high." The trader in him wouldn't let Jurzed overvalue his assistance. "If I remember that night, and I do, you gained experience that may come to benefit you in the future."

"Já." Jurzed's serious expression, which was never far away, returned. "But unless I find my tru-mate on Earth, my experience won't benefit me the way yours did."

A sound had them lifting their heads.

"I will have Bjorn take you to your men, then he can come back for me."

Jurzed didn't argue, taking the space behind Bjorn.

Before Bjorn could close the door, Skars leaned his head inside. "Thorsen told you the *boy* is in fragile health?"

Skars saw Jurzed tilt his head questionably to the side. Both of them knew Jurzed was already aware of Piper's condition. He had asked to talk to Trygve, and both clans were looking for the medicine she needed.

"Já?" Jurzed's eyes became piercing.

"We expect her to come back in good health."

"*Her*?"

Skars gave his friend a cunning smile. "Did I say her? My mistake. I meant to say him."

Straightening away from the nejim, Skars almost regretted telling Jurzed about the deception that had been played on him by the woman, then gave a fatalistic shrug as Bjorn flew them away. At least his friend no longer had such a serious expression.

CHAPTER 28
RAINE

F reshly showered and dressed, Raine went to the main room in Skars' ship to wait for him. Taking a seat on a soft cushion, she twisted her hands in indecision at what to do.

How could she stay with him after the lies he had told her, yet the baby's safety had to be taken into account. She protectively brought her hand to her belly. Earth wasn't safe for them, nor was there much food to be found. If not for the few items she had found, she would have gone hungry ... *they* would have gone hungry, Raine corrected herself.

The five days she had spent alone in the vault had shown herself something else. She didn't want to be without Skars. She had missed him, missed lying in their bed, talking into late at night, playing with his feet. Truthfully, she missed everything about him ... except when he was being a deceiving bastard or when he wouldn't let Milly stay with—

She corrected that thought; she had actually been

229

relieved she hadn't been cooped up with her again. Once was enough for her where that was concerned.

When the elevator door opened, Raine stood up, expecting to see Skars. Her mouth dropped open when Reva walked in dressed in a way that Raine had never seen her before.

She was wearing an old-fashioned gown that went to her feet, with long sleeves. Almost all her body was covered except for her face, which had bright purple circling her eyes, then spreading outward to cover her cheeks. Her blondish-red hair had been braided back, highlighting the bright splashes of color on her face.

"I thought you were Skars." Raine didn't know how to react to Reva's strange appearance.

"Skars won't be allowed to see you for the next two days and nights. It is our clan's custom to spend seven days apart before the marriage ceremony. You won't see him until he is standing with Thorsen as the wedding begins."

"I can't marry Skars." Raine fought back tears. She had never had a true friend to confide her secrets and fears to, and despite the strange makeup on Reva face, Raine could see understanding in her eyes.

"Skars told me when he found the survivors, that he helped them get healthy and find a safe place to stay on Earth. Milly told me she saw Skars, Thorsen, and you with the survivors. Instead of finding them a safe place to stay on Earth, the men were just sent back on their own. Even worse is, Milly said the women were traded to King Jurzed. I can't marry a man who would do something like that ... I just can't."

"Raine, did you ask Skars about what Milly told you?"

"I did, and he admitted it was true."

"You misunderstand me. What Milly told you is truth,

but did you ask Skars why he sent the men back and sent the women to King Jurzed?"

"No, because he lied—"

"He didn't lie. He just didn't tell you everything. I can assume he didn't because he didn't want you doubting his love for you."

"Skars loves me?" Raine didn't know if she should believe her or not, but God, did she want to.

"Very much." Reva took her hand. "Come sit down."

Raine let Reva lead her to the cushions. Sitting down next to her, Reva didn't release her hand, her clasp instilling a warmth she desperately needed.

"There is much Skars hasn't told you. The reason the surviving men and women were brought aboard the ship is to find out if any of them are of Viking descent. Has Skars told you about Xioarius and what happened on Raum?"

"Já."

"Did he tell you about our tattoos?"

"Já, that the tree of life disappeared the day Raum was destroyed."

"Good. At least that much he told you. The tattoo is our Viking heritage. It was a gift from the gods because we were taken from our homeland. It connects the Vikings to the Martian side of us, so we never forget our ancestral roots despite how many galaxies they took us to."

Raine listened intently, Skars' explanation becoming clearer.

"I told you the Viking centers the Martian side of us. For complete happiness, the Martians' needs must be met. For that to happen, we have to find our tru-mate."

"What is a tru-mate?"

"Your people call it a soulmate, but to us, it is much more. At a tru-mate's first touch, the Martian within us

231

calms. What one feels, the other does. One cannot survive without the other—the loss too unbearable for them. Many take their lives because they cannot bear the pain. You've been on board for several weeks; other than me, have you met any other Viking maidens?"

"No."

"Because there are only three. The other two have found their tru-mates. There are no maidens left. Skars wasn't looking for survivors; he's searching for tru-mates."

A hollowness in her stomach had her free hand going to her belly. "Did Skars have a tru-mate? Did she die on Raum?"

"Neinn."

"Then he hasn't found her yet?"

"I had a vision about Skars before he reached manhood. There is no tru-mate for him. There will only be *you*."

Raine truly wanted to believe in Reva's gift, but what if she was wrong? What if there was a tru-mate out there for him and he just hadn't found her yet?

Reva must have read from her expression what she was thinking because she told Raine, "I don't make mistakes. This is why Skars didn't want to tell you about tru-mates. He didn't want you to doubt his love for you."

"He hasn't even told me he loves me yet."

"Your wedding wasn't supposed to take place until after we left Earth. He asked the chieftain to make it as soon as possible, as our customs allow us to."

"Like not being able to talk to each other for seven days?"

"Já. We know our Viking men are lusty and charming when they want to be. With our customs, it makes the wedding night more enjoyable after they are deprived." Reva grinned.

At least she had that to look forward to, if she went ahead with the ceremony.

"When the survivors are brought on board, were any of them of Viking descent?"

"Neinn. No men, four women. The two Milly believed to be traded to King Jurzed ..." Reva paused. "And two Bjorn found hiding earlier today before the grones attacked.

"The first two weren't traded?"

"Neinn. When they didn't match with anyone from our clan, they were sent to King Jurzed. Because Thorsen and Skars used to be friends, his clan is given the privilege of possibly matching with someone from their clan. If neither of the women match, then they will be sent to the High Archuru."

"What if they don't tru-mate with anyone?"

"They will be given a choice of which clan they want to live with or return to Earth."

"What if the women aren't willing to be tru-mates?"

Reva's lips quirked in a smile. "We haven't had that problem since discovering our need for a tru-mate. The Martian side of us easily accepts their mates. On the other hand, the Viking side has had their ... difficulties. It is quite amusing to watch, but in the end, both succumb to their fate. Like I said, Viking males are lusty and charming. Our women share the same trait."

"Are you sure I don't have a small portion of Viking DNA in me?"

Reva's forehead puckered in confusion. "Do you mean because you are with child?"

"Let's go with that." There was no way she was going to confess that Skars brought out the lusty side out of her ... frequently.

Reva gave her hand a small squeeze. "I knew what you meant. I was teasing."

Laughing, Raine then quickly grew serious. "Where are the women Bjorn found today? Did either of them tru-mate?"

"They are waiting for me to begin the ceremony. I want you to come with me, to see what my clan struggles with daily. We lost Thane before we came to Earth. He couldn't bear the pain any longer, and he was our computer opera-tor. Our ship was damaged by a meteor shower, and, without Thane, we could have all have died. Thane was training Erik. Sadly, he isn't as competent, which is how Skars met you. He didn't trust the computer after the meteor shower about how long it would take our lungs to adapt to Earth's atmosphere."

"That was the day I met him?" Raine guessed.

"Já. Will you come with me? See for yourself what Milly saw so you will be able to make your own judgment?"

Twice she had nearly lost Skars before they had met. She would still be on Earth if he hadn't claimed her as his wife, still searching for food, or she could have been killed, like Dobbs. Ultimately, it came down to whether she trusted Milly or Skars more.

Remembering Milly's hate-filled face when she had been sitting in this room made the decision for her. Only one thing was holding her back.

Indecision flickered through her mind. Did she really want to be there if, by some chance, Skars' tru-mate had been found?

"Be brave, Raine," Reva urged her.

She was carrying a child. Her days of being a coward were over.

"I'll come."

CHAPTER 29

RAINE

"You must not talk to anyone, especially Skars," Reva warned her. "Afterward, I will take you back to your room. Whatever you see, remain silent. I will answer any questions you have afterward."

When Raine nodded, Reva moved closer to the door so it would open. Following her inside, Raine saw clansmen were inside, all of them staring at a clear plane of see-through glass.

Reva motioned her to the side, where she stood separate from the men, but would be able to see clearly what was taking place inside. As Reva moved away, she saw why Reva had situated her to the side. Skars was in the front on the opposite side.

She wanted to leave the room. With her luck, Skars was about to be tru-mated.

It was only when she saw Reva walk into the room that she could see through the window that she realized they were in an observation room.

Once Reva took a spot in the front of the room, the door opened again, and Skars' clan started filing inside. Row after row filled until there were twenty rows. Raine had been unaware there were so many on board Thorsen's ship. Their hair neatly cut at the back, their beards brushed and braided, and every single one of them stood without a shirt on.

After the room was filled to the back, another door opened, and Arne and Bjorn walked inside to stand in the front and to the side. Thorsen then entered the room, commanding everyone's eyes without uttering a single word.

This Thorsen was different than the one she had met previously. The gravity of his position and power was apparent in every line of his body as he walked to stand next to Reva.

Raine could practically hear the breaths being inhaled when the door opened and a lone woman was escorted in by two clan members whom Raine didn't recognize. Both men walked behind her to the front of the room and to Reva, and they were also the only ones who wore shirts, other than Thorsen.

"All you have to do is what I told you," Reva instructed her.

The strawberry-haired woman seemed to be in her early twenties and terrified out of her mind. She glanced at the door, as if all she wanted to do was take off running; it was everything Raine could do not to go running in there and hide her on Skars' ship.

Twisting her hands, Raine forced herself to remain still and watch.

As the woman went to the end of the front row, all the men dropped to one knee, bowing their heads. Startled at their action, the woman turned to look toward Reva, who gave her an encouraging nod.

Turning back to the kneeling men, the woman hesitantly reached out a lone hand to touch the first man's chest, where his scar was. Pulling her hand back, she moved to the next man to do the same. When she completed the first row, she stepped back as the row filed out to the back of the room and the next row moved forward.

She was on the third row when she suddenly hurried past one to quickly move on to the next.

"Wait," the clansman whom she passed shouted. "You went too fast. Touch me again ..." When the man tried to take her hand to move it back to his chest, her escorts quickly moved him back before returning to the woman.

Raine had to grit her teeth when the woman finished the fourth row and they filed out. She saw the sheen of tears on the clansmen's cheeks for not being picked. It was the saddest process she had witnessed in her entire life.

At the end of the last row, the woman's escorts gestured her toward where Bjorn and Arne stood. Taking their knees, they proudly bowed to her. Raine prayed one of them would be tru-mated, but then disappointment filled her when the woman finished and stepped back.

The looks on Bjorn's and Arne's faces tore at her heart. All of the men's pain was there for her to see.

Her escorts showed the woman out then brought in another one. This one seemed slightly older than the previous woman and more curious than frightened.

Raine forced herself to watch as the whole painstaking process started over. She almost asked to leave so she wouldn't have to watch.

Before the woman was on the last row, Raine somehow knew the woman wouldn't be a tru-mate to anyone in their clan.

As soon as Raine thought *their clan* in her mind, she realized her decision to marry Skars had been made.

Afterward, the woman was escorted out like the other one. The men in the room left to go into the room with the others who weren't chosen.

Staying where Reva had told her to stay, she watched Thorsen and the men comfort each other.

"I'll escort you back to your room," Reva said from the doorway.

Walking toward her, Raine could see pain etched on her face that no makeup could hide.

"How can they bear to go through that?"

"Some can't. We lost two clansmen last week. I fear we'll lose more in the coming days. We aren't finding many survivors now; they are finding better hiding spots, or they have already been taken."

They silently entered the elevator to return to Skars' ship.

"If you have a need of anything, just call for what you want, and it will be brought to you. I must go. Trygve and I will travel with the women to King Jurzed's ship."

Becoming excited at the news, Raine stopped her before she could leave.

"Would King Jurzed permit you to check on Piper? It would ease Lucas' and my mind that she's okay."

"I checked on him the last time I went. He is very well. Trygve reported to Thorsen and Lucas' that Piper's episodes are becoming less."

"Oh, that's good news. Thank you."

"You're welcome. Would you like me to pass along a message from you?"

"No, but if you have time, you might stop by and ask Lucas if he does."

"I will. While you were gone, I started making your dress. I need to have a fitting tomorrow to make sure it's ready in time for the wedding. Have you made your decision?"

Raine nodded. "Bring the dress."

CHAPTER 30

RAINE

R aine looked at herself in the mirror, seeing Reva smiling behind her.

"I never believed I would have one."

"A wedding dress?" Reva asked, straightening a fold in the dress.

Raine stared at the woman in the mirror who wore a long, simple white gown, with her hair pulled back at the sides in braids. She couldn't believe how her life had changed in a matter of weeks.

"Neinn. A wedding."

"You're not going to back out, are you? I have heard humans do that sometimes."

"You're the seeress, you tell me?" she mischievously teased.

Reva's hands dropped from the dress.

Apparently, seeresses didn't like their powers joked about. Raine tried to repair the unintended insult.

"I was just teasing—"

"I haven't had a vision since the day Raum was destroyed."

240

From Reva's distraught expression, Raine guessed it wasn't a good thing.

"They'll come back. You'll see."

"They won't. I was going to tell Thorsen my vision. I would have gone against my vision. The gods are punishing me."

"Do the gods normally punish you for a thought? Or is it the deed that counts?"

Reva frown. "The deeds."

"There you go. You have nothing to worry about. Your visions will come back; you'll see—no pun intended, by the way. You probably just feel guilty and aren't letting your mind relax enough to have a vision."

"You think so?"

"Absolutely." Raine place her hands on her hips. "Listen, I'm getting ready to get married in a few minutes, and I really don't want to come across as a bitch, *but* I'm going to if you don't chill out," she threatened good-humoredly.

"Very well. I will worry about it tomorrow."

"Atta girl. You can come over tomorrow, and we'll talk about it as long as you want to. Just do me a favor and don't come over too early. I really plan to enjoy my wedding night."

"You are going to bring laugher and light into our clan, Raine, really. When we leave Earth, it gets boring without other women around. This time, I will have another for companionship," Reva said enthused, linking their arms together as they left Skars' ship.

"Mmhmm," Raine responded noncommittally, her mind nervously springing forward to the wedding ahead. She wondered how many from the tru-mate ceremony would attend the wedding.

Raine came to an abrupt stop.

"You said the men are in pain without having their tru-mate. Does Skars feel this pain?"

"No. This is how we know you are a gift for him. He said, when you first touched him, when you believed he was unconscious, he felt a sudden warmth fill his heart."

Raine remembered feeling a similar effect herself. "You've eased my mind. I couldn't have gone through with the marriage if he were in endless pain without having a tru-mate. Humans aren't allowed to have more than one wife."

They could, but Raine wasn't going to give her that piece of information. Having a sister-wife, or whatever they called it, wasn't going to happen in her marriage. His love bud wouldn't be latching on to anyone other than her, or it would be pruned off.

Never envisioning she would ever be imagining how she would react at being cheated on, Raine almost didn't pay attention to what Reva was saying.

"I told you Skars had known since his manhood that he would never have a tru-mate, or have a son ..."

Raine stopped in her tracks again. "That's not true ... I'm pregnant; Skars told me. I saw his tattoo ..."

"He told the truth. You are pregnant ... with his daughter. Only tru-mates can have daughters *and* sons."

Sadness filled her for what Skars was giving up for her. She didn't bother to ask if it meant a lot to Vikings if they had sons; she knew the answer. It was probably everything to them.

Reva grabbed her hand. "Viking men idolize their daughters and sisters." Reva's eyes twinkled at her. "When you want to feel bad that you won't have a son, remember this"—Reva released her hand to place it on her womb—"the child will grow to become a tru-mate."

"True. I like your way of thinking about it more than mine." Raine nodded with a teary smile. "Have there been some women tru-mates who haven't found their match?"

"Yes, I haven't found mine. And before you ask, no, I won't be going through the ceremony with the other clans. As seeress, my loyalty will always remain with this clan."

"But that's not fair to you or him," Raine protested. "What if he belongs—"

"Then the gods will intercede when the time is right. Do not worry; my tru-mate will come."

From Reva's grin, she didn't seem concerned, and if she wasn't, then Raine decided not to be, either. There were more important matters she needed to focus on, and one was getting through her marriage ceremony.

Reva brought them to a stop in front of a door. "They are waiting for you. Are you ready?" Her gaze told her to take her time.

Raine drew in a deep breath. "I'm ready."

Soft, gentle music greeted her as she walked inside. The clan stood, all waiting for her, their eyes on her as she made her way toward where Skars and Thorsen were waiting. As she walked forward, she saw her friends and Lucas in the front row as she passed them to reach Skars' waiting hand.

His red eyes were lit with a warmth she could feel in the core of her being. She would never know what it would feel like to be a tru-mate, but she couldn't imagine it feeling better than this.

When Thorsen looked at her then Skars, she could tell he was going to start the ceremony.

Sending an apologetic glance to Skars, she raised his hand to stop him from starting the wedding. "We can't start the wedding until Skars signs a contract that he said he would."

Dumbfounded, Thorsen looked at them both again. "You can do this after the ceremony."

Raine shook her head, her nervousness easing when she saw Skars smiling. "We could have done it before, but Reva said your clan has a custom where we're not allowed to talk. I didn't find regular paper and pencil in Skars' ship, so I asked Silvia when she visited me yesterday if I could have a couple of pages from a notebook of hers and a pen."

Raine turned toward Silvia. "Did you bring them?"

Giving an anxious look to Skars and Thorsen, she pulled out a folded paper and a pen from the pocket of her dress and gave them to her.

For a second, Raine thought Silvia was going to stroke out at the glare she was receiving from the Viking men.

"Thank you, Silvia."

The elderly woman retreated to her seat.

Unfolding the paper, Raine poised the pen over it. "Are you still willing to promise I will be your only wife?"

"Já," Skars immediately agreed.

Seeing the Viking males' sympathy pointed at Skars didn't stop her from writing the promise. When she finished, she looked up at him again. "In return, I promise not to divorce you."

Raine nearly rolled her eyes at the Viking males' approval now centered on Skars.

Neatly writing in her promise, her fingers started trembling at what she was about to do.

"I want a few more guarantees before I agree to marry Skars, and some from you, Chieftain." Her voice might be coming out businesslike, but the paper she was holding in her hand was shaking.

Skars was no longer amused, and Thorsen was becoming angry.

"Chieftain, when humans marry on Earth," Raine sought to explain, praying it wouldn't end with Skars refusing to marry her, "the bride takes the groom's family as her own, and the groom takes the bride's family as his. When I marry Skars, I want your clan to become my family."

"That is our wish." Thorsen nodded.

"The problem is ... I don't want to leave Earth."

"Raine, I told you staying on Earth isn't an option for us." Skars shook his head, already planning to deny her request outright.

Raine could see her soon-to-be hubby wasn't the only one she was angering.

"I assumed you were a good trader, from the way you told me you managed to get the best deals from the planets you visited. You don't seem much of a trader to me if you're not willing to listen to my offer."

"Did she just insult Skars?" From the side, Raine heard Trygve ask the question to Brinn.

"She did," Brinn muttered.

Skars stiffened at the insult. Moving to Thorsen's side to face her, he crossed his arms over his chest. "What are you offering, and what do you want in return?"

Raine wanted to cry. She didn't want Skars angry with her on their wedding day.

Steeling her emotions, she accepted the cost of what she was going to pay to get the concessions she wanted.

"What I want is for your clan to make Earth your home. Why would we have to endanger ourselves to search for other planets when Earth has everything we need?"

"Except it doesn't. Not anymore," Thorsen said.

"But it could with your help." Staring pleadingly at Skars, Raine tried to get him to budge from his way of thinking. If she could move one boulder, maybe the others could be easier to move. "When I was exploring your ship, I saw you had plants and trees that I recognize from Earth. Do the other ships in your clan have the same ones?" Raine stared questionably at Thorsen.

She saw a flicker of unease at her question. He was getting that she wasn't going to be the pushover he supposed she was.

"A few," he carefully admitted.

"Then that's more of a start than Earth currently has. I also remember watching a documentary where seeds were kept protected in case something did happen on Earth. I don't know where it was, but we can find where they are and use them to start again."

"There is too much damage. The toxic bombs damaged the soil." Skars still wasn't moving.

"You mean to tell me, with all of the aliens that have been coming to Earth, with all their spaceships, and none of you know of a way to fix the soil and the air?" Raine shook the paper she was holding at the stubborn males.

"For God's sake, you're farmers—prove it!" she snapped.

Skars tried another tactic. "There are too many invader—"

"Ulf bragged you're the better fighters—prove it," Raine cut him off.

"We'd lose too many men."

"You're losing men now because they have no hope. Earth is your only hope of finding more women."

"What are you willing to promise in return?" Skars asked unemotionally.

Raine squeezed her eyes shut. Could she do this? She

couldn't ask them to take all the risks without willing to take her own.

Opening her eyes, she let them see the emotional turmoil she was in at what she was about to offer them. "I know who can fix your computers."

She didn't look back at Lucas when she heard him suck in a harsh breath.

"Don't you dare!" Lucas shouted.

Thorsen waved his hand at someone behind her back. "Remove him."

Raine wanted to break into tears at the shouts coming from Lucas as he was shuffled out of the room.

"If anything happens to Piper, it's on you, Raine! This is all your fucking fault!"

When she couldn't hear him anymore, Raine continued in a tear-filled voice, "Not only can they fix the computer, but there is a group of them hidden away in a think tank. There are over twenty people who were selected, who have the smartest minds on Earth. Their knowledge can be used to repair Earth. There are also several women in the group. I can't guarantee one will be a tru-mate, but there could be a chance one is. They also have computers there. I don't know if they still work. It will make your search for your ancestors much easier to locate. You also won't have to trade Xio for Piper. You will be able to keep your oath to your clan."

Their shaken countenance showed she had budged not one boulder but two. Looking over her shoulder, she saw the clansmen's then Reva's proud grin.

Turning back to Thorsen and Skars, she found no joy in her success.

"I also want written in our contract that you will convince King Jurzed to take Lucas so he can be reunited with his brother, *and*," Raine stressed, "I want his promise that he will treat Lucas well."

Raine didn't think she needed King Jurzed's promise. He had helped Skars save her life. He would see Piper and Lucas were taken care of ... once Jurzed got over his anger about not being able to use Piper to get Xio. If King Jurzed wanted Xio so damn badly, he could find him himself.

Thorsen nodded toward the paper she was holding. "Write down what you want, and I will sign. I swear I will fulfill the contract."

Finding a flat surface, she wrote down what she wanted and what she had promised. After signing her name at the bottom, she gave it to Thorsen to sign. Thorsen looked toward Skars for his reaction.

Her legs shaking, she moved to Skars to lay her head on his chest. "Please, I'm really afraid of heights," she pleaded. "I want my child to be born on this planet."

"Shh ..." He rested his bearded jaw on her head. "I look forward to the challenge."

Raine gave a shuddering sigh of relief when his arms closed around her.

"Which one?" she teased tearfully, guilt-stricken at what she had promised them. "Rebuilding Earth or having a child here?"

"Both."

"Sign the paper, Chieftain. My wife is a better trader than me."

Lifting her head, Raine watched Thorsen sign the contract.

"It is done. Who is this person?" he asked expectantly.

Raine felt a tear slip down her cheek when she told him, "My brother."

CHAPTER 31
SKARS

Skars trailed gentle fingers over the curve of Raine's cheek. Soft grey eyes looked up from studying his chest. She had been trying to convince him the scarred area was changing. The lumpy skin seemed more shrunken, the color changing from light pink to grey and black. Above the area which she thought looked different than when they had made love before was a line he could clearly see. It was a small tree limb, and hanging from the limb was a bud, which Skars had seen when another clan member had proudly shown theirs off when they had realized they were having a child, the bud representing a child in the womb. On his chest, the bud was slightly farther down and under the thicker limb with Thorsen's leaf. The lone leaf represented his only living immediate family member. Skars still couldn't see any of the roots or the tree trunk on the scarred flesh while Raine believed she could.

"I don't care what you say," she asserted, despite him contending he couldn't. "Those look like roots to me." Tapping a finger over them, she glowered at him. "Don't you see them? They're right under our baby's bud."

Skars loved how serious she was at trying to prove she was right.

"I believe you."

He was in too good of a mood to ruin it by arguing with her about something he knew wasn't there. From his vantage point, he couldn't see the roots under the small limb.

Giving up trying to convince her, he rolled over toward her when her hand on his chest slid sideways to smooth down his side.

"Today isn't the wedding day I wanted you to have." Twining a curl around his finger, he tugged on it. "I'm sorry."

"You weren't the one in the fault ... I was the one who turned our wedding into a bartering session."

Skars rubbed his finger over her lip to keep her from biting it.

"When will you go get them?"

"In the morning," he told her truthfully.

"Can I go with you?"

"Neinn. I won't endanger you or our child. We don't know what weapons they have."

Raine frowned. "Noah never mentioned weapons."

Skars tenderly caressed the naked curve of her hip before sliding to her belly.

"You aren't going, but I will bring him to see you as soon as I bring him aboard."

"Don't." She shook her head. "It will be better to wait a few days. He's going to be angry with me. We aren't as close you and Thorsen."

"Or as close as Piper and Lucas?" he probed.

"Yeah." She shied her gaze away from his. "Noah grew up in a different house than I did. He had a different father.

We really didn't have an opportunity to bond, especially with him being older than me."

"Then this could give you a chance to grow closer."

"He's going to hate me for telling you where they are hiding."

"Why did you?" he asked curiously. "You saw how bad Earth has gotten in just the short time you've been away. Why fight for it and expose those hiding?"

"Because someone has to. There's no one left, other than the ones who are like my brother, who the government deemed worthy to survive while the rest of us are left in the carnage left in their wake. Their time of hiding in their doomsday bunkers, buried twenty or however feet deep they dug for themselves, is over. They helped to destroy Earth; they can help fix it."

"I knew you were a shield maiden when I saw you."

"I'm a coward," she whispered into his neck.

"The woman who climbed that statue is no coward. She is a fierce warrior. You make me proud to call you my wife."

"I am a coward. I haven't told you I love you."

Skars turned his head on the pillow. "Do you?"

"Já."

"Then tell me."

"I love you, Skars."

"I love you." He grinned. "Now neither of us are cowards any longer."

"You aren't just saying it because I said it?"

"Neinn. I told you because I mean it. I love you with all my Viking heart." Skars saw the doubt in her eyes. "Why do you doubt me?"

"Just because you don't take part in the ceremonies, doesn't mean they aren't your tru-mate."

"This is why I didn't want to tell you about tru-mates. I

don't want you to spend years wondering if I have one. Sooner or later, the seed of doubt will destroy our marriage, Raine. You are the only bride I will ever want. You want to know how I know this?"

"How?"

Skars climbed out of bed to grab his wedding pants he had left on the floor. "I will be back."

Hurrying out of his bedroom, he messaged to Bjorn that he was on his way. He met his clansman, took Raine's gift from him, then rushed back to his wife.

Holding the gift in his hands, he saw Raine had tumbled off the side of the bed as she tried to get away from him.

Skars rushed to the other side of the bed, wishing now he had waited to put it back on the platform in the morning.

"Wife, are you okay?"

Raine pointed a finger a what he was holding. "What is that thing?"

Skars frowned. "My gift to you."

"Take it back. Get me a piece of jewelry or something else. Something that doesn't creep me out."

"This is a crinda that I told you about. Their eyes remind me of yours. I bought you one for a wedding present."

"How is this supposed to convince ...? How could you have known I had grey eyes?" she asked disbelievingly.

Skars set the furless animal on his bed to go to his chest to take out the drawings he had shown her. Finding the drawing he was looking for, Skars turned the lights on brighter so she could see what he wanted to show her.

"Come here."

RAINE

Raine hurried away from the bed, keeping wary eyes on the animal. Creeped out by the way its eyes followed her without moving its head, she situated herself next to Skars where it remained in her eyesight.

"This is the drawing Reva's sister gave her for me before she told me that I wouldn't have a tru-mate."

Taking the picture from him, she looked down at the drawing. She was puzzled by the picture, which was blank other than the charcoal color of the paper itself on both sides. The charcoal color appeared to have been applied to both sides of the paper. She could have drawn the same picture in pre-school once she had learned to use a pencil, to smear the lead onto the white paper. This picture showed none of the amazing drawing technique Reva's sister had shown on her other drawings. Having no idea how a blank drawing was supposed to prove what point Skars was trying to make, Raine started to hand it back to him.

"I don't understand how this proves an—"

As she started to hand it back, she stopped as the light hit the side that was facing up. Pulling the simple charcoal picture closer to her face, Raine peered carefully, able to catch the faint image the charcoal had been swirled over. Okay, she might not have been able to draw this in pre-K.

She shook her head; she had to be mistaken. There couldn't be an image of her in a swirling grey mist.

Bringing the picture closer to her eyes, she saw tiny lines and dots going in different directions, creating different patterns within patterns. Different shades of gray had also been used, some darker than others. The amount of time spent on the drawing showed the mastery of the artist's skill. Turning the paper over, she saw Skars' image cleverly hidden, as hers had been.

Skars took her hand and placed it on his tattoo. "If you believe you can see the beginning of a new tree growing on my chest, then why can't I believe this is you in the picture?"

She understood what Skars was trying to explain to her. What message Reva's sister was conveying to her from galaxies away. She and Skars not being tru-mates was only one side of the picture. That part wasn't important to the whole picture. What mattered was, if they searched for and found the intrinsic qualities which made tru-mates form an everlasting bond to each other, then it didn't matter if they couldn't see the proof on the outside of their bodies in the form of a mark; when the feelings they felt for each other marked their souls underneath.

"In her vision, we're tru-mates," she whispered.

"Já. When I touch you, I"—Skars pressed her hand more firmly down on his chest, over his heart—"I feel it here."

"I do, too."

Raine couldn't hold back her joy-filled sob. Their not being tru-mates had been nagging at her; every insecurity that she had dealt with her whole life because of her size and looks had preyed on her that he would drop her when his tru-mate came along.

She hadn't had the courage to believe he could truly love her the way she loved him because, if she did, it left her vulnerable to all the pain she had experienced from others. She was safe in her own little world of make-believe, so why chance heartache if you don't have to?

Carefully laying the drawing on his chest, she looked back to where her hand was held underneath his.

Because make-believe could never live up to reality,

despite how cleverly crafted love and pain have to be experienced to understand how they feel.

Her free hand went around his waist so she could fit herself snugly against him. "I finally get what you've been telling me, and I'm going to do it," she vowed.

"You do?" His arm went around her.

She nodded against his chest. "I'm not going to back down. I'm going to love you like no other Viking male has ever been loved, and I'm not going to worry, even if you find millions of Viking women descendants. I'll even add an amendment to our contract that I'm going to do it."

"Do what?" He forced her face from his chest to stare down at her in puzzlement.

"Be brave."

CHAPTER 32

RAINE

"Uh ... Nope. Sorry, not going to happen."

Raine giggled, rolling away from Skars' groping hand, making a sneaky attack toward an area declared off limits until she was able to catch a much-needed breather. Their wedding night had her body feeling as if she had come in last place in a fifty-mile marathon. In her extensive collection of romance books she had read, men needed a cooling-off period before men would be able to perform again.

His cooling-off period was non-existent. Clearly, Skars' sexual traits came from the more Martian side of his heritage rather than his human side.

Jumping up from the bed, she wagged a finger at him. "I'm going to take a shower. Then you're going to keep your promise to show me where you think it will be safe for us to build our home."

"I've shown you the map several times." Rolling over onto his stomach, he made a grab for her hand. "You can choose whichever area you want."

Dodging his hand, Raine giggled again, moving further away from the mattress, not trusting herself to be strong enough to resist his attempt to change her mind.

"I want it to have plenty land where all your clansmen can build homes, with trees, and mountains, and water. Water is very important."

Skars rolled onto his back to give her a heated look. "You know what else is important?"

Raine gave him an irritated sigh. "You really don't want to talk about this right now, do you?"

His eyes started to glow; Raine had discovered anger wasn't the only emotion that made his eyes do that in that particular shade of red.

Raine stopped in her tracks. Was she really walking away from the hunk of burning love sprawled naked just a few inches away from her? Unwillingly, her eyes traveled over a buff, tattooed chest to hips that she ached to lick; the smooth flesh like a mystery flavor in the alien of the month club. Appraisingly, her gaze went lower. Skars' penis rested comfortably on his muscled thigh, a centimeter from his knee, quelling her wavering libido with the suddenness of a belly flop in an inviting pool.

Tingles of discomfort from overused muscles brought her back to reality from the lust haze that Skars was intentionally staging to lure her back into experiencing more of the erotic pleasure he was so good at giving her. The problem was he might not need a cooling-off period, but darn, her body had said a Hail Mary the last time she had let him talk her into another go.

Raine gave him a threatening glare. "It's not going to work."

Skars slid his hand over his abdomen to come to a rest

on his thigh, drawing her gaze directly to the tip of his penis. "What isn't?"

She wasn't buying the look of pretended innocence either.

"Earth has this animal that lives in the water. It's called an alligator," Raine told him. "You don't see it until you're stupid enough to go into the water."

Skars' lips curled into a smile, which reminded her of the animal she had likened him to. "What does it do when you go into the water?"

"The alligator uses its teeth to drag you under until his prey is drowned, and then he devours it."

"I'm not like an alligator," he scoffed in amusement. "I want you very much alive when I devour you."

Sashaying toward the shower room, Raine decided to cut and run before giving in to the temptation in which Skars' sultry voice invoked—the memory of the last time he had devoured her.

"Yeah right," she tossed over her shoulder. "Behave yourself. I need a shower before I will even consider letting you ..." Raine couldn't bring herself to look back one more time, or she would find herself back in bed with him. Her willpower was already at the breaking point. "... devour me," Raine delicately finished.

"We call it ..."

Raine blithely plugged her ears, humming the rest of the way into the shower room.

Taking off the overly large shirt of Skars that she was wearing, she stepped under the water. Still in awe of the room, despite the numerous times she had made the excuse to shower in Skars' personal Garden of Eden, Raine lifted her face to let the water splash down on her. She didn't think she would ever get tired of the serenity and peaceful-ness she found in the room.

Realizing she'd forgotten the soap, she moved away from the water to the plants on the wall. Moving closer, she stretched upward, reaching for one that hadn't been plucked yet that was higher up. Plucking it, she dropped her gaze when she caught sight of the wall behind the plants.

As she peered closer, her lips firmed in a tight line as she pivoted to move the other wall closer to the bench where Skars had sat the first time she had showered.

"The dirty, rotten peeping ..." she mumbled, spotting the same mirrored tiles on the other wall. "I'm going to kick him where the sun doesn't shine," she threatened wrath-fully beneath her breath.

"Anything wrong?" Skars called out from the other room.

Spinning at his question, Raine was happy to see the doorway empty with the door still closed. How had he heard her? She had barely heard him, and his voice had been raised. She was irritated, but her voice had been muted.

Sitting down on the bench, Raine thought back to when he had been fighting with the Olggans and the reactions of the Vikings when she had screamed. Several other instances came to mind when they had reacted strongly to loud noises. Was their hearing sensitive to loud noises?

There was some dodgy stuff going on, which Raine didn't like at all. She couldn't blame the Vikings wanting to keep their acute hearing on the downlow. On the other hand, it also gave them a way to overhear conversations meant to be private. Trying to remember if she had said anything she hadn't wanted overheard by them, her gut clenched in worry for Piper.

She had to be mistaken. Could she be overanalyzing everything because she had found out Skars had deviously watched her shower? There was certainly a way to find out if Martian men had the ability to hear above the range of a human.

Going back under the water, she started to soap herself. Feeling silly, she gave a low moan.

"Is the water too cool? Do you need me to raise the temperature?"

Her jaw clenched in anger. "No, the temperature is fine," she replied in a normal voice then proceeded to tell Skars what she really thought about him to test him again.

"You dirty, rotten ..." she mumbled under her breath. She felt the words leaving her mouth, but even she couldn't hear them she spoke so low.

"What has you upset?"

Raine stared through the water falling down on her to see Skars standing in the doorway.

Envisioning her favorite latte, Raine gave Skars an inviting smile.

"I can't reach my back. Would you mind ...?" She trailed off provocatively.

The big lug of a Martian nearly tripped over his own feet to fulfill her request.

Taking the soap out of her hand, he started running the petal over her back.

Rubbing her back against his hand, she slowly turned around to give him a full view of the front of her body. Raine waited for his eyes to drop to her breasts before giving a blood-curdling scream that would have rocked a human's hearing, much less a Martian who she suspected had sensitive hearing.

Other than Skars staring at her questioningly, he didn't react.

Staring at each other, their gazes became challenging.

"Why did you scream?"

"I thought I saw a spider on the wall," she lied.

Skars narrowed his eyes on her expression. "Which wall?"

"The one behind you."

"There are no insects on my ship."

"That's good to know. I hate bugs." Pretending to shudder at the thought, she stared back at him.

"Why did you really scream?"

Fed up with the pretense, she glared at him. "I screamed because I wanted to know if your hearing is sensitive."

"Anyone would be sensitive to the noise you just gave."

"Then why didn't you react?"

"I've gotten used to your screams." He shrugged while reaching out to cup one of her breasts.

Angrily, she squatted it away. "So, your hearing isn't sensitive?"

"No more than yours is."

At least that was a relief ... if he was being honest. Which something told her he wasn't. She really couldn't blame him for not trusting her with the information. Not only could he be hurt if she shared the information, but his clan.

Raine came to the conclusion that she wouldn't be sharing her suspicions with any other humans. So, she moved on to calling him out on something he didn't have a good excuse for.

"I just noticed something new about this room."

Unperturbed from getting his hand smacked, he reached for her other breast. "What?"

Raine's hand went to his forehead to lift his eyes to meet hers. "The walls are mirrored."

A sensuous smile played across his lips. "I didn't look."

"You looked!" she snapped back.

"Prove it."

She couldn't, and the jerk knew she couldn't. Well, two could play that game.

Turning around, she gave him her back again. "My back, please."

His hand returned to slide silkily over her back. Hers went to the side to run down the length of his thigh. Encouraged by her touch, he moved under the water with her to nuzzle her neck.

Pressing her buttocks back on him, she felt his penis begin to stiffen against her. Taking a tiny step forward, she broke the contact. He hooked an arm around her waist and pulled her back into his arms.

Her hand went to the hand at her waist to move it to her breast. Erotic pleasure exploded within her chest at his touch. Losing ground quickly, she had to remind herself that she wanted to teach him a lesson to keep herself from sinking into the wildfire his touch could spark just by being near her.

Giving up the game she had started, Raine decided to cut and run while she still could.

"I'm good." Twisting out of his hold, she moved to stand over the blower. "Thanks for your help."

"I thought you wanted me."

Unwisely, she shrugged, forgetting she had just decided some lessons were too dangerous to teach. "Prove it."

Skars' expression grew cunning instead of angry at being sexually played. "Such a thing is easy to prove."

Moving to the blower, his hand went between her thighs, seeking the wetness the blower hadn't had time to evaporate. One lone finger easily slid inside.

Giving a screech, she went onto her tiptoes to evade the plundering finger. "You big jerk …" Raine had to bite down on her bottom lip to keep from moaning. Her head fell to his chest when he started inching his finger higher inside of her. Unable to prevent herself from licking the tiny nipple near her mouth, she smiled when she felt him shudder at her tongue on his flesh.

"Do you like that?" she whispered, licking him again.

"Very much," he groaned.

Becoming bold at his reaction, Raine nipped on the nipple before moving her mouth to the center of his chest. "Your body is so beautiful." Cupping her hands over his shoulders, she ran them down his arms, catching the wrist whose finger was thrusting inside her. She pulled it away to bring both of them to the back of his neck. "Don't move, or I'll stop," she warned.

She could tell from his facial features that he was battling the need to touch her.

Dipping her mouth lower, she let her knees go down to the blower, which put her mouth where she hadn't been brave enough to explore before. She had never put her mouth on a penis, and looking at Skars had her questioning her sanity about what she was about to do.

Smoothing her hand over his abs, she realized Skars had sucked his breath in and still hadn't resumed breathing.

"Breathe …" Letting the word whisper out of her mouth, Raine pressed a small kiss right below the bloom of his penis. Feeling the knobby texture had her knees clenching together.

Feeling the heat from the blower had her feeling she had just walked into a furnace. She scooted her knees to the side and maneuvered them back under the cool water. The water coming down on their flesh had both of them shuddering.

Moving her mouth from Skars' penis, she let her fingers take its place, experimentally touching him. Running her thumb over the opening, she felt it moistening and opening to spread like a flower blooming under the sun's ray. Pushing the skin of his penis down, Raine exposed the head. She licked her bottom lip and lowered her mouth over him.

The low hiss coming from Skars had her feeling like a goddess. This gorgeous man was under her control. She could do anything she wanted to him, and he would let her. A sense of freedom she had never experienced before had her mouth covering his penis more fully. Raising her hand, she clasped him in a tight grip. What surprised her the most was the arousal she was experiencing at his pleasure.

When steam started coming off his body as the cool water met his heated flesh, she moved closer to him to take more of him inside her mouth. Glancing up at him through her lashes, her eyes were unexpectedly caught by his.

Skars' penis might be Martian, but the man staring down at her was pure Viking. With his hands behind his neck, the muscles in his arms tense and easily seen, all showed he was holding himself back with iron will. No man, or woman, would ever be able to tame this man unless he wanted them to. He was just as wild as the flames he created inside of her. Skars was giving her the illusion of controlling him.

Stroking the inside of his thighs with her hands, she moved her mouth up and down over him, slowly building her speed until she felt more comfortable taking more. Her heart started pounding faster when his foot inched out to settle between her thighs, his toes bunching up to play hide and seek with her clit.

Raine didn't stop him, knowing his feet were just as sensitive as his hands and penis. Her body started quivering as his toes started pushing and rubbing against her intimately.

Holding on to his thigh, she felt his muscles quivering as much as hers. Small pulses started in his penis, showing he was about to come. The salty taste of him was on the tip of her tongue when Skars moved his penis away from her to bend down next to her and splay her out under the water.

"You weren't supposed to move." She reprimanded him in a hoarse voice when his mouth started suckling on her vulva.

Blinking the water from her eyes, she pushed the damp hair away from her face as a pleasure-filled scream filled the air. She placed a hand over her mouth in an effort to stifle the cry, not wanting to hurt his ears.

Skars caught her wrist while lifting his mouth from her. "Your screams do not hurt me." Rising above her, his head blocked out the splashing water from hitting her directly in the face.

He used his thumb to press against the corner of her mouth, parting her lips for his ravenous kiss.

Raine broke away from the kiss when her oxygen-deprived lungs couldn't take it anymore.

"It's a good thing you are half Martian and half Viking; I don't think I could handle either of you full-blooded." Raine couldn't prevent the spike of curiosity her teasing rose in her mind. "Just as a matter of curiosity, I wonder which of you enjoys sex the most. I think it's the Martian," she mused.

"Neinn. The Viking part of me is never satisfied." Skars gave her slow smile. "It's the Martian side of me that lets me keep giving ... over ... and over ..."

CHAPTER 33

RAINE

For a wedding day that had started out rocky, overall, she was more than satisfied with the way the day had ended. Except for one thing.

Raine raised up on her elbows to stare down at the floor. "Is he dead? He hasn't moved since you set him down."

"She's sleeping." Skars didn't raise his head from the bed.

"*She's* not staying."

"She's staying," Skars argued, rolling over to press on a mark on his arm. Raine had learned this was how they communicated with each other when it was important. They had their own built-in message system, which their AI translator would relay to their brain.

"She doesn't have any hair," Raine complained.

"She does, but she ate something she's allergic to, and it made her hair fall out. It'll grow back."

"You can bring her back when it grows back. Are you sure it isn't dead?"

"She's sleeping."

How could he tell? The blue color of the animal looked unreal. At first, she had thought it was black, but the longer she stared at it, the more she realized it was blue when she had moved around it to get a better look. As far as she could tell, it had no ears or nose, but when it did raise its head, she had seen the pure beauty of its grey eyes.

"She looks like she wants to eat me."

"She only eats plants."

"There's one plus," she groused.

"She's also very affectionate once she gets used to you."

Raine felt Skars jump off the bed to grab clothes out of his chest.

"Where are you going?"

The hairless whatever-it-was saw Skars moving around the room. When he came close to it, in a quick movement, it grabbed the bottom of Skars' pants and scurried up his body to rest on his shoulder.

Hell no! Raine screamed to herself that thing wasn't staying. Her friends would love it. She didn't want to hurt Skars' feelings by re-gifting it, but its gray eyes were giving her the same glare Milly had.

"Thorsen just messaged me that Ulf and Tayla escaped Volzon. Thorsen sent men to get them, but the grones are trying to get to them first."

Raine jumped out of bed to get clothes for herself. "I'm coming with you."

"Neinn."

"I am. I'm not going to argue—"

"You know how I told you that some species from outer space don't eat humans?" Skars pulled his shirt on.

"Yeah ...?" Raine paused putting on her pants.

"Yeah ..." Skars mimicked her. "They do."

Raine let her pants slip to the floor, going back to bed. "Have a safe trip."

EPILOGUE
RAINE

"Where are we going?" Skipping to keep alongside Skars as they left the elevator, Raine was surprised to see he was taking her to the lower level where the nejim were.

Waving his hand, the hood raised, and Raine hopped in place when she realized they were leaving the ship.

"You're letting me go down with you?" she asked excitedly.

"Já." Grinning, Skars pressed a kiss on her lips. "I thought you deserved a treat after last night."

Her excitement vanished. Last night had been rough. Skars had taken her to talk to her brother, at his request. It had been the first time he had asked to speak to her since Noah's arrival on Skars' ship the week before. The meeting between them had been short and brief, with Skars making her leave when Noah's brewing anger had found the outlet he had been searching for.

Raine looked down at her slippers, blinking back tears. "He hates me."

Skars hooked an arm around her shoulders to pull her closer. "For now."

"Forever." Raine laid her head on his chest.

"Neinn. He will get over it with time. They had two months of rations left. He is angered because you took the control out of his hands. He asked Thorsen to see the navigation room this morning. He will come around."

Raine gave a hiccuping laugh. "He always did love computers."

Skars tilted her head back. "We are going to forget him for the rest of the day. I have a present for you."

She narrowed her eyes on him. "It's not another crinda, is it?"

"Neinn." Shaking his head, Skars laughed at her. "They don't do well with two in the household."

"I wonder why," she scoffed, climbing onto the nejim.

The small animal was a complete diva. It didn't even want her in the room, preferring to keep Skars' attention to herself. Raine felt the same way, which was why the two were developing a hearty dislike for each other.

Burrowing her forehead between Skars' shoulder blades, Raine managed to make it to Earth without passing out.

"We're almost there. Keep your eyes closed until I tell you to open them," he instructed her.

Tightening her arms around his waist, she felt the nejim begin to slow then descend. Listening, she heard Skars raise the protective shell then felt him getting off.

A small, surprised squeal came out of her when she felt Skars lift her from the seat and into his arms.

"Keep your eyes closed."

Raine couldn't prevent the small giggle from escaping her.

Even with all the turmoil Earth was going through, and her brother hating her, she had never been happier. She no longer worried about crashing and burning with Skars. Her big husband would protect her and what the future held for her.

"You can open them."

Raine felt her feet lowered to the ground.

"I told you that you would feel the ground at your feet again that we can call home."

Opening her eyes, she stared around the empty area that he had brought her to. Then she glanced at him, not understanding what he was showing her. There was nothing around as it was a bare wasteland but ...

Then it dawned on her. Her eyes went misty when she saw how he was watching for her reaction.

"I can build our home here ... or"—Skars pointed to a spot farther away and to the side—"there. Tomorrow, we'll bring soil from another area so we can plant crops here." He turned and pointed behind them. "The area is large enough for the clan. It has ample supply of fresh water once we—"

A sudden blast had Raine practically jumping into Skars' arms.

"What was ...?"

Skars' teeth gleamed through his beard. Taking her by the shoulders, he turned her so she was facing one of the surrounding mountains.

"That was Thorsen blasting close by. We only wanted one way into this area unless on foot or air."

Raine couldn't hold back the tears any longer.

"You aren't pleased?" he asked, his smile disappearing.

"I am," she sobbed, turning to throw herself into his arms. "How could I not be? You just moved a mountain for me."

GLOSSARY OF CHARACTERS AND TERMS
VIKINGS FROM MARS

Spoilers ahead...

Arne:
Martian Viking. Warrior, Part of Skars' inner circle. Often guards Raine.

Astrid:
Martian Vikings' seeress. Reva's older sister that died.

Bjorn:
Martian Viking. Warrior. Part of Skars' inner circle.

Brinn:
Human. Co-worker of Raine's at the bank. Somewhat close to retirement age but pretends to be younger. Raine is concerned for her health. Her fiancé never came to get her when the bombs were fired. Friends with Raine.

Bruulls:
Alien species that Raine wanted to sacrifice. Green and mushy with squished-up faces.

Crinda:
Small creature that is extremely rare, with a gentle spirit and an affectionate nature. It is used as highly prized pet. It

dies easily if not taken care of properly. Its grey eyes remind Skars of Raine's eyes.

Dobbs:

Human. Deceased. Former co-worker of Raine's at the bank. He died during an alien encounter when foraging for supplies with Lucas.

Doth:

A purple vegetable that tastes like a potato.

Emma:

Human. Co-worker of Raine's at the bank. Close to retirement. Friends with Raine

Erik:

Martian Viking. Computer systems trainee of Thane's. Can't figure out how to work the Vikings' computer systems after Thane's death. Skars and Thorsen consider him useless.

Ferajorin:

Species from another planet.

Fwetasip:

A fruit from an alien planet. Tastes like cantaloupe.

General Dartar:

Olggan. King Jurzed's general. Usually leads his king's warriors into battle.

Grones:

Alien species. Particularly vicious. Uses its strong tail as an advantage in a fight; often used to serve a death blow. Flesh eaters.

High Archuru:

Top warrior. Male Viking who is the crowned victor of the festival of competitions. The current High Anchuru is lethal and cunning; Skars believes he stops at nothing to achieve his goal.

Hilda:

Martian Vikings' seeress. Reva's oldest sister and wife of Ulf that died.

Hithea:
Alien food. Tastes like chicken.

Iaslamire:
The planet where snowdrops grow, the flower Raine likes.

Já:
Yes in Norse

Karina, Kaz, Kennedy, & Silvia:
Other retirees who were in the bank vault.

King Jurzed:
Neptunian Viking. Bounty Hunter/Guardian. Leader of the Olggans because he saved their planet. On the hunt for Xioarius. Cousin species of the Martian Vikings.

Lanree:
Alien animal. Known for its howling and screeching. Skars compared Raine's screaming to that of a lanree.

Leron:
A planet. Known in the galaxy as a place where any sexual encounter can be had between any species.

Lucas:
Human. Manager at the bank. De-facto leader of the group who hid in the bank's vault to find shelter. Has been taking care of his sister, Piper, since their parents died. Friends with Raine.

Manitorz:
A place on planet Leron.

Milly:
Human. Customer service representative at the bank. Most hated employee. Hates Raine and has it our for her. Raine is afraid of her because she reminds her of her schizophrenic mother, who abused her when she was a child.

Nei & Neinn:

No in Norse

Nejim:

Small carrier vehicle the Vikings use as a transportation device on Earth because it is agile enough to maneuver through small and tight spaces. Equipped with thermal radar. Raine thinks they look like motorcycles inside balloons.

Njal:

Martian Viking. Warrior. Part of the inner circle.

Noah:

Human. Raine's half-brother. They aren't close. Highly skilled with computer systems. Part of a government think tank.

Okrakratus:

Small alien creature without teeth that is used as pet.

Olggan:

Species from another planet. Grey and black skin. Lead by King Jurzed.

Ozion:

Alien planet.

Piper:

Human. Lucas' sister. Has been protected by her brother her whole life. Has a health condition called neurally mediated syncope, a malfunction of her heart. Disguises herself as male from the aliens.

Raine:

Human. Main heroine. Works at the bank as a teller. While foraging for supplies, she saves Skars' life, who then claims her as his wife. Big-hearted and caring, gentle. Brave but believes herself a coward.

Raum:

Home planet of the Martian Vikings. Destroyed by Xioarius.

Since its destruction, the Martian Vikings have moved from planet to planet in search for a new home.

Reva:

The Martian Vikings' seeress. The only Martian Viking maiden left. Knew od Raum's foretold destruction but was forbidden to tell. Foresaw Raine becoming Skars' wife and saving their species' future.

Seeress:

Viking psychic who can see the future. Highly respected by the Viking clans. Deeply bound to their duties. Can sense tru-mates.

Skars:

Martian Viking. Main hero. Fierce warrior. Claims Raine as his wife when she saves his life. Came to Earth on the hunt for Xioarius and to find any tru-mates left. Self-confident and arrogant. Battles with himself and his feelings as he falls in love with his wife.

Skitr:

Shit in Norse

Sorn:

Alien species that is destroying the Olggans' planets.

Tayla:

Human. Co-worker of Raine's at the bank. Pragmatic and calculating. Gets captured with Bjorn by the Vozen.

Thane:

Computer Operator who committed suicide due to the pain he suffered without finding his tru-mate.

Themoter:

Controlling device the Vikings use on the humans.

Thorsen:

Martian Viking. Fierce warrior and leader. Lost his wives and children when Raum was destroyed. Skars' brother. On the hunt for Xioarius to exact revenge for the destruction of their home planet.

Tispe:

Norse for women who are spiteful toward their own sex out of jealousy or envy.

Trippe:

Alien type of meat/food.

Tru-mate:

What the Vikings call their soulmates. The Martian part of the Vikings calms at their tru-mate's first touch. They feel each other's feelings and can't survive after the other's passing; the pain is too much to bear.

Trygve:

Martian Viking. The clan's healer.

Uatera:

Alien planet.

Ulf:

Martian Viking. Warrior. Part of Skars' inner circle.

Volzon:

Alien species who capture Tayla and Bjorn.

Xeturn:

Alien planet.

Xioarius:

Villain. Destroyed Raum, the Martian Vikings' planet, and all its inhabitants with it. He was on Earth and couldn't escape before the bombs were deployed and destroyed most of the planet. Hunted by all the Viking clans but especially the Martian Vikings. Thorsen has sworn his revenge against him.

Ziea:

Jurzed's sister.

www.ingramcontent.com/pod-product-compliance
Lightning Source LLC
Chambersburg PA
CBHW070853180626
46817CB00003B/764